TOO CLOSE
TO
BREATHE

TOO CLOSE
TO
BREATHE

OLIVIA
KIERNAN

DUTTON

DUTTON

An imprint of Penguin Random House LLC
375 Hudson Street
New York, New York 10014

LIBRARY OF CONGRESS CATALOGING-IN-PUBLICATION DATA
Names: Kiernan, Olivia, author.
Title: Too close to breathe : a novel / Olivia Kiernan.
Description: First edition. | New York : Dutton, 2018.
Identifiers: LCCN 2017039972 (print) | LCCN 2017051310 (ebook) |
ISBN 9781524742621 (ebook) | ISBN 9781524742614 (hardcover) |
Subjects: LCSH: Women detectives—Ireland—Fiction. |
Murder—Investigation—Fiction. | BISAC: FICTION / Mystery & Detective /
Women Sleuths. | FICTION / Suspense. | FICTION / Literary. | GSAFD:
Suspense fiction. | Mystery fiction.
Classification: LCC PR6111.I43 (ebook) | LCC PR6111.I43 T66 2018 (print) |
DDC 823/.92—dc23
LC record available at https://lccn.loc.gov/2017039972

Printed in the United States of America
1   3   5   7   9   10   8   6   4   2

Set in Electra LT Std
Designed by George Towne

For Grace and Matthew

TOO CLOSE
TO
BREATHE

WHEN I THINK of him, he's gone. He's at the bottom of a river. In my mind's eye, I see him, submerged, standing against the current, black hair buffeted about by underwater winds, his cheeks pushed back into a smile, teeth glowing in the green depths. I want to take the bus into the city and stand on the bridge, right over the spot where we dropped him. People would walk past. Smile. They wouldn't know what we'd done. I'd smile back. A smile can hide many secrets.

You greet me with a hard kiss when I open the door, step straight inside, out of the sharp sea-breeze night, eyes black as the devil. I meet your inky gaze and try to remember when evil outstripped good. In your grip there is a rope. Brown, grainy, and rough. Already, I can feel the rasp of it against the perfumed skin of my throat. A thrill of something ripples on the edge of my breath.

CHAPTER 1

THERE HADN'T BEEN a suicide note. The victim remains resolutely tight-lipped, stone-cold silent; the best and the worst witness of her end. A note would allow mourners to hold on to something. Assert blame. Be angry at what's written. Tear the fucking thing up if they wanted. Without it, there is nothing. Grief battles alone. Even so, I imagine I see a ghost of a smile at the corners of her swollen mouth, the kind of smile that speaks of secrets. Secrets she'll take to the grave.

The narrow-faced pathologist begins the autopsy. She walks the length of the victim's body, reporting her findings in clipped, clinical tones.

"Time of death: approximately 20:00, 19 October 2011. Cause: suspected asphyxiation by hanging. Manner of death: pending. Victim: thirty-nine years old, female. Autopsy performed by Dr. Abigail James; also present, Detective Chief Superintendent Frankie Sheehan and Assistant Commissioner Jack Clancy."

We are in Whitehall. Dublin city's state-of-the-art supermortuary. The viewing area is fondly nicknamed "the Waiting Room," a sour reminder that there's a good chance of ending up on some patholo-gist's chopping block one day.

I look down on the doc. She's peering into the victim's mouth, a penlight in her hand. She's another unfamiliar face—the doc. Another adjustment. Although change is fair game when you've been away for months, it makes me feel cheated.

"She's new."

Jack Clancy stays focused on the victim below. He sticks his hands in his pockets, rocks on his heels. "Still as sharp as ever, I see. I hope your detective skills aren't as diabolical as your observation skills, Sheehan."

"See that?" I point to a half-drunk cup of coffee, smiling. "Unfin-ished. No lip till that mug's empty. What happened to the last guy?"

"He fecked off to Australia, like the rest of the bloody country," he says.

"Detective Harwood?"

"Back at the office."

"I thought he'd moved to Special?"

"Ballistics."

"What happened? Couldn't keep away?" I flash a smile at him.

A cloud of worry grows behind Clancy's eyes. When he speaks, every part of his face joins in: His eyebrows punch up, down; his mouth flattens, puckers; and the skin trembles over his jawline.

"We had to move some staff around, Frankie. Your team, intimi-dated as they are, turn out to be as loyal as beaten dogs, but we don't have another detective at your level to work with you."

"I prefer to work alone," I reply.

The remainder of my coffee is a cold sludge of half-dissolved sugar, about as welcoming as the day began and as predictable as it would continue.

I bring the subject back to terra firma. "What are we doing here for this fluff then? We're a bit much for an open-and-shut suicide."

The expression on his face tells me he doesn't think I'm much for anything at the moment. I straighten. Meet his eyes.

"The coroner had an uneasy feeling about this one," he answers. He raises an eyebrow at the phrase "uneasy feeling." "The commissioner is twitchy."

"Twitchy?"

He doesn't answer.

"About me?"

Silence. There is a tang of bile at the back of my tongue.

"Fuck 'em." I glance sideways at him, hoping to see some agreement in his face, but his mouth remains a hard line, his eyes forward.

After a while, he speaks: "What are you thinking then?"

"Of the victim?"

He sighs. "The suspect."

"Now that's a philosophical question." A tight grin. "You obviously don't think this is simply a plain old 'I'm checking out of this shit hole by myself' job?"

His shoulders shift beneath his jacket. "There is always that."

I turn. The doc, Abigail, is narrating the woman's story:

"The cranium is intact, no sign of fracture. There is a right lateral shift of the occiput on C1, which is compatible with significant upper-cervical-spine displacement from hanging. Lateral C spine radiological examination shows bilateral pars interarticularis fracture, or hangman's fracture, which suggests a sudden drop of the body onto the rope."

"Seems to be the death of choice these days," Clancy says from over my shoulder.

I'm aware that at some point during Abigail's postmortem, my hand has moved to my neck. Mouth tight, dry, my breath still and small in my chest.

I swallow, and the walls of my throat stick together. "You know, it's still an unusual choice for a woman. More of a man's death."

Clancy is tense. I can feel it rippling from him in waves.

I cough, try to sound like I've got my game face on: "Histori-cally, when women kill themselves, they tend to use less immediate methods such as pills or blades. Hanging, although not uncommon, is not usually their first mode of exit." I throw in a smile for good measure.

Clancy steps up to the window, looks down on the victim in the room below.

"Maybe this wasn't her first choice," he says.

"Maybe." I lean on the intercom. "Dr. James? What's on the left arm there?"

Abigail glares up at the window.

I let out a brief whistle of air. "Someone doesn't like breaking out of her routine."

Clancy nods permission at the doctor, and with stiff shoulders she moves down the body and continues to narrate her findings.

"On the left forearm, just distal to the cubital fossa, there is a lin-ear cut through the skin, appears to have been created with a very sharp instrument like a razor blade. There is dark coloring along the edges of the skin. Maybe an old tattoo mark or paint residue from the blade or cutting device used."

She stops briefly, takes up a specimen tube, and swabs the area. Dates and labels the contents, then continues: "The opening of the wound is two centimeters in length. However, no major blood vessels are disrupted."

"Bingo," I murmur, half to myself, half to the victim. "An attempt at slitting her wrists didn't work, so she hanged herself."

It's enough. Enough to hope it's as far as it goes. Small steps. Tak-ing up the case file, I move toward the door. "See you back at the office?"

"Sheehan . . ." He sighs. "You should—"

I have to drag the lightness into my voice, into my frame. I turn, drop my hip, my hand slipping from the door. "Come on, Jack. You and I know I got this. I'll clean it up good. Trust me. No loose ends."

He studies my face for what seems like a full minute, tongue pushed against his cheek, chest high with tension. I know he sees beyond the high-collared white shirt, the fresh cut of hair sharp along the jaw and newly lightened. I know he's seeing the hollows. In my face. Below my eyes. The dark crease of the case file against clenched fingers. The pink scar running from hairline to left temple.

Finally, his shoulders fall, he lets out a long breath, and a dimple in his right cheek deepens. He looks like he's aged an entire year in that moment.

"All right. But if it gets too much."

I'm already moving out the door. "I know, I know. I'll call you in or something."

ONCE FREE OF Whitehall, I turn left and head a short way down the pavement before ducking into a nearby side road. The road is more of a public driveway, an entrance to a sports ground. The dugouts are empty and littered from weekend matches. The pitches beyond are scarred brown at each end, but there are no cars parked. A good way down the driveway, breath seized in my chest, hands clinging to the case file like a lifeline, I stop, bend double, and throw up in a gutter.

It takes a moment for the retching to subside, and when I straighten, nose running, sweat trickling from my brow, I lean back against the wall, light a fag, and wait for my hands to stop trembling. As I look back up the drive, pedestrians march by, cars are dark speeding blurs, and somewhere beyond that, out in the streets of Dublin city, there are more dead bodies being found. More uninvited deaths for me to uncover.

"Fuck." The fag drops, and I crush out the smoldering stub, then leave the sports ground. At street level, I check for Clancy's presence, then quickly head for where I parked this morning. Inside the Waiting Room, Clancy will be ordering the tox reports I should have remembered. He's pissed. At himself. Frustrated with me. In my mind's eye, I see him run a large hand through his graying hair.

"I'm too old for this shit," he'll say. And when he sees me later, he'll have to fill me in on all the questions I couldn't bear to ask.

CONED PARTY HATS, no matter how jauntily positioned on the head, lose all sense of frivolity when greeted by someone who hates small talk and has a fresh corpse to deal with.

My arm is still outstretched, holding the door open. I intended on walking quietly into the office, giving a nod or two to a couple of my colleagues, then heading straight to my own corner of the building, closing the door, knocking the dust from my desk, and putting down a plan of action for the suicide case.

Helen, the only other woman on the team, steps forward and draws me into a hug. An action that reflects, no doubt, what all twenty-odd bodies in the room feel toward me at that moment: pity. I trained as a forensic scientist and profiler for four years, worked my way up through the ranks of Gardaí to detective super for fifteen, and have been a detective chief super for two years, and in all that time I've never seen anyone bestow a hug on another officer. Plenty of backslapping, shoulder-punching, knuckle-touching, and understanding nods, but never a hug.

Suppressing horror and anger in equal measure, I struggle out of Helen's determined grasp. Stocky, her head only to my shoulder, an immovable bank of fat and muscle. She pulls away, eyes studiously avoiding my temple. The fluorescence of the office a shining circle of light on her forehead, hair so tightly wound that I can see where the teeth of her comb have scraped over her scalp.

"We wanted to show you how happy we all are that you're back," she crows, then turns, sweeps a hand around the office. Includes everyone.

I can't get my mouth to work fast enough.

"Thanks, everyone. It's good to be back." There is resentment in my voice and the whining sound of defensiveness. I swallow away my discomfort. They're waiting. "It's very kind of you all. But I thought fun and kindness were outlawed here?" A bark of laughter that no one returns.

Pitying eyes stare back from the corners of the office, a few understanding nods. Christ. How long do I have to stand here for? There's a large chocolate cake by the vending machine. Paper cups, plates; the lot. It answers my question.

Had Clancy known about this? I can't imagine it. I ignore the cake. The desire to reassert myself rises inside me.

"So, now that we've got that awkwardness out of the way, let's get to business, shall we? We have a suicide to tie up. Excuse the pun," I say, genuinely not having meant to reference the hanging. "Cake can wait till home time."

Helen shakes her head. "But—"

"Inspector, you should know me better by now. I don't suffer pity parties for my staff, and I certainly don't suffer them for myself. Am I clear?"

Helen is relatively new to the team. A year or so, and that *is* new in this job. Stripes are earned only by hard work and how long you've waded through your caseload without stopping for more than a fag and a coffee. She will make an incredible detective one day, but for now she's efficient to the point of grating, has yet to learn which fires to snuff out and which flames to fan, and so throws everything into every detail.

She produces a small spiral notebook from a pocket at her knee, flips to a clean page.

"Yes, Chief," she murmurs, and makes a note.

Addressing the entire room, I raise my voice.

"By all means, if you can't bloody resist the chocolate cake, fill your party hats and go at it, but for fuck's sake, then get to work. Who's on the case-building team?"

"I'm with Stevo," Helen says. "The rest are following our lead."

"Have they recovered any phones from the scene?"

"No."

"We need to find the victim's phone."

"Forensics are still there. I'll call them."

"Anyone on CCTV?"

Helen shakes her head. She seems somewhat confused, and I don't blame her. "I didn't think there was a need."

"The manner of death hasn't been decided yet, Inspector."

"Sorry. Yes. I'll get started with street cameras." She ducks out of my path to the other side of the office.

I turn to Steve, a thin tech-head with a mighty obsession for detail. Steve was born staring into a laptop. His face wears the signs: pale skin, lavender smudges under his eyes. His chin, so pointed you could open a tin with it, sports a ginger goatee. At his elbow, a constant companion, an energy drink to power him through the day. Steve doesn't need a strong right hook to take a criminal down. He can do it all from the tap of his keyboard.

"Steve, a list of relatives, please. Any background info you can get on her husband."

He nods and I look out at the rest of the room. Gray determination and the odd slicing glance of coldness come swinging my way. That's better.

"Seems like a lot of man-hours for a suicide," someone mutters.

I let the comment go and turn for my office.

It has become a storeroom. Boxes of files stacked in the corner, solved, minor or major crimes, each one a fingerprint smudge against humanity. My eyes catch on a file at the top. The name: Tracy Ward. Case number: 301. No one has made an effort to move it. Weirdly, I find that hurtful. I shrug the emotion away.

I start up my computer and wait for it to whiz to life. My staff are right. This is a lot of manpower for a suicide. But I can't risk letting something slip. If the powers that be are as tetchy about this death as Clancy would have me believe, then I can't afford any complacency. Although, to be fair, complacency has never been my problem.

Truth is, the moment the plastic sheeting was drawn back from that woman this morning, I'd already begun shaping her personality in my mind. Short, classic, elegant hairstyle; the scent of the morning's hairspray lifting up from her fringe as if she'd just breezed by.

I see her hand, poised, then waving overhead, fingers depressing a nozzle; sticky vapor clouds the air before landing like shimmering dew over ash-blond hair. A beat for the hairspray to dry, then a quick comb through to soften the effect along the chin.

Jewelry had been absent, removed prior to autopsy to prevent radiological interference. But in the soft pad of each purpling earlobe were identical puncture marks, where, undoubtedly, up until a few hours before, a pair of tasteful earrings were housed. My guess would be studs. Pearl. Luminescent to complement her pale skin. A medium ball, nothing ostentatious.

A slim-fingered hand with a neat French manicure pushes the butterfly back onto the gold-stemmed post. A glance in the mirror to check how they look. The pearl reflects the white glow of her shirt.

The case file tells me I'm right. There, in the photo stack, item number four: two pearl earrings with gold-plate backs.

Settling into my chair, I pull my notebook forward to build Eleanor Costello's picture. The next photo shows an overall shot of the scene as found at 10:16 A.M. today.

A neighbor had become worried when the victim didn't emerge for work. Did he always notice when she didn't leave on time? Well, yes. He had a routine. Breakfast at the window. Eight a.m. The victim would walk by his house. For the morning train. Like a religion, it was. Hard not to notice that. But no, he didn't notice anything unusual the night before—he'd been out late. They'd been neighbors for seven years. They shared keys; he often locked himself out of his house. Didn't all neighbors hold copies of each other's keys? No, he hadn't been aware that Mrs. Costello suffered from depression. If she suffered from depression. Although, between him and me, he wasn't altogether sure whether the marriage was always a happy one, if I knew what he meant. I didn't. But he was not one for dropping anyone in it.

This was Neil Doyle: unmarried, intrusive, and exactly the type of person I'd cross the street to avoid. Everything about him was weak and soft, from the delicate bones of his elbows that appeared just below his sleeves to the small potbelly that rounded out the bottom of his T-shirt. He worked from home. A consultant, whatever that meant.

The husband, Peter Costello, is unreachable. But the helpful neighbor supplied us with enough information on the guy to set up a bank account in his name and take out a mortgage. Although a mortgage would probably be rejected. Peter Costello is unemployed and has been for a long time.

The next photo shows the victim's hands; the fingers curled in, like long petals, on the palm; the tips blue, as if dark ink were pooling along the crescent-moon nail beds. The photos are labeled, left hand, then right. Apart from a small detail on the skin, both look very similar.

On the index finger of the right hand, above the knuckle, there is a line of purple-brown dots. Petechiae caused by minute vessels bursting under the skin. The rope rips upward, grips her throat. Sudden, hard, and terrifying. She is gulping, her body kicking for air. She fights, her right hand pushing against the rope, working its way under. But the rope bites down and something pulls her arm away. Or someone.

My breathing falters, chest squeezing like a fist on a fly. My head, the scar running along my temple, feels newly sliced, oozing pain, sharp enough to make my eyes water. Anxiety is churning through my veins, thumping away at the undersurface of my stomach, pushing sweat into my eyes and down my back. I can feel fear swirling inside me. I could sense it this morning. My subconscious, ahead of my conscious, preparing me for the task ahead. The investigation *not* of a suicide but of a murder.

CHAPTER 2

THERE IS AN unsettling truth to be learned when profiling a killer. That is: how incredibly alike all humans are; how worryingly similar our desires, our drives, our fears. There is a sliding scale, of course, but it never ceases to alarm, how even at each end of the spectrum, there is still some part of me that can see evil's point of view. Even if it turns my stomach to admit it.

The victim, on the other hand, so often overlooked, is more important. The victim, a by-product of the perp's obsession, rage, or envy, is dusted off for evidence or clues, then allowed to fade into the shadow of the killer. But the question is not who committed the crime but what type of person becomes a victim of it.

The team will be resistant to the idea. No one wants another murder case, least of all me, but the pebble is in the shoe, and we either hunt it out or endure the constant rub.

Eleanor Costello's fingers fill the large screen in the case-building room. I move the laser beam over the arc of her index finger.

"Here. The petechial hemorrhage suggests that at some point between dropping onto the rope and dying, she struggled to free herself, right?"

"Instinct? But she eventually succumbs to the suicide attempt?" Helen suggests. She is eager to please after the misjudged party this afternoon.

I nod. "A need to survive? Perhaps."

The flashback is blinding. Eyes squeeze closed, shut tight to the memory, but it plays out anyway. A hard thump at the side of my head. I am trying to run even though I'm already falling to my knees. Sudden pressure in my gut, stars, white flecks of lightning spark across my vision, then darkness and pain.

I look out at the office. "Yes. Survival instinct. She's worked her finger beneath the rope. It's tightening as a result of her body weight. But both hands were found by her sides."

The team is predictably blank. Fuck, we're such a cliché. Then from the back a hand rises, the voice deep, scratchy, and instantly recognizable.

"Someone else was there."

I search the team. Spot him. A lean lank of a man who manages to look perpetually disheveled despite a suit and tie.

"What happened to Special Branch, Detective Harwood?"

Baz moves forward. An ally, a sparring partner, and, apart from Jack, the only person I can call a friend. Not that I'd ever tell him that. He has a hard enough time carting round his substantial ego.

"Ballistics were fun for a while but, ultimately, not my thing," he says. "How could I miss all this?"

I smile. "You did a good job of missing it when you were here before."

"Two days absent. Two. Days. You ever going to forget that? I'd the flu."

"Man flu."

"The deadliest kind."

Shaking my head, I suppress another smile. "The jury's still out if you're any better, to be honest." I turn to the team. "Both hands found by the victim's sides. As Detective Harwood said, someone else was there."

Helen speaks up. "She could have just pulled her finger out," she announces.

The statement raises laughter from the office. "If only," one of them jibes.

I lie down on the floor. Silence falls over the room. They think I've lost it.

"Helen, maybe you'd like to attempt this? Steve, an approximation of my weight and height, please. Don't be a dick, though—I'm still your superior, remember."

He stares down at me. Grins at the others, asks for support. "Five nine . . . erm, maybe one hundred forty pounds?"

My eyes widen. He puts up both his hands. Backs off. "No fair, Chief. There's no right fucking answer to that question."

"Pipe down, Inspector. Five eleven and one hundred thirty-three pounds. Helen?" She moves closer. "Why don't you try lifting me?"

My height and weight are close enough to the victim's. I want to illustrate how Eleanor Costello would have had to lift the entirety of her body weight to release her index finger from beneath the rope.

Helen's mouth turns down. She squats and her trousers rise to her shins, revealing solid beat-wearing footwear. She prepares to slide her hands beneath my back. I shake my head. "No. Only your fingertips."

There is comprehension developing in her eyes. I get up and face the team.

"Effectively, Mrs. Costello's entire body weight was squeezing down on that finger. Her legs are scissor-kicking, her jaw is locked, mouth open, tongue desperately trying to scoop oxygen into her lungs. Each muscle twitch is tightening the noose, pulling her weight further onto her finger, onto her throat, killing her. That is the force that caused these hemorrhages. But the body was not found with a finger trapped under the rope. Both hands were by her sides. Someone removed her hand from beneath the rope. It would have been impossible for her to release it herself."

And there. It is done. The case has opened up like an old paint tin, changed from suicide to murder with a few purplish bruises.

The team swarm over the pictures. Make notes, calls; begin the setup. Someone writes, "VICTIM: Mrs. Costello, 39 years old, married eight years, no children, microbiologist," on the whiteboard and pins the photo of the fingers beneath the declaration.

Baz is at my side. "Clancy suggested we should work together."

"Great."

"You sure?"

"It's fine." I throw him a half-smile.

He sighs. "He didn't tell you."

"He danced around it." I shrug, gather up my bag, my coat. "Clancy has trust issues. I'm broken, a possible liability in his eyes. I would've done the same thing, probably. He thinks I need a chaperone. I don't."

"I'm not here to mind you. I'm here to work. Fuck what Clancy thinks."

"You see, we're already agreeing on something. Could've done with someone a little more experienced in the field. But"—I look around the office—"beggars can't be choosers."

"Funny. Just put me on interview." He tugs the sleeves of his jacket, straightens his suit.

I smile, fold my arms. "I've seen your attempts at interview. You barely scrape in at a grade three."

"I scrape in at a grade two, actually. Clancy reckons the pope lies better than me."

"The pope lies better than anyone. You seen God lately?"

He laughs, and something not insignificant lifts in my chest; something that was threatening to pull me inwards has lightened, and the relief is mighty.

"Chief?" Helen interrupts. "We've had a call from autopsy, initial thoughts and a possible artifact. The pathologist reckons it could be significant. Firstly, severe erosion of tooth enamel, posterior incisors and molars, possibly due to bulimia. Secondly"—she checks her notes—"there was a dye or something found along the edges of the cut on the left arm."

"Yes. I remember."

"She said the tox have come back and it's a specific shade of blue. Potassium hexacyanoferrate or, more commonly, Prussian blue. It's been used by artists for years."

"A paint?"

"Yes." Helen smiles. "She said the way the compound coated the edges of the wound"—she looks down at her notes again, reading the pathologist's statement—"'appeared purposeful and consistent with postmortem application.' There was also a minute synthetic hair found in the wound that Textiles are working on, but to the naked eye it might belong to an artist's brush."

"Thanks, Helen. Fill in the team."

I move to leave the office but stop at the door.

"Well?" I say to Baz. "You coming?"

COSTELLO'S HOUSE IS at the bottom of a cul-de-sac in Bray. The type of street that makes developers grit their teeth. Prime location, a stone's throw away from the beach and local amenities, but populated with unadventurous detached town houses with bland square gardens and boxy garages. Put up in the seventies and predominantly inhabited by the gray brigade.

The quiet suburban house is theirs, not inherited, not rented or leased. Sought out in 2004, bought and lived in since. Inside the living room, it's neat, minimal, the only clutter a few books on art stacked below the coffee table.

I hear Keith Hickey's voice before I see him.

"Detectives. Back again so soon?" he says.

He walks from the kitchen and into the living room toward us, moving on the balls of his feet, anything to add a few inches to his height.

"Keith," Baz says. "How's it goin'?"

He stops before us, chin up. "We've got a good lot of the tagging and processing done now," he says. "Dublin's given us a team of four SOCOs. Quality lads now. Should be out in a couple of days. Tops."

"Any phones yet?" I ask.

"Nada. A laptop, though. Ready for you to take to your guy."

"Can we look around?"

"Sure." He holds up his palms. "But you know the drill: Keep your hands and feet inside the cart at all times."

I dangle a pair of gloves at him. "Of course," I say.

"I'll be in the bedroom if you need me." He winks, then heads off across the room.

I turn to survey the Costello home. The scenes of crime officers, SOCOs, are hard at work, scouring the house like white-suited miners. Every now and then a camera clicks and there is the rattle and shake of an evidence bag. The front door is open, showing a darkening autumn night; the screech of seagulls cuts through the cold air.

I linger over the coffee table, put on a pair of gloves, reach down, and select one of the books on art. Chagall. The cover is striking. It shows off a long stained glass window, sunshine blasting through shocking reds and oranges. It's vibrant. I turn it open. There are notes in the margin, phrases like "perspective," "medium," and "egg tempera."

"The paint or stain found on the body? Significant? I wouldn't have imagined she was much of an arty type." Baz looks over my shoulder.

"She doesn't seem bohemian enough for you? Are science buffs not allowed to appreciate art?"

"All right, all right. She didn't seem the creative type is all. She seemed like she would've been a bit more tightly wound. Stiff, you know?"

I raise an eyebrow at him. "She was dead."

"Fair point," he says.

He nods at the painting on the first page: a woman, a goat playing a violin. "There's a print of that in the downstairs loo. Looks pricey enough. One of the lads says it's framed by some fancy uppity company in Blackrock. A few hundred at least."

"So she was the arty type."

"Could be the husband's?"

"Maybe we can ask him when we find him."

He shakes his head; the corner of his mouth tucks in with a half-smile. "Though there has to be a link. Right?"

I shrug. "A painter's pigment found on the body and a possible interest in art? Sure. It's something."

I move toward the room. She chose the bedroom. Or her killer did. Probably because of the aged oak beams that run across the ceiling. They aren't a period feature but rather the kind that has been added to fit in with a nautical theme. The wood has the appearance of driftwood and in places isn't flush against the white ceiling.

There are three SOCOs working systematically through the room. They're finishing up, getting ready to collate, add to the picture. The real work can begin now. The walls, window ledges, and door handles are covered in black dust. The sheets have been carefully removed, placed into plastic bags, the pillow cases collected. I bend, check under the bed, although I know that too will have been cleared.

One of the SOCOs glances up from dusting the headboard of the bed. "There's a laptop in the office. We've swabbed and taped it. You'll want your tech to have a look?"

"Thanks," I mutter. I'm staring up at the ceiling. I can see her hanging there. As she was found, rigid and cold.

Baz joins me. "I've had them dust the Chagall in the toilet."

"Fingerprints?"

"A couple. It's a long shot."

"Sometimes a long shot is all you need." I look up at the beams. "How d'you think she got up there?"

His hands go to his hips, push his jacket back from his sides. He looks around, takes in the generous expanse of room. It's light, airy. There's no way a woman of Eleanor's build could climb up to hook herself on one of the beams without a stool.

"The window is too far away. As is the bed. The dresser would've had to be moved. Probably what set the coroner twitching," Baz murmurs.

Something wobbles inside me, but I hold it together. I turn to the SOCO at the bed.

"Anything on the husband yet?"

He shakes his head. "Not much."

My teeth bump together; frustration twists in my gut.

"The office is down the hall, on the right. The small boxy room," he says.

THE OFFICE IS gray, cramped, dull. The desk is some kind of odd plastic that's supposed to mimic steel. The shelves are aluminum and glass. I flick on a lamp.

"Whoa, that's bright!" Baz exclaims. He blinks.

"A daylight lamp," I murmur. I flick it off, turn on the main light. "It's a type of treatment for winter blues, or seasonal affective disorder. Dark evenings, gray skies, can leave some very low."

"People need treatment for that? Don't we grow up used to gray-ness in this country?" He laughs.

"You'd think, but for some it leads to clinical depression. It can have a profound impact on a person's life."

"So, we're in the bowels of one of the gloomiest and soggiest Oc-tobers in five years, Costello here may not be himself, and now we have a suspicious death."

I've moved on. I'm searching through drawers. I can't help feeling somewhat confused when I find it. His passport.

"I really thought this would be gone."

I sift through the stiff pages. No stamps. It's never been out of Eu-rope. I'm surprised to see that he is of Italian heritage. Born in Naples. Dark-haired, strong-faced, but with soft round brown eyes. He is hand-some. Even in the grainy passport photo he looks powerful. How would a man like this cope with unemployment? How much he would have sickened inside at relying on his wife for money, for security.

It's late. After midnight. The streetlights are orange orbs on the other side of the dew-lit window. Time is creeping by, eating through the seconds since Eleanor was found. Each minute takes the case fur-ther away from a quick resolution. Each minute means degradation of evidence, time layering dust over witnesses' memories.

Peter Costello's not coming home. I can feel it. The house is ex-pecting no one. It has been opened up, scraped clean, relieved of the secrets it holds. It's no longer a home to this couple. For one it's a grave; the other, a net.

The laptop is on the desk. It commands attention. It's taunting me.

"Have they tried to get in?"

Baz shakes his head. "Keith says no. We'll send it back. Have Steve look at it."

"The password is right here." I only need to glance at the wall and he sees it. Tacked to a calendar, which is still open on the month of

May, is one of those mini Post-its. Written on it is the artist's name: Chagall.

Baz takes a glove from his pocket and lifts the laptop carefully from the desk.

I follow him out of the office, back down the hallway, and out the front door. The sea breeze lifts the hair from my forehead, rushes up my nose. The raw saltiness of it stings the gritty tiredness in my eyes. Baz passes the laptop to one of the investigators, and I see them nod under his instruction. It's packed carefully in a box and driven off into the night.

I take out my torch, look over the front door. There is nothing to suggest someone tampered with the lock to gain entry into the house. Either the killer had a key or had gotten in elsewhere, or Eleanor knew them and invited them inside. I cast the light over the house; the windows are tight against the late-autumn weather. In the distance there are fireworks cracking across the black night, early Halloween celebrations.

I step down from the porch, away from the bustle of the investigation. I check the eaves of the house, follow the guttering round the side and finally into the back garden. In the limited light, it appears that the garden wasn't used much. A simple lawn stretches into overgrown straggling bushes. I bring the torch round, to the edges of the house. A bucket beneath the gutter, a drain thick with leaves. I push the leaves away with my foot; then, placing the end of the torch in my mouth, I crouch down and lift the grate. The round eye of a terra-cotta drain looks back at me, nothing hidden, nothing lost inside.

"Anything?" Baz makes me jump.

The torch falls from my mouth down into the drain. "Christ."

"Sorry," he says.

I fish the light out and stand up. "No. I'm hoping CCTV will show something. I can't see there being many cameras about here." I look out into the street.

He's shaking his head. "Helen came back on the cameras already. There's nothing in this area, the closest is an ATM on Quinsborough Road. Best we can do is put an appeal out on social media for commuters passing the main road there." He points out beyond the cul-de-sac to a road that runs parallel to the coast.

"We're in a black hole," I say.

"Tell me about it."

By the time we leave, the Bray coastline is filling with dawn birdsong even though the sky remains black as deepest night. The temperature has dropped, and our breaths cloud up before our faces. I carry a box of Eleanor Costello's stuff to my car, open the door, and slide it onto the floor in front of the passenger seat. Baz leans up against the boot.

"You sure you don't want me to help out looking through that?" He makes a pass over the stack of bills, junk mail, and papers that I've rescued from different areas in the house.

"Hell no, this eye-drying monotony is all mine." I walk round to the driver's side. "I need to get back to the office. Call me with anything new."

"Will do, Chief," he says.

I'm already pulling off, foot too heavy, too fast on the gas. I wheel-spin away, and in seconds, the house and Baz are swallowed up by the October darkness.

Beside me on the passenger seat is my new hobby, a recommendation from my doc—the shrink who finally cleared me to return to work. Return to normality. Or normality as I know it. *You've suffered a great trauma*, she whined. *You should take time to let your mind heal*. My hands tighten on the steering wheel. Panic rises in me. Exhausting, unrelenting waves of panic. Panic that wrings the air from my throat.

Changing down a gear, I lower the window, let the sea air strike blood into my cheeks, tunnel icy passages through my hair. The scent of death clings to the inside of my nose. My mouth fills with saliva. I gag, stop the car just short of the promenade on Strand Street. It takes a couple of minutes to settle my stomach; to let the sweat rise, cool, then dry on my forehead.

My eyes settle on the passenger seat. A bonsai tree. The barometer of my mental well-being. Another method of absorption. Something about controlling an entity's growth seems appealing. Blowing air slowly out through my lips, I pull away from Bray and back toward the office.

CHAPTER 3

THE CASE ROOM is a hum of phone chatter, fax machines, and tension. Anyone who thinks the not-sleeping, not-eating, and subsisting-on-caffeine detective is a fictional cliché has never suffered the fever of a murder investigation. Especially one in the first twenty-four hours after a victim is found. There is not one face that isn't pinched in concentration. The need, the urgency to scrape together this case, trembles in the warmth of the room.

When I step onto the floor, Helen, like a dog out of the traps, is at my side.

"Chief, we've got something on the cameras. I think you should see it."

I walk to her station.

"As I told Baz, there's no CCTV around her house," she says. "But I did get some from the university she worked at, UCD. They've a digital system over the gate that runs 24-7. The night porter was happy to courier us the most recent recording. It arrived only half an hour ago, but . . . we've got the victim leaving work."

She flicks the screen over on her computer to a clear image of Eleanor Costello midstride, about to exit the university grounds. The date on the top-right corner of the image displays "Wednesday, 19 October 2011." I lean in. Her clothing is the same. She's laughing, her hand at her ear holding back waxen blond hair. The white collar of her shirt peeks out beneath a pale pink scarf. Her coat—black and to her knees—is blown back behind her by some perpetual breeze.

There is a man with her. His smile matches his companion's. He's youthful, but there's something in the way he holds himself that displays a quiet confidence.

"We don't know who the man is yet," Helen adds, pointing her pen at the screen.

I move to the nearest computer. Open up another window and search for the university's website. From there I open the staff profiles. A list of their lecturers, professors, and student representatives. Scrolling through the biomedical school, I stop at a man's face, check the screen for likeness, then take a screenshot.

"Lorcan Murphy. PhD student under Eleanor's supervision and teaching assistant in microbiology." I get up, offer the chair to Helen. "Good work. I'll need a background check, criminal records—that kind of thing—and anything else you can scratch together in the next few hours. I suspect he'll be taking over Eleanor's lectures, so I'll pay him a visit this morning."

"Yes, Chief."

I move to the top of the room, to the whiteboard, and as if I'd signaled to the entire staff, the team stop what they're doing and turn their chairs to face me.

The question is always the same.

"How are we doing?" I ask.

One by one the answers come in, the dividing and conquering of knowledge, the sharing of information, the setting of new goals.

Between them, my team relay Eleanor's movements up until her death. She worked yesterday until approximately four p.m. She had one lecture on the division of mast cells. According to three different witnesses, there was nothing unusual about her delivery.

She finished the lecture at one, then worked in the lab until three p.m. Her lab work consisted of preparing twenty petri dishes with agar solution for her students' classes, followed by work on a paper she was writing for the *Dublin Biochemist's Partner,* a science journal. Lastly, due to the CCTV footage and the identification of her teaching assistant, Lorcan Murphy, we believe she might have caught up with him to review his postdoctoral thesis.

Then the room falls silent. Eventually, a voice speaks up from the back, Paul Brady, a round-faced officer whose shirt is consistently too tight.

"The trail goes a bit cold after that, I'm afraid," he says. "We know she sometimes or usually took the number 145 into the city center and then got the train out to Bray, but we've checked all the footage around the stations and on the train and we can't locate her."

"It's possible Mr. Murphy may have driven her home," I suggest. "Helen, can you see if he drives? Then follow up on more CCTV footage."

"Yes, Chief."

"How about Cell Site? Phones? Anything on Peter Costello, his movements, his phone?"

"There were a couple of phone bills seized at the house last night but no phone. The bill is in the victim's name. We've contacted the phone company; they're both on the same contract, one phone assigned to Eleanor and the other to her husband. Cell Site picked up Eleanor's phone on a mast in Bray just before six on the evening of her murder."

"So, assuming that she's with her phone, she went straight home after leaving the university." I add that to the board. "It's crucial we find Eleanor Costello's phone. It may have been disposed of near the crime scene. Check street rubbish bins, the coastline. Extend the search.

Also, if someone could put an appeal out on social media for Peter Costello to come forward for questioning. We'll see what Lorcan Murphy has to add to the picture."

I search the team for Steve, who begins speaking before I find him.

"The laptop rolled out some deets that could be relevant. Empty of almost anything telling, apart from the start of what seems like a terrible novel, an ancient game called *Crusader Knights*, and, interestingly, the Tor bundle."

"Any closer to deciding which of the Costellos used the computer most?"

"Initial fingerprint analysis shows both sets of prints. Last log-in was early yesterday afternoon, when the user accessed the Dark Web via Tor."

I address the room. "Tor is a package used to enter secure networks that are mostly untraceable. In urban language, people use it to access the Dark Web."

Helen speaks up. "So the last user must have been the husband, yes? Eleanor was working then, right?"

Steve shrugs. "Nothing to say she hadn't taken it with her. In the footage of her leaving work, she's carrying a large enough bag. Also, the laptop is one of those where the VDU can be removed and used as a tablet. Very portable."

My fingers want to snap through the pen in my hand. "Is there anything else you can take from it?"

Steve shakes his head. "I'll keep trying, but the Dark Web usually spells a dead end."

"Right, in the meantime: Peter Costello. Find him. Find Eleanor's phone. She was still in her work clothes when she was found the morning after her death. Who was there? Who put that rope around her neck?"

I step away from the whiteboard, and the team return to their posts, eager, focused, and hungry for a lead, a suspect, a name. I print out the smiling images of Eleanor and her colleague, then stick them up on the case board. I take a moment to study their expressions. They look happy, as if their laughter was the kind born of a shared secret.

GRAFTON STREET IS the worse for wear after a raucous Thursday night. A few revelers stumble down the echoing streets. Drunken laughter and the occasional shout drift up into the dark morning. I've come back to change my clothes but can't help lingering in the quiet of the flat.

Up four floors, I enjoy the bustle of the city but at a pleasant hum that feels like a distant, comforting friend. The lamp is still lit from when I was called in this morning. The sofa cushions are smashed up against the corners. I massage my neck muscles, remembering that I'd woken on the couch again.

I make a large mug of coffee and crack open the window. Lighting a cigarette, I check myself and realize I've eaten sod all in the past twenty-four hours. I check the cupboards, find a porridge pot, add water, and set it rotating in the microwave.

On the coffee table is the box I removed from Eleanor Costello's house and copies of whatever the team have gathered so far, a sizable stack of faxes and paper. Sitting cross-legged in front of the table, I push the box aside. Under the table, sandwiched between last month's *New Scientist* and this month's *Hello!* mag, is a creamy manila file. The file is a copy; the original sits, waiting for closure, in my office.

Tracy Ward's case was pinned down within a month. It should be open-and-shut, when the trial comes around. One advantage of nearly being killed along with her is that it gave us enough to hold the suspect in custody until we could gather the case together.

A previous victim of Ward's killer had stepped forward. Rachel Cummins, a redheaded, fragile survivor who was clearly broken. She testified that he'd attempted to kill her and had almost succeeded. I remember Clancy asking me to visit her. It was barely a month after the attack; the wounds on my neck and on my head were newly joined. Clancy had advised: "You've both shared an experience, it might help her talk."

And I asked her to look at the face of her attacker once more. I remember the shake in my hand as I rested it over hers when she selected his face from a line-up of e-fits.

I know little about the killer, apart from his psych profile. Of that, I remember every miserable, wobbling line. I lift the cover of the file, and tingling starts up in my fingers. The coffee trembles in my hand. It's too soon. I slide the file back between the magazines.

Inside Eleanor's box there are maybe ten unopened letters, the sort with shiny envelopes that give themselves away as junk from banks, garages, and opticians. Still, it provides the whitewash for the foundation of her life.

There is one from a car manufacturer inviting Eleanor to the launch of their new sports model. I check the background information that the team have provided. Eleanor sold an A3 hatchback four years ago. No car since.

The microwave pings, makes me jump; my knee cracks against the table, and coffee threatens to pitch over my case notes. I catch the mug just in time and move it to the floor.

I eat the stodgy meal by the window, admiring the narrow branches on my new bonsai tree and gazing out over the darkness that still swamps the early morning. There is a tremulous silence from the city. The type of silence that's filled with possibility and makes you question whether you have invented all of humanity and its stinking crap. Somewhere in the blackness spread out beyond my window, someone knows about Eleanor Costello's death.

Finishing the porridge, I chuck the container in the bin, then reclaim my seat in front of the coffee table. I take a pad of sticky notes and a pen and prepare to immerse myself in all the details we've accumulated about Eleanor Costello.

Occupation: microbiologist, part-time lecturer, occasional freelancer for pharmaceutical companies. Hobbies: unknown, although I scribble "amateur artist" on a sticky note and tack it onto the page. Her old family home address is cited as Eshgrove Estate. I grimace. The estate is a thin-walled concrete forest in the north of Dublin, marshaled by gangs of drug pushers and petty criminals.

I picture Eleanor Costello's smooth white skin, her blond hair styled to perfection. Talk about a phoenix rising from the ashes. Her dismal history goes on. She left home at sixteen. Stayed with an aunt, now deceased, in Kilcullen. The date her aunt died would have correlated with the year Eleanor graduated in biosciences from Trinity College Dublin with distinction.

She moved permanently back to Dublin, this time to Templeogue in 1997, and there were numerous work posts around the city, none lasting more than six months, until finally she took up teaching and contract work at University College Dublin almost seven years ago, shortly after meeting Peter Costello.

I lean back against the sofa. There are other surprising elements to Eleanor's past. She was done for shoplifting at thirteen, a harsh sentence that resulted in a couple of weeks at juvie. A single letter from a social worker to her doctor about the possibility of abuse at home. At the age of twenty she was arrested for assaulting a fellow student. My eyebrows pinch together: An assault? The charges were later dropped.

My breath tickles the paper; the corners of the notes bat about gently under my chin. Each line of her file draws me close. What can one really know about a person by looking at their dead body? Only so much. I know this. But before I could stop myself, I had built Eleanor Costello in my mind.

I light another cigarette, take a long drink of coffee. The nutty flavor melts over the back of my tongue. Looking at her history, it's a fair assumption that, for all of Eleanor Costello's outward fragility, she's a scrapper, a "dust yourself off and get going again" kind of person.

In some ways, her past might have worked against her, making her accustomed to abuse, possibly expecting it or, worse still, more comfortable in that environment. Sadly, she might have recognized her role in a violent relationship: that of victim.

CHAPTER 4

SO SHE WAS a girl done good." Baz is thinking aloud.

"Looks that way. Although it appears she knew how to fight her own corner," I say, referencing the alleged assault.

He shakes his head. "But those charges were dropped. It might not've been anything. Besides, we're all different beings when we grow up."

We're in my kitchenette. The city is rearing up for the day. Cars clog the streets, lights on, horns blaring, even though it's barely six and sunrise won't be for another two hours.

Baz is pouring coffee into large mugs. He's never been in this flat, but within minutes of arriving he understood the place, knew where he was welcome and where he wasn't. It's so like him to choose the neutral ground of the kitchen.

With some persuasion, Abigail has given him more information on the ongoing autopsy. Old fractures of the left carpal bones—wrist fracture—about eighteen months ago. Some scar tissue in the lower abdomen, possibly from surgery; significant decay of the teeth, hinting at an eating disorder. Cracks are appearing in the perfect veneer of Eleanor's life.

"The tox reports?" I ask.

"Ongoing," he says.

"Did you check through the drawers in the office again?" I ask him, swinging the conversation back to the Costello home. I'm searching for her passport.

"Yes, as predicted, it was tucked in at the back. The same drawer you found the husband's in." He shakes his head, pushes his hands through his hair. "Fuck. The Dark Web, huh?"

"What?"

"The Dark Web. Steve filled me in. She was into some dodgy shit then?"

"Maybe."

"She looked so bloody normal yesterday."

I give him a half-smile. "Define 'normal.'"

"Well, a bit anal-retentive, you know. Everything about her life, from her clothing, the house, her hair—everything was so ordered. It all seems"—he pauses, searching for words—"fake now."

"The computer may not be hers—both sets of prints were found on it, remember? And, if she was using the Dark Web, it might be that she was simply uptight about security. Not everyone who uses the underweb is dealing in crime."

Baz checks his watch. I glance outside. There's a gentle lightening of the sky, a blue-gray hue stretching out along the cityscape. Mist is clouding around Dublin's buildings, yesterday's cold freezing in the morning air. Somehow, two hours have slipped by.

"I should shower." Baz points his thumb over his shoulder, toward the door.

Getting up, I take a sip of the coffee. It's gone cold. "I've a lecture to attend."

He raises his eyebrows. "Lecture?"

"Lorcan Murphy. The victim's understudy. It's been a while since I brushed up on microbiology."

He laughs. "Sounds riveting. Rather you than me. I'm off to Peter's old workplace."

"They won't know anything. Social media is a wonderful thing. I did a search on him already, I've a list of his friends and followers. Here." I pass him the list. Triumphant. He should have thought of this. I smile. "If it were me, I'd start with his sister. She's in Sandyford. Not too out of your way."

"Feck off, Sheehan. You're an arrogant piece of work sometimes." He yanks the flat door open, glares at me, but I can see the smile in the lines around his mouth.

He stuffs the page into his pocket, steps into the hallway.

"You're welcome," I call out, and the door slams.

IT WOULD PROBABLY be a fair guess to say that the lecture hall in University College Dublin has rarely been as packed with students on a Friday morning as it is today. Most of the students will have arrived at the hall with prior knowledge of Dr. Costello's death. Her assistant, Lorcan Murphy, is remarkably confident in his delivery, and the subject matter seems morbid enough for the morning it's in.

His eyes barely slide in my direction as I slip into the dark room. He points a remote and the screen lights up. The image displayed shows rows of fuzzy yellow orbs on a blue background.

"Anyone recognize this little devil?"

"Strep A," someone offers from the back.

Murphy smiles. "That's right. Streptococcus A. A major protagonist in necrotizing fasciitis. Or flesh-eating bacteria, to the layman."

He presses the remote again and a gruesome image of an ulcerated leg fills the screen. There are groans from the front row. Hardly sensitive teaching matter, considering the demise of their lecturer.

"You can see here the proliferation of the infection, aggressive bacterial colonization will be seen on slides, the inflammation extends via the fascial tissue through to the deeper structures, often compromising vessel walls, resulting in intravascular thrombosis."

He presses the remote once more and a purple slide appears—an image of the infection as seen through a microscope.

"Here." He points to the network of thin lavender lines on the image. "Can anyone tell me what the significance of this dye is?"

A hand flickers at the front. "At the lab, two dyes are applied, the first violet, second red. Strep A retains the violet dye and is shown up as purple histologically."

Murphy nods. "Good. Gram-positive."

I've had enough and stand, catching Murphy's attention. I walk toward the door.

He hedges; then, addressing the room: "Okay. A list, please, of the epidemiology of this disease, then the distinctive features you might look for under the 'scope."

The students shift in their seats, look to one another, but gradually there's the shuffle of paper and they set to work.

In the corridor, Murphy's less gloomy. All smiles. His hand extends. "Detective Sheehan. Good to meet you. I'm Lorcan Murphy. Elean—" He stops himself. "Dr. Costello's PhD student."

I place my hand in his. Despite his outward calm, his skin has that too-hot, damp feel to it. Immediately, I want to wipe my own hand clean.

"Sorry for your loss," I say.

He shrugs, but there is a paleness that stretches around his mouth. His nostrils flare, suppressing emotion. He's not able to meet my eyes when he says: "What can you do?"

He's not asking. For the briefest of moments he looks lost, as if he's the type of man who clings to the ordinariness of his life when things get fucked up. I set my jaw.

"Quite a lot, actually, Mr. Murphy," I answer the nonquestion.

Confusion crosses his face. "Please, call me Lorcan."

"I like to keep things formal. Everyone knows where they are then."

"Right so, of course, yeah." He points down the hallway. "There's a coffee shop. I don't have an office of my own, per se; I used to share with Elean—" He sighs. "Sorry, Dr. Costello."

"An office? I thought she lectured part-time? Wasn't most of her work consultancy and agency-based?"

"Yeah, but it was solely on behalf of the university. She never accepted contracts anywhere else. She's too busy here."

Our twenty-four hours since the victim was found is almost up, and not one member of my team has been to her office. Anyone could have been and gone from there. Including the husband. I call it in. The team will take an hour or so to get the necessary warrants.

"Has anyone been in her office since?"

"I've a set of keys, but no one else would enter, not unless the school manager let them in." He stops. His expression is hopeful. "I can get him for you? He's probably in the library about this time."

I walk on. "Let's get that coffee. My team will be here shortly. They'll fill him in. I'm afraid Dr. Costello's office is now a crime scene."

"A crime scene? I thought—" He drops his voice to a whisper. "I thought it was a suicide?" He mimes the word "suicide," as if his mouth might become contaminated if he says it out loud. Such is the effect of Catholicism on a country: educated, sensible people become blithering eegits in the face of mental illness.

"Poor Peter," he murmurs.

Letting the thought stew for a few moments, I turn in to the small café. It's brightly lit and overlooks the sizable sports fields that stretch out behind the university. There are women smashing into one another in the soft ground, practicing rugby drills. They pivot, dodge, and crash up the pitch. They partner up, shoulders drive against shoulders. It looks cathartic, empowering.

I step up to the counter. The woman behind it is young, keen, and too happy for a morning, in my opinion. She can't be more than twenty-odd. Shouldn't she be hungover? I order a plain black coffee, and before Murphy can make his request, the girl beams and chirps: "Latte and an extra shot, right?"

A ferocious blush sweeps up Murphy's neckline and into his face. "Sure." He makes a shrugging gesture at me, as if to say, *What was that about?*

We collect our cups and sit at the back near the window.

He has barely shuffled his feet beneath the table when I ask my first question: "How long have you known Dr. Costello?"

The paleness is back. "Probably four years or so. Not long."

"Not long? Four years seems extensive enough."

He laughs, then bites down on his lip. "Not in academia. I've been working on my PhD for six. She's been my tutor for three; before that I had another tutor, but that finished and Dr. Costello stepped up."

"Oh? Why's that?"

"Why did she step up?"

"No. Why did you finish with the first tutor? It seems odd. A PhD is a big investment for both student and tutor, isn't it?"

"It was nothing dramatic. He retired. Eleanor had studied under Professor Muldoon, and he thought she'd be best qualified to continue." He takes a gulp of the coffee. "And he was right. She was an amazing tutor. Very passionate."

"Passionate?"

The blush rises again. "About her work."

"I see." I close my notebook, lean back. "How would you describe Eleanor, personality-wise?"

His eyes narrow briefly. There is a flash of uncertainty in them. "I dunno. She always seemed so together to me. Professional. She was a consummate professional." The pitch of his voice teeters toward bitterness.

I see them leaving the university grounds on the evening of her death. Something in their body language suggests more than professionalism to me.

"Do you drive, Mr. Murphy?"

"I have a car, but I bus it home. Guess I haven't quite left my student days behind." He laughs again.

"On Wednesday, do you know how Eleanor Costello got home?"

He shrugs. "I assume she got the train. It's what she usually did. We walked out together—we sometimes do after a tutorial—we walked to my bus stop, which is about fifty yards down the road. She left me there. She gets her bus from the south side. She likes to walk."

On the sports field, the women are jogging around the pitch, legs red against the cold, clouds of breath streaming out behind them.

"You ever go for a drink together, after work, perhaps?"

He pulls back a little. "The odd time, but it wasn't a habit, no."

There is a defensive note to his voice. I back off, give him a smile. Trust is hard-earned and worth keeping with witnesses and suspects alike.

"Do you know if Eleanor had any enemies? Was she in any trouble?"

His bottom lip juts out; shakes his head. "No. I don't think so. She seemed happy, if that's what you mean."

"Money trouble?"

"I don't think so. But she probably wouldn't discuss that kind of thing with me."

He frowns, face softening into an expression of regret. "I'm sorry, Detective. But I really should be getting back to the lecture hall. The end-of-term exams are coming up, and the students have already suffered a huge upheaval."

I stand, offer my hand. "Thank you very much for your time, Mr. Murphy. Would you mind pointing me in the direction of Dr. Costello's office?"

"Of course. Thank you, Detective."

"I'm afraid I'll probably have more questions once we know a little more." See which way the spinning bottle is pointing.

He fishes about in his pocket, produces a stiff business card. "Here. My card. I will help any way I can. Truly. Call me day or night."

"Thank you. I might have to do that."

I take the card. There is fear in his eyes, and I can't tell whether it's for Eleanor Costello or himself.

ELEANOR'S OFFICE IS not how it should be. Apart from a few tubes of lipstick and a bottle of perfume in the top drawer, there is little of Eleanor Costello here. The laboratories that she worked in are also predictably clean, as one would hope a microbiology lab would be. Her field was medical microbiology, specifically the effects of drugs on various pathogens. There are rows of petri dishes displaying diseases in all stages of progression and suppression held behind brightly lit incubators.

The scenes of crime officers have arrived, and they remain, dissecting Costello's office. Clancy has asked to check in. Or for him to check on me rather.

I'm passing the coffee shop on the way out when the young woman, the barista from behind the counter, calls out. At first I think I've left my purse behind or, worse, my notes, but as she approaches, hands wringing, face creased, I realize that she wants to tell me something.

"Hi," I say, and put out my hand. "Detective Sheehan."

She gives my hand a brief, gentle shake. "Nicole. Nicole Duarte." Her eyes slide to the floor. Nervous. "Dr. Costello? She's dead?"

Her teeth chew over a dry flake of skin on her bottom lip.

"Yes. We believe she was murdered."

She peeks up at me, dark brows pulled down, skin blanched. "Murdered? Sorry." She shakes her head. "I mean, who would do that?"

Her hands weave worried knots in her apron.

"That's what we're trying to find out. Nicole, was there something you wanted to tell me?"

She looks at the counter. Takes a step back in that direction. "No. Sorry. It's not important."

"Are you sure?"

She looks up at me, shakes her head. "I thought . . . I thought she killed herself is all." Her eyes redden, water. She sniffs.

I step forward. "Nicole, are you okay?"

She nods. "I just wasn't expecting that."

"But you expected suicide?"

She wipes the back of her hand over her eyes. "No. Goodness, no. I reckon I was thinking of my own stuff. That's all." She sighs, and it hiccups in her throat. "I saw her leaving a therapist's office in town months ago. When I heard suicide, I guess I thought she might have had depression or something." She shrugs. "I don't know."

A stream of students comes round the corner, gathers in a line before the counter.

"I have to get back to work," she says.

"Sure. Here," I say. "Take my card. If you've anything you'd like to tell me, then contact me, anytime."

She tucks it into her apron. "Good luck, I hope you find whoever did it."

I nod. Watch her return to work, see how her eyes slide occasionally in my direction, waiting for me to leave.

The afternoon is the gray, misty sort where it feels like night has not really left the sky and the day is darkening before it began. It's gloomy but no matter. October has always been one of my favorite months. The sharp angles of the trees are surprising in the landscape rather than depressing; a few stubborn fiery leaves flap about on the branches, holding on until the first storm rips them away and winter begins in earnest.

Pausing at the university gates, I inhale the dank, earthy smell of autumn; feel the cold reach into my chest, tickle the base of my lungs. I am checking for anxiety, but there is none.

STEVE WALKS OUT from the kitchenette, guiltily shoving a flaking slice of chocolate cake into his gob while looping his scarf around his neck. He stops abruptly when he sees me.

"Chief!" Crumbs fall from his mouth. He glances around furtively. "My cover will be here shortly."

"Get out of here, Adams, while you still can."

"Yes, ma'am."

He rushes to the door.

"And Steve?"

"Yes."

"The reports are done?"

"On your desk, Chief."

"Thanks. See you tomorrow."

He ducks out of the room, pulls the door behind him. I can hear his heels clopping smartly down the linoleum hallway toward the lifts.

The night shift are settled into their tasks, working in the half-light of computer screens. I retreat to the isolation of my office. The reports are laid out neatly; photographs peek out from between the pages. I run my hand over them, ease the pages apart. "Victim." "Cause of death." The words and phrases of crime, of murder, lift out from the text. A familiar sensation spreads over the side of my head, an itching, like a nettle sting. I trace my hairline, fingers featherlight over the scar, and a thin layer of moisture rises like hot breath over my skin.

Reaching down to my right, I open the middle drawer of my desk and move the files forward. A soothing wash of relief runs through me when I touch the glass. I don't have a drinking problem, but there are some days when I could happily succumb to alcohol's warm, soft oblivion. I lift the bottle away, unscrew the top, and take a few burning mouthfuls. Already, I feel safer. Or maybe the alcohol simply makes me care less.

That was the shining pearl of wisdom my shrink impressed on me before she gave the green on my return to work. Learn to care less, she'd said. I'm not sure whether she grasped the irony of her statement. I spend my days hunting people who have learned to care less, who have little or no empathy, to whom conscience is a foreign entity.

Frequently, empathy, caring, conscience, are the only weapons I have at my disposal that a killer doesn't. In my world, empathy is the secret weapon. I spend my time tracing other people's movements, questioning their motivations, striving to understand the importance of a particular but sickening ritual a killer has subjected their victim to. But I couldn't say this to the doc.

I told her, yes. I would learn to care less. I told her that I knew how to do that now. She looked so relieved. I had ticked the box for her. She could close my file. Write me up. Cured. Fit for work. She couldn't wait to get me out of her office. I couldn't wait to leave. Our minds in mutual denial, we almost fell over each other on the way to the door. "Call me if you have any more trouble," she'd said. I agreed, happy in the knowledge that neither of us meant a fucking word of it.

I spread the pages out over the desk and stare down at the contents for some time. My fingers rub small circles at my temples, but gradually I feel the urge to make some notes on the killer's profile.

I've barely started when the phone flashes on my desk.

"Sheehan."

There is a click and then silence. I push my notes away. Tension grows across my shoulders.

"Hello?"

The line goes dead. I put the phone down and stare at the screen for a few moments. It flashes again and I snatch it up.

"Hello?"

"Frankie. It's Baz."

Air rushes out of my chest. "Baz. What is it?"

"Priscilla Fagan. She'd like to come in tomorrow. To make a statement."

I rub a hand across my forehead. "Sorry. Who?"

"Priscilla Fagan. Peter Costello's sister."

Clarity. "Oh. Right. Of course."

A pause. "You all right? You sound a bit distant." I can almost hear him checking his watch for the time, see him frowning when he realizes it's barely five thirty.

"I'm fine."

"Right so."

He rings off, leaving me staring at the blank screen on my phone. I wait a few more moments to see if it will ring again, but when it stays mute, I drop it into my pocket and decide to leave.

CHAPTER 5

THE MORNING HAS been chewed up with paperwork and warrants. Frustration crawls over me, digs needling claws beneath my skin so that even a few hours' sleep does not free me from the feeling. I'm meeting Clancy in his favorite watering hole. It's lunchtime, but the pub has yet to fill with punters looking for a warm meal.

Clancy is buried in the farthest part of the room: a deep wood snug in low lighting next to the fire. I've not been here in months, but some things don't change. The same scrawny-faced man is behind the bar. He nods at me as I pass.

"Just a coffee, please, Enda."

He plucks a cup from a rack behind him. "No bother, Detective. I'll bring it over."

Clancy is focused on his pint. The long dimple in his cheek is sucked inwards, trapped between teeth.

I sit across from him. "Thanks for ordering the tox reports. That was remiss of me."

He shrugs. "No harm."

I'm not sure how to bridge the tension that's been growing like a tumor between us.

"Jack, I know you've taken a big risk putting me back on cases, but let's be honest with each other . . ."

He glances up. "Go on then."

"I may be unpredictable at times, but I'll do what it takes and you can't afford to lose that."

He leans forward, eyes round and intent. "Did it cross your mind that I actually fucking give a shit about you, Sheehan?" He shakes his head, takes a messy gulp of stout.

His voice is low as he speaks, as if we might have an audience, even though there is not a sinner in the pub apart from scrawny-faced Enda.

"Fuck. I know you, Sheehan. I knew that night when I was screaming down the radio for you to sit tight and wait for backup. I knew that you couldn't wait five fucking lousy minutes, you had to go in by yourself. Face a lunatic with only a phone as your defense. I knew that as sure as I know now that if you don't get back into work, you're lost."

It takes me a moment to clamber over the violent tumble of his words. Enda approaches, places my coffee in front of me. I grab at the cup and take a burning mouthful.

"I'm sorry," I murmur. A breath in the face of a tornado.

"Christ, Sheehan. I'm not looking for a fucking apology. There's a lot on the bloody line, 'tis all."

He doesn't need to spell it out for me. Sympathetic leave for me, only this time of the permanent variety, and early retirement for Clancy if things go arseways.

Silence spans out between us. Our relationship is not built for honesty; it's built for files, suspects, knives, gruesome, cruel acts. On our yellow brick road, the tin man doesn't want a stinking fucking heart; he wants an AK-47.

My phone rescues us both, and the expression of relief on Clancy's face nearly makes me laugh.

"It's Baz," I tell him, then answer.

"I've taken Mrs. Fagan down to the station. Or rather, she said she'd meet me there in fifteen," he says down the line. "She suspects one of them was screwing someone on the side. She didn't say which one, just mentioned a third party in the relationship."

My voice goes up a note of disbelief. "And she's still willing to give a statement to that effect?"

"Yup." He sounds ridiculously pleased with himself.

"She knows it might incriminate her brother?"

"Well, I didn't linger on that fact, but I'm sure she knows it won't paint him in the best of lights."

"Jesus. Whatever happened to blood is thicker than water?"

He laughs. "Depends how much shit is in the water. You wanna be there?"

"Yes. Definitely. You'll do the interview, but don't start without me. Give me half an hour."

Clancy is finishing off his pint. "So?"

"The husband, Peter Costello, it's probable he was having an affair, or perhaps she was. His sister, she wants to make a statement."

"Odd."

"Yeah. We'll take it slow, make sure it's not just a toy-sharing squabble left over from childhood." The pub is filling slowly. Road workers, filth and mud caked along the soles of their boots. High-vis jackets swinging open. They order pints of beer before food. Liquid lunches—no wonder the roads are gone to fuck.

"There might be evidence of domestic violence," I add. "An update from the postmortem. The pathologist said that the only way Eleanor's wrist could sustain that kind of fracture is if something had crushed it or smashed through the bone. The wounds in her abdomen, stab wounds—possibly the result of rage or frustration."

"Your money's on the husband killing her then?"

"There was nothing in her medical records at all that could explain those injuries. You have to be hiding something not to go to hospital when you've been stabbed."

"Shame?"

"I think so." I pick at the corner of a beer mat. "The very nature of domestic violence is that victims are often shamed into not reporting it. A successful, organized woman to the external world, Dr. Costello would have felt immense pressure to keep her abuse hidden. Factor in the likely bulimia—almost a confirmation of her own self-loathing—and you have someone who is extremely vulnerable to emotional manipulation and physical abuse." I meet his eyes.

"And him?"

I spread my arms. "Where is he? I'm not saying that an episode of domestic violence resulted directly in her hanging, only that evidence suggests someone was hurting Eleanor Costello on a regular basis."

"Why kill her by hanging, though? Surely if she'd died at his hands it would most likely be the climax of a rage-fueled fight. A crime of passion, so to speak. Hanging seems, well, a little passive."

I shake my head. "He could be into other stuff. We found something on the computer that suggested one of them used the Dark Web."

"Interesting." He's reluctant to offer support. He's scared. For me.

"Maybe she found something and he needed to make her death look accidental. Maybe he used the underbelly of the internet to hire someone to do it for him. It must've been so difficult, sitting in every day on your unemployed ass while your beautiful wife, who has her shit together so tightly that she can make herself throw up her lunch every day, heads off to work to pay the mortgage. Which by the way was just one year short of full payment."

He's laughing. The long dimple that runs down his right cheek deepens, and I get a glimpse of a younger man, a secret charm, a looker with a clever word. His head is bent, shaking from side to side. "I'm not sure he was that unhappy if he was balling some other bitch while she was putting her nose to the grindstone. Sounds like a good enough deal to me."

I throw the beer mat at him. "We don't know yet if he was the one doing the balling. And you know, there's not enough fucking"—I make quotation marks in the air—"'bitches' in this department, that's the only reason any of you pricks get to the top."

He's still chuckling, the wrinkles on his face darkening but at the same time softening, so unlike the dragging lines that pulled at the sides of his mouth the other morning.

"Go on," he says. "Whoever is at the other end of this doesn't stand a chance. If they weren't a murdering fucker, I'd feel sorry for them."

I can't feel sorry for anyone. I can't even afford to feel sorry for Eleanor Costello, even though the image of her slim, smooth body lying on the autopsy table is cataloged at the front of my mind. A flash of blond hair on the street is enough to make me see her congested face on that rope and from there imagine the struggle of her death. I can't feel sorry for her. To do that steers the investigation.

A piece of evidence is like a precious card, the face of which you must never reveal to your opponents until the last fanning out of your hand. Each interview you have the chance to gain a card, but you can only do that if you act like you're playing with nothing.

This is what I am organizing in my mind as I speed along Dublin quays toward the station. Traffic is heavy, and the occasional car creeps up from the underground car parks at the back of the Custom House, hovers on the roadside waiting for a gap in the convoy. I wave the odd one forward, mind half on the road, half already on the interview with Peter Costello's sister.

THROUGH THE REFLECTED window, Priscilla Fagan is knitting. There is an aggressive motion to the needles; she looks mightily pissed with something. I know she is working herself up in her head. This is a woman with stuff to say. Baz is pacing the corridor. He is practicing his lines. His questions. I've never seen him this anxious. I consider pulling him from the exercise altogether. Peter Costello's sister may crack open a window on this case. If he puts her on edge, that window will snap shut and no amount of prying will lever it open again.

This woman needs to feel in control; she needs to lead. By the end of her speech she'll well and truly believe she has solved this case for us. And she may well have done, but just not in the way she suspects.

"If you need to vomit, go ahead. I won't tell anyone." Banter. It earns me a dark look from beneath his eyebrows.

I want to distract him; he needs to get through the order of questions on the sheet I gave him. The exact order. If he fluffs it, we may need to call her in again, and a second statement can bring about all sorts of other issues. Like lawyers.

The pacing continues.

He takes a deep breath, blows it out, waves the three pages of questions through the stifling office air, glances at them again, then passes them to me. "Right. I'm ready."

"Great. She'll have run out of wool otherwise. You sure you don't want a fag? Very calming."

He's already at the door. I push a bottle of water into his hand. It helps to have a prop. He gives me a quick backward glance of thanks, and then he is in the room.

Priscilla Fagan looks like she's never cooked, eaten, or recommended anything other than pasta for dinner. Rolls of fat ring her middle, her breasts could comfort at least ten heads, and her arms are baker's arms, chubby, wide, and strong. She's in her midfifties, and there is not one rib of whitening hair on her head. Thick black waves arch back from her forehead and continue into a practical cut to her ears. She's the type of woman who'd roll up her sleeves and not blink an eye at gutting a fish; would know the correct way to pluck a pheasant, hang it, use every piece of flesh on its carcass and then some.

When Baz slides into the seat across from her and offers her his best charming smile, she gives him a look that says: *No point in trying that smile on me, sonny. I've more use of a new saucepan than I do the likes of you.*

The confidence dims on Baz's face. "Mrs. Fagan, thanks for doing this."

"I want to clear up a few things." She widens her mouth. A breath. She is about to launch into her statement.

Baz holds up a palm. "Would you mind if I record our chat?"

Her eyebrows shoot upward. "Isn't that what I'm here for, Detective?" No-nonsense.

Nodding. "Yes, yes." A green light sparks up on the side of the recorder. The cassette wheels start spinning.

He reads out the date, the reason for the interview; she is waving him along with her hand. Impatient. Before he takes a breath for the first question, she takes control. A smile creeps across my face.

"That woman was an out-and-out bad one. She was quite controlling, you know." She gives him a "Well, what do you make of that?" look.

Baz recovers well. "How long have you known Dr. Costello, Mrs. Fagan?"

She is relieved that he's not poured cold water all over her statement; that he appears to be joining her side, allying himself to her opinion. She leans back in the chair.

"Well, Peter met her at a charity auction—you know the ones, a nobody celebrity does the auction, et cetera. I can't remember what this was for, but his company was investing in a new drug and she was part of the research team. At the time, of course, she was a nobody and he was a somebody. Plenty of money to splash around on her, and like gum to a shoe, she made sure she stuck to him."

He waits for her to come round to her answer.

"He was well and truly smitten from the off, I could tell. He brought her to mine for the Sunday roast only the weekend after."

"So you knew her since almost their first instance."

She purses her lips. Disgust. "Unfortunately."

"When was the last time you saw Peter?"

"We used to meet up every couple of weeks in town, but now, with one thing or another, I haven't been in touch and I'm afraid it's been a bit longer than usual. Time gets away from you very quickly when you're my age, Detective. It must be over six weeks since I saw him."

"You didn't speak to him? On the phone?"

"It isn't a usual thing with us, chatting on the phone. I've tried him a couple of times. Left a few messages with *her*. She said she'd pass them on, but I've not heard a dicky bird."

There's a break in her voice, and Baz gives her a few moments to collect herself.

"How did he seem to you?"

Her eyes narrow. "Fine." She's defensive. "In fact, he seemed happier than he'd been in a long while. There was a bit of a chance of work coming up for him. He was pleased about that."

Baz shares her smile, a natural lead to the next question. "How did Peter lose his job? Was it the recession?"

"That and the rest."

Baz nods. Encourages.

"He invested in her stupid drug, didn't he? Lovesick fool. Worst investment he's ever made and maybe his last. No decent company will give him work after it." Her forehead crumples between her eyebrows. "It's really affected him, that. Over the last couple of years especially. He's proud of his work, you know. I'm sure that's what's made his health deteriorate."

"Peter is ill?"

She pulls a tissue out from under the cuff of her sleeve. "Terrible. Nothing they can pin down, but when I saw him last, he was awful shook."

Baz resists being led any further from his line of questioning. Mrs. Fagan is tiring fast and we need a body of information to work from.

"How about art, Mrs. Fagan? Was Peter an art enthusiast?"

"Strange you should ask, but he's gotten into a bit of painting over the last coupla years. Goes to a class once a week. Not that he's gifted, mind, sure he'd tell you that himself, but he likes to know how the greats did it, he appreciates the history, you know?"

"And Eleanor? Did she share the same interest in art?"

She shrugs. "Wouldn't know."

"Were they happy? How would you describe their relationship?"

She rubs her nose vigorously, the tip left glowing red when she finishes. The tissue is stuffed back up the sleeve again. Relaxed, honest, unconscious movements. Signals of truth.

"Strained. When I last saw them together, he could barely meet her eyes. But then—" She stops suddenly; her lip catches between her teeth.

Baz leans in. "Yes?"

"Sorry," he corrects. "You are probably parched. Here." He opens the bottle of water I gave him, fills a plastic cup, passes it to her.

She takes a sip. "Thank you. The air's dry in here." She's back on track. "Peter has had a few other problems."

"Oh?"

"They're a bit personal and he'll be angry for me saying, but when you said you had to take the laptop, I thought I'd tell you so you wouldn't get the wrong idea. He's just a man. They're all at it." She stops, remembers who she's talking to, then: "Sorry."

Baz spreads his hands. "No offense."

"The last time I was there—must be a good six months or so ago—he was in the kitchen making a cup of tea and I saw his hand-computer thingy, the tablet, on the side. I was considering getting one so I picked it up, and I don't know what I touched, but the screen filled with this"—she recoils as if confronted with the image again—"filth, is all I can call it. Porn."

"You didn't talk to him about it?"

Her eyes widen. Round. Horrified. "Would you? He's my brother.

No, no. I put the tablet yoke back and that was that. Never mentioned it. Just want to vouch for him, though, in case it puts him in a bad light. He's as straight as an arrow in every other way and the gentlest of souls. Peter wouldn't hurt a fly."

"And you think that Mrs. Costello was seeing someone else?"

She makes a snorting noise. "No! I'm not sure another man would've tolerated her snootiness. No. Peter. Peter is seeing someone else. He says it's nothing serious, but I can tell he's smitten. Maybe now he's free of that . . ." She pauses, then quickly blesses herself. "I guess one shouldn't speak ill of the dead, should they?"

"Have you met his new partner?" He's being charitable again. "Partner," not "lover" or "mistress." Words can win another's trust in many ways.

"No. And she's not that new. It's been going on quite a while. I've no idea why he hasn't moved in with her and sought a separation from Eleanor, but as I said, she was controlling. I was never happy with the power she held over him. Oh, she came across all meek and demure, but I can tell an actress at work. Sure haven't I had to do enough of it over the years."

Baz raises his eyebrows at her and it's enough to set her off again. "You don't stay married next to thirty years, Detective, by telling the truth, let me say that." She rocks back in her chair again, pleased with herself. "Amy. That was it. He mentions her a lot. Don't know a last name now."

"Do you think he might be with her now?"

She laughs. "I hope so."

CHAPTER 6

THE BONSAI IS already suffering. Eleven days since I brought it home. Twelve days since Eleanor Costello's death. Mrs. Fagan's interview was at once useful and useless. We have been unable to trace the history on the laptop or discover who his lover might be. There is still no sign of Costello; he has disappeared like a stone dropped in the ocean.

I have positioned the tree beneath the window. It has the best of Dublin beaming through the pane at it. It looks like it may well die on me. I stare down at it, armed with a glass of Rioja and a cheese biscuit.

The ambers and yellows of Dublin's nightlife play on the windowpane. Silver fog rolls up off the Liffey and into the chill city, a suitable backdrop for the night: Halloween. A few sirens sound off in the maze of streets below. Fireworks screech and pop in the distant damp sky; backyard fireworks that are launched by the light of family bonfires, children hidden behind plastic ghoulish masks. Trick or treat.

There are clippers on the floor at my feet, a tiny spool of soft thin wire, and a sachet of plant food. They've not moved since I brought the tree home.

Sighing, I put the glass down and collect the plant from the window. I thumb through the not insubstantial hardback I've bought on bonsai care. There is one chapter on maintenance. I should've checked the contents before buying it. It shows how to bind the tree, steer its growth. It talks of deciduous and evergreen.

I check the triangular label that's wedged into the soil at the foot of the plant. Evergreen. Of course it is—we're almost in November, and the foliage is still high. Ligustrum bonsai: full name. They are not unlike everyday trees, I'm surprised to learn. They're not dwarflike miniatures but are created by manipulating growth, pruning, so that they become shrunken versions of their optimum selves. On one hand, it feels wrong to restrict a natural thing's growth, to bind it and cut into its leaves so that its shape may be admired for neatness. On the other, I'm entranced by the aesthetics of it all.

The image in the book shows how my tree could look. I compare the two: Mine is unchecked, wild, unsculpted. Taking up the copper wire, I clip off a length. I lean back from the tree, take in its height, its shape; then, not really sure what I'm doing, wind the wire around a branch. Once the branch is secure, I bend, move the narrow wood, encourage, coax, persuade nature to work with me.

Afterward, I feel surprisingly satisfied, calm, in control. I fill a small jug with water, mix in the sachet of plant food, and tip it into the base of the pot. There. The tree already seems happier. I replace it on the windowsill, throw the remaining wine down the sink, and head for bed. It's only nine, but my body is heavy with exhaustion and sleep is tugging at my limbs.

My eyes have barely closed on the darkness when my phone rings. It's Clancy.

"You up?"

"Of course I'm up."

"What's new!" He sighs. "Listen, there's another body to look at. I'm not able to get there. At a blasted anniversary do and I've had a few too many. Pretty grisly this one, from the sounds of it. Take an empty stomach."

I push my legs out of the bed. "Right."

"And Frankie?"

"Yes?"

"It's quite close to your folks'."

It takes a moment for this to sink in, and when it does it feels as if an invisible hand is gripping my throat.

THE FIRE IS still smoldering, even though it's sitting in a pool of water. A pool that probably contains precious evidence and is now trickling away into the undergrowth, seeping into the warm earth, and feeding the scorched grass. The man responsible for the bonfire is apologizing for drowning the area so assiduously.

He had not reckoned on a murder scene, although what the fuck came to his mind when he saw that there was a body in the middle of his bonfire I don't know. I can understand where his instinct came from—he had thought only to try to save whatever or whoever was burning within—but it's clear that whoever is in the midst of the broken-down bonfire is dead.

The man, Mr. Quinn, grabs my hand, shakes it hard. I know his face as well as I know that beyond the whispering grass that brushes my legs is the very sand where Ireland's last high king defeated the Vikings. I know, in the winter, flocks of oystercatchers pick their way through cockles thrown up by the waters of Dublin Bay. I know, when the tide is out, at the southern end of the promenade there's a good chance of spotting the blackened wreck of the *Windrise* sinking for eternity in the brown sands. Clontarf. Home. My child self runs out from the darkness, into the summers of yesterday, tumbling, screeching toward the rolling bay. I hear her laughter fade into the darkness, fade to the sting of nostalgia.

"Frankie, how've you been, love? I thought it might be you." Mr. Quinn's face is grim.

I know every stretch of this coastline, every leaning tree and hedgerow that stands up against the might of wind tearing in from across the Irish Sea. I know Mr. Quinn is seeing the wobbling, sensitive child who cried so hard when her brother pinched her arm that she threw up.

Mr. Quinn works at Keegan's Garage in our little neighborhood. A grease monkey. He can't be more than fifty-five, but he's worked at the local garage since he was pimple-faced and sweaty-palmed. He's no family, not many friends apart from the Keegans, who have tacked him onto their life like a shadow; he's always there, always trailing somewhere behind.

His hands have kept my folks' old banger on the road for two decades. Even above the smell of the doused fire, I pick up the sour, metallic scent of oil that blackens the nails on his hands.

I remember those hands. One summer day I found a tiny brown rabbit alone along the side of the road. It sat quivering on the curbside outside Keegan's. I crept closer, saw its eyes were red and swollen. It didn't move, frozen with pain, ears flat on its back. Its rib cage flickered thinly beneath brown fur. I thought it had been struck by a car and, unwilling to leave it alone, called out to the nearest adult. Tom Quinn was bent over the bonnet of a van, but he emerged from under the hood, dirty-faced and smiling.

"You all right there, Frankie?" he shouted.

From my crouched position, I waved him over. At my side, he understood quick enough what the emergency was.

"He's got the myxi, love," he said.

In one swift movement he scooped the baby rabbit up. He didn't see that I followed him back to the garage, unwilling to be separated from my new charge, already imagining the rabbit well and deciding the best place in my room for it to sleep. I had no idea then what Tom was about.

If I close my eyes, the sound of the animal's screech still haunts me. My hands, too late, flew to my ears. The sound was brief, but the echo bounded about my head for the rest of the day, turning me inside out with fear. After, the rabbit dangling from his hand, he dropped its supple wasted body in the bin outside, and as he returned, he squeezed my shoulder.

"You saved her from a lot of suffering. Well done." Even at that young age I could tell he was speaking more to himself than to me. Solutions don't always greet us in the shape we imagine, but no matter the shape, they solve a problem.

The crowds must have been here for the bonfire, but now I can see more making their way down the promenade to join the queue of rubberneckers. My parents could very well be somewhere among the masses.

In the background, the sea is rolling on. The sound of waves turning on the shore, an eerie reminder that whatever heinous thing we discover here, not one ripple of the sea will be affected. It's humbling and oddly comforting. No matter how you've fucked up, your existence makes not a blind bit of difference to Mother Nature. And thank fuck for that.

Tom Quinn leads me toward the scene.

"It was a shocking sight, I tell you," he says. "I'd the parents take the childer away before they realized what they were seeing, but I can't promise ye that some of them didn't get an eyeful. Shocking. Just shocking."

The bonfire is an annual Halloween event for the town. Even though bonfires have been illegal in the Dublin area for years, in Clontarf the tradition rolls on and the Gardaí cast a blind eye. Local children build it on the wide stretch of sandbank sheltered by Bull

Island. I remember. The gathering of anything that might burn begins sometime in the middle of October. Businesses and neighbors contribute spare tires, fallen bracken, trees, pallets. It's all dragged toward the site, ready for Halloween night. The Keegans have always taken ownership of the event, and Tom, their trusted friend and colleague, lights the tinder at eight p.m., manning the fire until the last glittering ember goes cold.

"There was a bit of a heavy shower yesterday evening, and I reckoned on the stack being a bit damp, so I'd used a bit of petrol to get it started." He shakes his head, visibly paling. "I didn't know. I mean, I couldn't see anything in the stack. Now, though, you know yourself, there were pallets and the like thrown in and it was pretty dense all right. By the time I came up here this evening, sure, the night was already set in."

I put my hand out, squeeze his shoulder, a shadow of his actions years ago. "Don't upset yourself, Mr. Quinn. It wasn't your fault."

"Who'd do such a thing? People these days, there's some odd ones about. She must've been dead, though—surely? Whoever it is."

His face is pleading. He wants reassurance.

"She?" I ask. The sound of the dying rabbit echoes in my head.

He rubs a hand over his face. "It's often women, isn't it?"

I lift my eyes, try to read something other than confusion in his gaze. "Sometimes," I answer.

I lift the ribbon of crime-scene tape, duck beneath it, and wait for him to follow.

"How long after you lit the fire did it take to get to full blaze?"

"Well, 'cos of the petrol, now, not long. Maybe ten, fifteen minutes. There was a fierce northeasterly wind come across the bay and it took the flame to the side, like. That was the only reason I got sight of the body."

I turn, face into the wind, and walk toward the remains of the fire. The smell of burning flesh hits me in patches on the salty seaweed air.

A young uniformed officer greets me. I can see he's struggling with keeping his hand from his face. He wants to block the stench of charred flesh entering his nose. But professionalism or fear stops him.

"They're ready now, Chief."

Paramedics are standing, redundant, nearby.

"Should we send the ambulance on?" the officer asks. "I guess the city's van is on the way."

"No. The ambulance will do," I reply.

Scenes of crime officers move slowly over the area, collecting, gathering up the scene on film, in bags, on paper. Massive spotlights have been erected around the scene, and I spot Keith Hickey putting up a screen at the back end of the bonfire, but the wind is getting the better of him and the plastic flaps about unchecked.

I give Tom another smile, then turn my back on him. I know he'll creep forward. Curiosity or morbid fascination, whatever the fuck makes people want to stare at death, I don't know, but today that desire is playing on my side. I can't ask him to look, but I want him to see. There is little more telling than watching potential suspects view the victim. Their reaction can be enough to sway entire cases. In my view, there is no better test of guilt.

A white sheeting is laid down on the grass. I take out a tissue and press it over my mouth. The smell would not be so galling were it not for the knowledge that it's human flesh I'm inhaling, microscopic particles of the deceased clinging to the inside of my nostrils, lodging in my throat. I swallow.

They remove the outer layers of the bonfire, charred branches, half-burned pallets, the skeleton of an old mattress. Immediately, the forensic team are investigating, sharing thoughts with the fire department. Examining the course of the fire, the suddenness of the flames. Finally, they extricate the body. The arms are flexed in a pugilist attitude; bent at the shoulder, elbow, and wrist. Nitrogen, oxygen, human gases—the mysterious ingredients that go to make a person—expand;

internal pressure, along with muscle shortening and contraction, has pulled the limbs into the defensive state.

Along the rib cage there are long pink striations, gashes where the skin has shrunk and the underlying tissue has broken through, the subcutaneous fat becoming fuel for the flame. The hair has fizzled away. The head is flexed, chin almost to chest; more muscle shortening, or maybe an indication that the victim was dead before the fire was lit. Hope rises in my chest. It's a cruel kind of hope, but it would be merciful for the victim to have died before burning. The feet and lower legs are blackened but relatively whole and suggest that the victim was indeed female; the shoes are present, low-heeled, probably pumps. The ankles are thin enough to wrap a hand around. The team lay the body down gently as if the remains could light off on a breeze.

I move closer. On the wrist is a thick bracelet, partially sunken into the skin. It's one of those charm bracelets that have become popular over the past decade. Whoever has deposited the body was not so worried about the identification of the victim. A cold shadow passes over me. Whoever did this wanted a big show. It could be the killer acting out a fantasy. I sigh. Or it could just as easily have been a convenient manner of disposal.

I can sense Tom behind me, stretching, craning his neck. I move a little to the side.

The young officer approaches again. "Sorry, Chief?"

He's waiting for instruction.

I nod. "Yes. Get her to Whitehall. I'll follow as soon as—"

There is a deep groan at my ear. Tom is shaking his head. Stepping back. His eyes are on the charm bracelet. He holds out his palm, as if he can push away what he sees. Then all of a sudden his face crumples and he rushes forward so fast that I have to grab him to stop him falling onto the body.

"Amy! Amy! Amy! *Amy!*" he shouts. Over and over again. Each time getting louder.

The young officer helps me drag him from the scene, then hurries back to direct the remains away.

A tall, thickset man has pushed under the tape. He strides toward us, his face pale, his hands clenched. Eamon Keegan. The owner of the garage, community pillar, a constant at Sunday Mass, at the local, pint-and-chaser kind of man. His hands have worked over cars in Clontarf since before I was born.

"Tom!" he shouts. "Who is it? Tom?"

I turn to Tom. Keep my voice low. "Is that Amy Keegan?"

He doesn't have a chance to answer. Eamon Keegan has him by the shoulders. "Tom? Who is it?" He roars into Tom's face, tries to shake the answer from him.

I push between them.

"We don't know anything yet, Mr. Keegan. Please, step back behind the tape."

But Eamon Keegan pushes on toward his daughter and I'm a discarded thought in his wake.

"Amy? Amy?"

I run after him, pull at his arm. "Please, Eamon. Please, there's nothing you can do."

Whether it's fear, denial, or both, Eamon Keegan stops and I stand weakly beside him, a pathetic grip on his arm. The team pull a sheet over her body, and in a few swift moves they lower her onto the stretcher.

Eamon falls to his knees on the damp sand.

"Amy?" he whispers. Tears coat his face, shine wetly in the darkness.

Along the boundary of Garda tape, residents hover, watching, stricken at the hand of evil that's swiped at their neighborhood. I have a sense that the killer could be among them. I can feel the movement of their eyes as sure as if they were my own. The ambulance, light blinking silently, trundles across the bank and heads slowly southwest toward Drumcondra.

I rest my hand on Eamon's shoulder, feel the throb of grief quake under my palm. Amy. Amy Keegan. His daughter. I resurrect her from my memories. Round-faced, pale, a generous helping of freckles across her nose and forehead. Dark hair, the color and sheen of tempered chocolate. Later, older, I recall meeting her at the local one Christmas. I was on leave, visiting the folks. Almost thirty and a seasoned detective, by all accounts. I was skinny, casually dressed in a sloppy sweater and baggy jeans. But when Amy walked in, I recall feeling a flood of heat in my cheeks. She couldn't have been more than twenty, but she glowed with sophistication. Gone was the round-faced girl in wellies that I remembered. In her place was a petite, narrow-faced young woman, with stylish short hair and long smiling dimples.

My mouth is dry. It's all so close to the bone. Scraping, shuddering terror. I tip my head back. Just for a second. Inhale. My lungs, throat, seek air that is not tainted with the smell of burning flesh, but I can't rid the stain of death from my tongue. Amy. I try to think of what it was she did for a living. Something corporate. I recall my mother telling me on the phone that she'd had to move back in with her folks. An early casualty of the recession. Obviously, she'd not managed to move out since then. Or maybe she had and she'd been visiting.

Why would anyone want to harm her? And why subject her remains to this? Defilement. Eleanor Costello smiles at me. She is turning; the breeze blows her white-gold hair into her eyes. Laughter, then nothing. Amy. Peter Costello's lover. Mistress. Victim. Affair. Amy. Amy Keegan.

I lead Mr. Keegan's shaking form to the row of neighbors.

Tom stumbles behind. "Oh God. Oh God," he murmurs. "Moira. Oh God."

As I get closer, Moira Keegan's face emerges from the crowd, white and tight with fear. Terror rattles in her voice.

"Eamon? What is it?" she whispers. She swallows. "Eamon?"

The young officer is at my side. Face solemn. I am grateful. He breaks the news. Low-voiced and sad. A beat of silence and then a long trembling howl rips free from Moira Keegan's throat. She falls, like her husband did, crumples like a paper house.

I turn, move away, and the officer's voice trails after me. "Mr. Keegan, I'm sorry, but when you're ready, we'll need you both to answer some questions."

I walk from the scene toward my car. I shut the door, rest my arms, head, on the steering wheel. It's dark, a starless night; sharp eastern winds rock against the car, whip a light sheen of rain across the windscreen. The smell of burned flesh clings to my nose, my hair. I wipe a shaking hand over my face, open the window a crack, and breathe in the cold air that cuts into the car. My phone lights up, casts a white glow across the dashboard.

"Sheehan," I say, hand over the ignition.

No one replies.

"Hello?"

I wait for the answer—Baz, Clancy, checking in—but nothing comes down the line. I close the window, press the phone more firmly against my ear. Peering out into the blackness, I look beyond the hedgerow to the crime scene. Study the rows of people still gathered on the promenade, stupidly look for a light, a phone to an ear.

"Hello?"

In the vacuum of silence, a breath, a scratch of air.

"Hello? Who's—"

The call finishes. The number is blocked. I note the time, the duration, then pull onto the road slowly and head in the direction of the Keegan house. Once there, I park in a spot down a side street, lower the window, and light up a cigarette. It doesn't take long for Baz to find me. He parks, gets out of his car, and slips into the passenger seat.

"That was grisly," he says.

"Yep."

"Your hometown, huh?"

"Cozy, isn't it?"

"The mother. She's taken ill. Hospitalized." He turns in the seat.

I squint against the smoke rising from my fag and look out the driver's side window.

"I'm thinking she may be the Amy your Mrs. Fagan was on about," I reply.

"The affair?"

"Yes. Although we've shag all to connect the two. Here's hoping that Amy's mobile hasn't dropped off the planet too."

"I wouldn't be holding my breath," he says.

"I know."

In the rearview mirror, I see Eamon's broad figure coming up the road, head bent, shoulders rounded and low. Tom Quinn holds up one side of him, the young officer the other.

I go to step out of the car, but Baz holds me back.

"Frankie, maybe we should leave it? Until tomorrow morning maybe? You're not getting much out of them tonight. That scene was enough to break a man."

I pause, stare out at Mr. Keegan. A man I once thought a giant now looks like a child's breath could knock him down.

I nod at Baz. "I know. You're right. They're my neighbors, for Christ's sake. But the first twenty-four hours after a victim's body is found is crucial to a case. Our ears and our mouths work for one person and that is the victim. Nothing can get in the way of that. Not manners, not sympathy, not neighbors."

I wait for him to join me on the pavement, then walk toward the house.

Eamon stands at the door. The keys are in his hand, but for a moment it looks like he's forgotten how to be, how to move. He looks at once numb and wild. His eyes stare unblinkingly forward; his mouth hangs at the corners, his face pale, taut with sorrow. Every now and then, a tiny muscle jumps in his jaw and I hear the dragging sound of his breath.

"Eamon. I'm so sorry," I say.

I don't mean to, but my voice catches, and I have to mind myself, stamp down on a wave of emotion. I swallow. Heat prickles along my hairline. Then I say the words I hate, but I have to; memory is a slippery thing with little immunity against time. We need the answers as soon as we can get them.

"Eamon, do you mind if we come in? We need to ask you some questions."

Tom moves closer, puts a protective hand in front of his boss. "Frankie? Can't it wait, love?"

A bloom of shame heats my face. I'm disgusted with my own need for control, the desperate pull for answers, but I think of what's waiting for Abigail in Whitehall. Amy, or what's left of her.

I look at Eamon, then to Tom. "No," I say. "I'm sorry, but it can't."

Tom shakes his head. "Unbelievable," he mutters. He takes the keys from Eamon's slack fingers and opens the door.

CHAPTER 7

BAZ IS FROWNING. He's feeling the frustration of the case. A desperate part of me feels a certain happiness at his misery. His sense of impotence at being one step behind. Of what I felt when I saw Tracy Ward's murder. Watching a person die because you answered the clues a moment too late. I wince. It's wrong.

He drops back against the headrest. Sighs.

"She could be totally unrelated to the Costello murder. How are we going to connect the two?" he asks.

"Cell Site. Steve is following up with the phone companies. We have Peter's and Amy's numbers. We get a mast that both phones pinged from simultaneously and we have a link. Whether that makes her his lover is less concrete."

Amy Keegan was only twenty-nine. Eamon had last spoken to her on 10 October. She was studying medicine and working part-time in the city. She was busy. He tried to answer more of our questions, but shock slowly took over his speech, and eventually he sat in his living room numb and still. His regret at not checking up on her was all he could focus on.

Her phone was not found at her family home or her flat. In the few hours since discovering her body, we've been unable to locate it. Her wallet, her bag, and her phone charger are also missing. Her laptop was lying on her bed at her flat and had last been used three days previous. Despite the late hour, uniforms are already knocking on doors in Dublin; pulling statements from Amy's friends, classmates; catching any crumb that may lead us through her last movements.

"Maybe it's a coincidence that she has the same name Mrs. Fagan mentioned," Baz says.

"Nothing's a coincidence at this stage."

"We're dealing with a serial killer then," he states.

"Maybe," I reply. "If they kill again."

In my mind's eye, I see him in action. Delivering pain. He smashes down on Eleanor Costello's wrist. Her fingers are trapped beneath his palm, white with effort. The hammer bounces from the bones, recoils—the force is so strong. She screams, a hollow, ripping sound that's torn from the ends of her being. Neighbors will hear, but she will stay quiet about it. An accident.

When she passes out, he sits on the kitchen floor, her head cradled in his lap. His fingers mend, bind up her painful hand. He flinches as he touches the puffy flesh. It looks raw, sore. When she stirs, he offers her whiskey. She sips, groans, then passes out again. He carries her to their bedroom, lays her down, brushes her soft blond hair away from her sticky brow. He feels like a hero.

Could Peter Costello have done all this, to his wife, his lover?

I share a pained look with Baz. "It doesn't look good," I answer. "Sorry."

I know he doesn't want it to be true. He liked the sister.

"How we gonna find him?"

"He can't leave the country without his passport. I've had Steve notify all ports, airports, et cetera. At the very least we can probably say that he was around up until yesterday evening, when Amy's body would have been hidden in the bonfire."

"If he killed her," Baz replies.

"Anyway." I lighten my tone. "It's no longer our only lead."

"Oh?"

"We have Amy's computer." I put the key in the ignition.

He rolls his eyes. "Let's hope it gives us more than the Costello computer then."

Nerves are worming away in my chest, closing up my breath. It has to be enough.

IT'S WELL AFTER midnight by the time we get back to the city, but it could be trading hours in the case room. All hands are on the rolling deck, holding any scrap of a lead down until we can find a way out of the storm.

"Hey!" I call out. "Amy Keegan's body is with the pathologist and we should receive initial reports on the autopsy any moment. I want to get this out quickly, really get the public on our side, put pressure on our suspect, Peter Costello. Helen, you're on press, get on social media, keep updates light and frequent—every hour. Mention age, that she was a medical student, and we have the family's permission to use her name, so use it. Appeal for any witnesses to come forward."

Helen gives a sharp nod. There's not a bit of fatigue about her. The rest of the team have their top buttons open, ties loose, sleeves rolled up, and then there's Helen, shirt bolted up to the neck against the heat of the office.

I find Steve; despite the red-rimmed tiredness circling his eyes, he's in a more-than-usual smug mood. He's obviously had some good luck with Cell Site and Amy's phone and thinks I'm the kind to allow myself to relax in light of success. I'm not. But I humor him. He reaches over my head. From his fingers he dangles a note, torn from the yellow pad on his desk.

"You're so gonna owe me, Chief."

I walk by him, add new words to the case board.

> **Victim:** Amy Keegan. Remains found in bonfire in Clontarf. Possible connection to Costello murder. Student at UCD, medicine. Last seen by classmates 23 October.
>
> **Suspect:** Peter Costello. Forty-four-year-old Irish-Italian, approximately six foot three and of slim build. Missing but likely nearby.

I give him a half-smile. "I doubt I'll owe you anything, Detective. You're on the payroll. For the moment anyway."

He flaps the note around. "Cell Site came through. We've both Amy Keegan's and Peter Costello's phones pinging off masts all round Dublin city in the last four months."

He stoops over his computer.

"I've overlaid the hits on the map here. The last hit together was O'Connell Street six weeks ago. Nothing after that. We've got more than enough hits to connect them, though."

I peer into the screen. A break in a case is a gift. "Six weeks ago. So long?"

"It doesn't mean they weren't meeting in the last six weeks. He could have got wise. Changed his number. Changed his contract and no one knew about it."

I lean over, switch his screen back to the Cell Site lists. I shake my head. Peter Costello's phone stops hitting masts almost within a few days of the six-week period, but Amy Keegan's phone continues to be picked up at masts in Clontarf and UCD over and again up until she disappeared on 23 October.

Steve continues: "When Eleanor's death was proclaimed a murder, I ran Cell Site on Peter's phone almost immediately, and not a blip in the twenty-four hours prior to Eleanor's death. I hadn't reason to run them over a longer period up until now."

I'm nodding. "Right." Tight-lipped.

There's no denying the evidence is mounting, and there's nothing more damning than a suspect who's hiding, but I'm making mistakes somewhere. Wrongs are slicing across this case and I can't see the cuts.

"Don't look so dejected, Chief. We'll get him. On the Amy Keegan computer, I've managed to scoop out a treasure too."

I meet Steve's eyes, can't help the half-smile that's creeping over my face. "The Tor bundle?"

"Better. Her history was pretty clear, which got me suspicious, but a quick search gave me a hidden file with bookmarks and links to a number of chat rooms that she was pretty active on."

He opens up a minimized tab on his screen.

"This is one. Don't have her username, but I can trace the IP address of her computer to this site to the night before she went missing. The twenty-second. In short, the chat room shares concerns about suicide and death fantasies, and there was mention of the Dark Web, in particular a site called Black Widow."

I give Steve a wide smile. "You're worth your payroll after all."

He grins back at me. "Told ya."

"Get the Tor bundle set up on my laptop, please. Check out the Black Widow site and send me a summary as soon as you can."

"On it."

I hesitate over his desk a moment, remove my phone. "Steve?"

"You want the summary by this evening, right?"

"When it's ready." I tap the top of my phone. "Could you get in touch with my service provider? I've had a couple of calls through. One heavy breather. Blocked numbers. The provider might need a warrant to release the number. Let me know and I'll get the paperwork."

"Will do." He jots down my mobile number, tacks it to the bottom of his screen.

There's a soft knock on the door that somehow, even in the bustle of the room, silences the lot of us. When I turn, I see why. We have an unusual visitor. Dr. James stands in the doorway.

Briefcase in hand, she crosses the room with quick "don't mess with me" steps. The heads in the office follow her progress, but she doesn't blink an eye at any of them.

She places the case down on a free desk, clicks it open, and produces an envelope.

"Detective Sheehan," she says, "I thought you should see these right away, so I brought them round on my way back from Whitehall."

Baz is now at my side. I take the envelope, tear it open. Inside are numerous photos of Amy Keegan's body during autopsy.

She tilts her head, looks down at the first photo. "The lungs were clean. As was the larynx. No soot," she offers.

I lift my eyes from the photograph. "She was dead before the fire?"

"I still need to run CO hemoglobin levels to be certain, but yes, it appears that way."

"Cause of death?"

Abigail reaches out a pale hand, lifts another photo from the stack. "Here." She points to a wound on Amy's burned skin. "She had numerous injuries, cutting marks, knife wounds throughout her body. I would be tempted to say she bled to death."

I study her face. Brows drawn down over the bridge of her nose. Eyes flicking over the image still searching for answers, for clues.

"You don't sound very confident about that," I say.

A small purse of lips, then: "In a fire, the skin can split." She moves her finger down Amy's torso. "But here, there was some indication of vital reaction around the edges of the wound." She glances up to see if I follow. "The early stages of healing. These are recent stab wounds or deliberate cuts." She pulls back from the photo, meets my gaze full on.

"There were forty-seven injuries of this nature. That I can find. All antemortem. Before death. There could be more, but some areas of the limbs were too badly burned to examine fully. I need to put some samples under the scope to be sure."

"Okay," I say. I glance over her shoulder at Baz. He shrugs.

"Anyway," she continues, "this caught my eye." She pulls a photo from the bottom of the stack, holds it out, finger and thumb pinching at the corner. She gives it a little shake, indicating that I should take it.

Holding the picture in my hand, I look down at the image. It shows Amy Keegan's open mouth, lips blackened and thin.

Abigail points to the teeth. "Here. I ran a swab. Tests show hydrogen cyanide, but there's the remains of a paint along the gum line. Prussian blue. Heat would create a chemical reaction, reacting with the substance and converting it to hydrogen cyanide. Highly toxic, but a side effect of the fire; the paint was most likely applied postmortem. There's no trace of either compound in her blood or organs."

I look up, meet Baz's eyes. "I think we've just gone beyond coincidence."

Two victims known to the murderer. The term "serial killer" turns over and over in my head. A third murder will earn the killer the monstrous title. Do we truly have a serial killer on our hands? The need to lock our suspect down is charging inside me. The need to bring him in before he kills again.

THE BONSAI IS alive—that is something. I've bound more branches, curved copper wire through the thin arms of the tree. Guiding life where I want it, unveiling the tree's true potential as I see it. I've cut some of the branches back over the tiny green canopy. I'm not sure if I should find it worrying that I enjoy the process. I'm interested to see how the tree flourishes without what I've decided are unwanted appendages.

I remember seeing a cross section of a tree trunk in a war museum years ago. It showed a small explosion of blackness nestled among the tree's concentric rings. A black scar. I recall lingering over the wood; that dark smudge of suffering captured me, pulled me into its past like no other object in that museum. I wonder what scars my bonsai will preserve for me. What ones have I already cut out. If only humans could cut out their own suffering as easily.

Tracy Ward's file is on the coffee table. Open. Challenging. It's been more than four months, and I've yet to look through it. Alcohol can only go so far in bolstering my courage. A porcelain shield in the face of a terrifying army of nerves. I reach out and I see the tremble in my fingers against the pages. I'm careful to bypass the crime-scene photos. Skim over the statements, my statement. Not quite able to read through the detail. I can't remember giving it, but there at the bottom of the paragraph is my signature scrawled on the page.

There is a pocket in the file, titled "Evidence." I remove the contents, photos of the knife, rusted brown with blood, Tracy's blood, my blood. There are close-ups taken at the autopsy depicting abrasions, bruising, ligation marks, the victim's hands, her nails. Beneath three of the nails on the right hand, what looks like black soil or dirt, caked and pushing downwards into the sensitive nail bed. It could be blood, congealed, blackened. I tilt the photo, and there, I think I see it: a flush of blue along the nail bed. I bring the photo to my face, squint down, but whatever trick of light plays devil's advocate is gone and I don't see it again.

I feel a closing in on my chest, that shiver at the base of my lungs. For the briefest of moments, I see a different case, where Neary is not the killer, where he didn't hold that knife and savagely murder a young woman. The file shakes in my hand, and I close it, wipe my palms on my trousers, and get up.

I collect my glass and go to the window, light a cigarette. Breathe away the fear. I can't remember much after the attack. Clancy and Baz filled in the dark spots. Made the arrest. But without much effort I can still feel the knife slice through my skin. I touch the scar along my temple, a jagged ridge some emergency room doctor rushed to mend. Eventually, it had to be reopened, drained, to let badness and infection out.

All other injuries are of the invisible kind; the tip of the spinous process from the C7 vertebra has never rejoined and floats among the muscle, a constant, aching reminder.

I close my eyes. Remember. He smashes the heel of the knife against the back of my neck. I'm falling, like a house of cards, tumbling down. In the end it's what saves me. The fall. His next strike is with the blade. He aims for the jugular but gets the temple, just above the ear, enough to slice the scalp from the skull, to send the sound of the blade grating through my head for good. A sound that wakens me still, in the dark, in the day whenever a silent moment threatens.

He fled then, no time to finish the kill, although the desire was there. I could hear it in the groan of his frustration as blue lights lit up the dark hallway. The stink of Tracy Ward's blood was in my nostrils, iron, rotting stench, warm and wafting from the bedroom. The ambulance came and Clancy rushed forward.

Before I slipped into unconsciousness, I tipped my head back, saw Tracy's open throat, dark and smiling at me from the end of the bed. Her legs, arms spread, her head lolling, eyes wide with shock. Blackness was merciful, squeezing inwards, blocking out the horrific sight. I was too late. I couldn't save her. Couldn't unwind the seconds even though her screams still echoed around the house.

The wineglass shakes in my hand. My fingers are yellow-white against the stem. I put it down on the ledge. My statement. It's disjointed, repetitive, but remarkably professional-sounding.

Ivan Neary, the suspect, the killer. Caught at the scene, knife in hand, not even a minute after slaughtering that young woman.

Nothing can stand in the way of his conviction. As a killer, he has a worrisome profile. This is likely not his first kill.

Clancy has protected me from so many details. I'm made up of two parts: One side wants to know everything about this guy, from where he went to school to which hand he holds his dick in when he pisses. The other side of me is too scared to ask.

He needs to be sealed away tight for as long as possible.

The team is sure we've enough to convict him. I am a firsthand witness. My statement in court will put iron bars around the rest of his miserable future. Minimal words but maximum effect. The memory of the attack is a barely joined wound, opened with the merest of scratches. The defending lawyer will go straight to the weakest point. They will attempt to discredit me, my occupation. Pull up past wrongs. I'm not afraid of that. I'm afraid of seeing his face. Fuck knows I don't want to remember it.

I'm the only living witness to the horror he sliced out that night. There is something binding in that truth. The attraction to seek me out will grow in him the further time gets away from Tracy's death. I'm a living token of the murder. Proustian memory. I'm a direct path of access to the thrill of the kill.

Closing the file, I tuck it into my briefcase. In my bedroom, I check the suit I've had pressed and dry-cleaned for court tomorrow. Navy blouse, trousers. I remind myself that, although I'm part of the criminal proceedings, I'm doing this for Tracy Ward. I'll unwind those few seconds after he cut her throat. I will not run.

Climbing into bed, I pull my computer onto my lap and open the newly installed Tor bundle. Steve has set up a profile for me already.

I am TeeganRed. Seventeen. In the final year of school. I can't wait to leave my parents' house. I self-harm and have already been in two abusive relationships. I don't drink, smoke, or do any drugs. When I'm not at school, which is often, I spend most of my time on the internet, researching ways to draw the pain I feel out of myself. To match the physical pain with the emotional.

I have death fantasies. Several times a day. But I'm not suicidal.

Sometimes I go as far as buying equipment. I have a drawer under my bed. It contains ropes, pills, blades. Thinking about the different ways I could be killed makes me feel relaxed. Calm. But I do not want to die.

This is the feathered fly I cast out on dark waters. A lure for a predator. The persona is built with Amy Keegan's killer in mind. And it doesn't take long for my bio to attract a bite. I ask if they know somewhere I can meet other users, users with similar desires. They send me a direct message with a recommendation of what they claim to be the number one site for all fantasies and unusual desires. That site is Black Widow.

I leave the conversation quickly and, fingers cautious on the keyboard, open up Black Widow. The site has hundreds of threads. I'm not sure where to start, but as Eleanor was found hanged, I settle on a chat centering around suicide fantasies.

There are discussions on Cotard's syndrome, what death might feel like. I click on the first thread. There are almost 250 replies to the original poster's question, which asks simply whether their desire to experience death but not die is normal. The users spell out their fantasies, how they imagine their last breath feeling, the mix of euphoria and pain that might come as a result of it, how their family and friends would grieve. Many of the replies say that it's normal to want to feel missed, but a few get it. A few connect fully with what the original poster is asking. They too want to experience death but don't want to die.

I lie back onto the pillows and sigh into the white screen. The hunt for Amy's killer may not come from this lead; the search may become too time-consuming and yield little. But cases have been broken on less—whether it's a flake of skin, a strand of hair, or a digital footprint, all leads have to be followed to their end.

Over the next two hours, I manage to get through most of the members' usernames listed in the chat room. Numbers and obscure internet names swim before my vision every time I blink. Amy Keegan will not have given herself away easily.

I'm unable to find any name that hints at her own. Either she was not a member, or I can't see her. I let my hands linger over the keyboard for a moment, then go to the meet-and-greet section. I post a message introducing TeeganRed, then go straight to the last thread I was reading. The last person to add to the thread did so a day ago. Long enough in cyber time. I type out a response quickly, add to the thread. My hands are fast and nervous on the keys.

> Hey, I know what you're saying. It's like I want to know what it will feel like to die, and then to be nothing. Nothing but empty afterward. Must be weird. But probably kinda peaceful too.

I hit the return key. There is hotness over my cheeks. I feel self-conscious and scared all at once, as if I've invited some invisible danger into my home. The cursor blinks. No new comments. I close the program and the computer.

CHAPTER 8

STEVE IS AT my desk first thing. He's spent the early hours of the morning hounding my mobile provider, pulling the tail of whoever has been phoning me. The paper he holds trembles in his thin fingers. Overcaffeinated or excited, impossible to tell which.

"The number's pay-as-you-go. Recognize it?"

I take the sheet of paper. Shake my head. "No way to connect it to anyone?"

He holds up a finger. "Not the number, but most companies intermittently send signals to phones, collect information such as the IMEI number."

I scan down the page. See a fifteen-digit code at the bottom. The serial number of the handset. "And?"

"The phone belongs to Peter Costello. I've already checked the masts, where he made the calls to you from. First was off one at Ormond Quay and the second in Clontarf."

"That was the night Amy was found." A coldness steals into my bones.

"I'll keep Cell Site on the number."

The thought that Peter Costello was there that night. Watching his handiwork frowned over, picked through, studied. Seeing the confusion, the shock on faces. The detective bent over the wheel of her car, fighting down nausea and fear. The killer not able to resist a call, to get closer, put an ear up against the grief, the anxiety.

"Chief?" Steve tips his head, narrow chin angled to the side.

"Sorry, what?"

"Do you want me to send someone to watch your place?"

I grimace, shake my head. "No. They're only phone calls. I'll be fine. Just keep on that number. We find that phone, we find our killer."

"It's only been active on those two occasions, Chief. My guess is the SIM and battery are removed once the call is over."

"Just keep on it."

"Of course." He collects the paper and goes to leave.

"Steve?"

He turns.

"Good work. This is our first solid lead on Peter Costello's whereabouts."

BAZ TAPS ONCE on the door, then steps inside. "What are you doing in? I thought you had court today?"

"Not until eleven. We've no spare moments here." My scalp itches; heat floods out through my pores. I shrug out of my jacket, hook it over my chair.

"I've been reading through Eamon Keegan's testimony, and I've come up with a small discrepancy. Amy's phone records show that she called him on the eighteenth."

I'm removing my laptop, checking my status on Black Widow.

I look up. "But he said he hadn't heard from her since the tenth."

"As they say, that's the weird thing about murder inquiries, people tend to lie. Especially when they've something to hide."

I tip my head back, blow air out through my lips. "Goddamn human nature," I say.

It takes a particular kind of evil to murder their own. The image of Amy's hand comes into my mind, blackened, charred fingers straining inwards. No. Eamon Keegan couldn't do that to his own daughter.

"You're sure?" I ask him.

He shows me the printout from the phone company. The highlighted line clearly shows Eamon Keegan's number. The call lasted fifteen minutes and seven seconds.

Baz gathers up his stuff. "I guess this puts Eamon Keegan on our suspect list."

"He'd just discovered that his daughter had been murdered, her body dumped in a bonfire. No. I can't believe he could do this. Maybe I shouldn't have interviewed him so soon."

"He seemed pretty sure of the last time they spoke, Frankie. I replayed the interview. You asked him the question twice. According to friends at the uni, she was last seen and heard from on the twenty-third. Eamon says *he* last spoke to her on the tenth, three weeks before she turned up dead. Now we find that he did in fact talk to his daughter, only a few days before she disappeared. On 18 October, the day before Eleanor Costello was murdered."

I click open the Tor bundle, go to the Black Widow site, check if there've been any nibbles on the line.

Baz continues. "So, should we get Keegan in for questioning this afternoon?"

"No," I hear myself say.

"We shouldn't ignore that he lied. Even if it was his grief talking—which, fuck, you know, you're right, would be understandable—we can't ignore a missed step in the timeline."

"All right. Send one of the officers to check it out. A few questions, that's all. I'm not going to put him through the wringer with this again."

Baz sighs, drops his notes on the desk, looks down into the screen. "Any luck with Black Widow?"

"Nothing to go with yet." I scroll through the thread, one hand on the track pad, the other massaging an ache over my temple. "All these people wanting a lick of death. Why?"

Baz moves to the chair on the other side of the desk. Sits. "An adrenaline spike? The desire to relinquish control?"

He pauses; the muscles in his face drop, soften. "When we were kids, there was a spot in Glendalough, where the river passed through two mighty walls of rock. The drop must have been near on fifteen feet. Me and my friends, we'd sometimes spend the day there, taking turns leaping into the water; weightless, terrified, and freezing our nuts off. Every time I went over that edge—every time—I wasn't sure if I'd come back up. If I would die. But every time, I surfaced, Christ, the buzz, and I'd be outta that water like a scalded hare to throw my skinny, short life to the gods again. It was some rush."

My fingertips roll over the thin ridge of scar tissue. Seek out pain. Ease pain away. "Maybe there's a part of me that wants that."

I stare into the screen, the numerous threads asking for pain, the thrill of pain. Describing in desperate, frightened words their fantasies and the confusion that comes with them. I think of the court case today, the zigzag of emotions that draws jagged lines across my nerves, but also the pull, the urge to see it through, the desire to push ahead, pursue, get a foothold.

I drop my hand, leave my temple aching.

Baz tips his head. "What do you mean?"

I search for the right words. "Maybe I seek out fear. Sometimes, it feels as though I can't help but look over the precipice."

"Looking is not jumping."

There's a timid knock on the door.

"Chief?" Paul's round face appears. "We've had an e-mail with a link to an attachment," he explains. "It's a video. It appears to show Amy Keegan in some distress." His voice is desperate, if not a bit scared.

When I reach his desk, he pushes back from his computer. Paul manages PR, all the ins and outs with the public. All the bullshit and the abuse, rarely the good. On his screen is a video he's paused, mid-shot. I lean in, lighten the screen. Baz stands behind me.

"When did it come in, Inspector?" he asks.

I hear Paul swallow.

"We've been swamped. I'd been dealing with the calls first and only got to the e-mail in the last hour."

"When did it come in?" I ask again.

"Five past five this morning. Probably one of the first responses, it got a little buried in the rush. There's no trace on the IP address, so I guess it's encrypted or something."

"It's come from a Dark Web user," I say. "You've attended all our briefings, Inspector?"

"Yes."

"Well, then, pay fucking attention. You played it?"

"I wanted to wait, Chief. It looks like . . . like it might be a snuff movie."

A coldness runs across the back of my neck. "If so, Inspector, we're about to witness our biggest piece of evidence. So hold on to your stomach and hit play."

As if captured by the devil, Amy Keegan's death plays out before our eyes. A live recording. The date, a white flicker in the corner.

If there was any doubt about the authenticity of the video, the final seconds of Amy's death as filmed by the killer discount it. He remains hidden behind the camera, but I can hear his breath slow, deepen; his face close enough to hers that he snatches her final exhalation. Her pupils constrict; then the black center widens, languid and sure, stretching over the light blue of her eyes. Fixed dilation. An almost certain symptom of death. There is a bounce in the camera as the killer fumbles to turn it off; then everything goes black.

"Fuck me," Baz murmurs through his hand.

We're all captivated. With horror. With shock. Nausea is churning in my stomach. Heart thumps in my ears. There are dots shooting across my vision. I blink.

Baz turns suddenly. I must look pale because he presses his lips and asks, "You okay, Chief?"

No one could guess how much effort it takes for me to smile. "Time of death is no longer a mystery," I say.

Baz nods. "Sunday, 30 October. After Eleanor. Makes the window of opportunity pretty tight. To get the body in the fire, all the way to Clontarf. If, indeed, they had to travel."

The room in the video had blue walls. A bedroom. The decor seemed a little dated. Quaint. The killer hadn't bothered to hide the design of the duvet cover, a dark blue floral swirl on a white background. There was clear plastic sheeting spread over bed and carpet.

Amy remained silent as she climbed onto the bed. There was an edge to her movements, but also the briefest flit of a smile tracing the line of her mouth. Then came the moment when the balance seemed to tip. Tied down, her struggle increasingly frantic, a desperate kind of shrinking when the knife approached, her eyes white orbs of fear.

From somewhere to the right, there must have been a window, as a thin strip of white-gold light split the bed diagonally from the top of Amy's pale toes right across her body to where her left hand was tied, wrist raw and bleeding. During the video, when the pain seemed to overwhelm her, her face turned toward the light. I imagined she was willing the world to find her, to rescue her. Then a gloved hand would steer her face back toward the camera, toward further torture, and her body, arms tight as cable wire, would press into the mattress.

Besides the horrific nature of the film, another thing was startlingly obvious. The room looked nothing like the interior of the Costello home.

"Worth rechecking the Costello house, see if there are any similarities with the rooms?" Baz asks, still staring down into the blue room.

"No point. The date is after we discovered Eleanor Costello. We've had two uniforms there since."

"Unless the video wasn't recorded live," he counters.

"Steve?"

Steve shakes his head. "Looks like the genuine article to me, but I'll check."

"Break it down. Scene by scene. It has to give us something," I say.

I see Steve swallow.

"You okay?" I ask.

He frowns, all manly, makes a pathetic kind of snorting noise. "Sure, why wouldn't I be?"

"Right, so. Get on with it."

I move to the case board. The frustration at not locating Peter Costello is a titanic fucking ball bearing banging round my head. He can't hide forever. I draw him up on the board. Under his name I write, "Dark Web," "Cell Site connecting him to Amy." I bring the pen to my lips, study the information. Then I add the two silent calls from Costello's phone, the locations, the times. I move toward the door, shrug into my coat, and Baz arrives at my side.

"Tom Quinn? You want me to cancel his interview?"

Tom. I see the tiny rabbit cupped in his hands; then the body, dropped in the bin, discarded like a worn dishcloth. But then I see him standing in Keegan's Garage, a full smile white against the dirt and oil on his face, sleeves to the elbows, arms folded. A hard worker. The face of home.

"We need to start somewhere, Frankie," Baz urges.

"Bring him in, but I'll do the interview. Peter Costello is still our prime suspect. Our pursuit of him mustn't waver." Frustration and anger press my hands into tight fists.

Baz is following my thoughts. "Maybe he did switch SIMs or got another phone. Eleanor was onto his affair, so he got rid of the old one?"

I want to say yes, I want to agree, but something's not quite right.

I close my eyes and Amy's lifeless face looks out at me. He, the killer, reaches up, switches off the camera. He likes to have a moment with the body afterward, linger over his work. The stink of her struggle, her panic-soaked breath, is heavy in the room. He rubs sweat from his eyes, then leaves her, lets her tired body rest. He makes a cup of tea, smokes a fag. Imagines how else he can draw out his pleasure.

The idea comes to him as he lights the gas for the kettle. He finishes his fag by the window. Outside, kids are dragging driftwood up the beach toward an unlit bonfire. He remembers Amy mentioning that her village celebrated similarly. Kids, families, loved-up couples, warm against the chill Halloween night enjoying the bonfire. Jealousy is sudden and violent around his throat; bitterness stings his mouth. He moves quickly.

My head is shaking. "So, if Peter Costello murders her, then crams her body into an as-yet-unidentified vehicle, drives north to Clontarf, where he might easily locate the bonfire. Waits for his window, which is no more than three hours between when it gets dark and when the fire is lit. He drags the one-hundred-twenty-eight-pound body of Amy Keegan out of the car and spends time in the dark hiding her deep in the firewood. It's raining slightly, so there's not many out on the promenade, and anyone there assumes he's adding to the fire.

"He buries her in the midst of the bracken, wood pallets, tires, and the like. Stays among the crowd for some fucked-up kicks, then slips away in the mayhem that ensues?"

Baz rubs his chin. "It sounds mad enough to be true."

He breaks away, collects his coat. "I'd better get out to the Costello house, see what's what. Tom Quinn will be here by the time you get back."

We're both mentally and emotionally drained from what we've witnessed, and it's barely half past ten. In a normal job, you'd be awarded a course of psych therapy for what we've just watched, but instead I move to the door, pick up my bag, prepare to leave for court.

"I'll walk you down," I say to Baz. "I've a half hour to get to court. Clancy will be smoking himself into emphysema if I don't hurry." I make light of it so I can feel some thin rein of control between my fingers.

"From one sociopath to another," Baz says as he opens the door. I step out into the corridor.

When we get to the exit, he squeezes my shoulder; his long square fingers pulse briefly against the skin and bone of me. I try not to pull away, reward him with a tight smile.

"Call me with anything new," I say.

"Will do, Chief," he answers.

WHITE VANS ARE crammed up along the quays, satellite disks spinning on their roofs. The reporters wait, twitching, anxious, eager for a shot of the perp or his lawyer. The prosecutor stands for a few seconds on the steps of the court, addresses the crowd. Cameras collectively swing about, seeking anything of interest. We are sitting some way down the quay, Clancy and I, watching the commotion, the hype.

"You could go in the back way?" Clancy's voice is hopeful.

I have to swallow before I can speak; my lips are so dry, they sting and peel apart when I answer.

"No. The public need to know that their streets will be safe from at least one more killer. The case needs to get some coverage. PR is always good."

"Fuck fucking PR," he growls.

I get out of the car and squint against the cutting wind that's rising from the Liffey. "Come on, Jack. You know how these things work."

"It's different this time."

"Why? Because I'm one of you? Not a faceless woman that we've scooped up from the floor, untangled from a beam, or dredged from a lake? You always make a statement after one of these cases and today should be no different."

He flicks his wrist. Checks his watch. The prosecutor has gone in. The reporters have turned their backs on the steps, lit fags; are leaning up against their vans.

"We'd better get inside."

I walk away from the car and the movement draws attention. A photographer kneels, balances the lens at the right angle. Click. It sets off a series of flashes, and a cacophony of questions roars out from the reporters. Clancy shields me with his arm, but I try to stay ahead of him. I want to appear tall, confident, uncowed, even though I can feel the tingle of panic sparking in my toes and fingertips, the trip in my breath and the way my throat is sticking at the back of my mouth.

THE ROOM IS packed. The press have done a good job of teasing out excitement from the public, of whetting the appetite, stirring hunger for justice. It has helped that Tracy was young, only twenty-two, just returned from her gap year, the world at her feet and she about to step on it. Her parents have shown a united front in the media, the mother red-eyed and pinched with grief, the father hoarse with sorrow and determination.

Prosecutors couldn't ask for a better case. Throw in an assault on a senior member of the Gardaí, not only that but a female member, and you've got the kind of drama that movies are made of. Both public and law firmly on one side, the villain on the other. But the job of the court is not to play into that drama.

In reality, court is a monotonous trudge of facts and silences as lawyers scrabble to catch up with their notes and judges read through evidence and statements. However, if there *is* drama to be had, cases such as this are where it's at. A killer caught weapon in hand, fleeing the scene, witnessed by another victim but still professing innocence, will call on the lawyers to use all their legal trickery to win. There is a good possibility that this monster will smile as he's led away after a verdict of not guilty. And that is something that can't happen.

MY HEAD ACHES; my forehead feels like it's knotted into folds of lead above my eyes. The crowds of people we managed to dip through on the way in close around us, but Clancy barrels onwards, shooing away cameramen as if they were flies.

"That was a fucking joke. What are we working for, eh?" he snarls. "A bunch of Mickey Mouse arseholes in suits."

I can't answer.

"I mean, we were right there. Weren't we? Self-defense, my hole," he continues, yelling over his shoulder. "We were right fucking there. Seen him with our own bloody eyes." He pulls a packet of cigarettes from his pocket and jams one in his mouth. "Fucking pile of shit, that's what it is."

I push forward, reach his side, say anything to get him to shut up. "It doesn't mean anything. Of course he'll say he's innocent."

He gives me a fierce look out of the corner of his eye. "The fucker was caught red-handed. It's absolute bollocks." He slices the air with his hand. "Four months waiting for that bullshit. Look at the evidence!"

"The judge has to look at all angles. At least he was denied bail. It's a wobble, that's it. All cases have them."

"It's a fucking insult. Here, the car's over there." He nods to the car across the road. A couple of reporters are leaning up against the hood.

We are breaking through the swell of people outside the courthouse, stepping onto the road. They are waiting for any glimpse of the suspect, who has long since been led out of the room and shepherded safely out through a side door.

Clancy darts across the road, waving at the traffic as if the will of God would stop cars for him. The dark navy of his coat flaps around him as he waits for me on the other side. My foot has barely left the pavement when the crowds, seeking Neary's lawyer, swell around me again. I struggle to keep my balance, putting my hands out in case I fall. Someone grabs me, stops my tumble. They stay close.

Icy waves roll down my arms, my back. I turn, but whoever was there has rejoined the crowds. Collars are up against the cold, backs turned on me, facing Neary's lawyer, who's making a dramatic speech from the steps.

I hurry across the road and stand in front of the car. From this vantage point, I get a clearer view of the madness unraveling outside the courthouse. No one looks in my direction.

"You right?" Clancy barks, impatience straining in his voice.

"Yes," I say. "Fine."

I get into the car, eyes peeled, not quite sure who or what I'm looking for. I watch the damp streets of Dublin drift by through the pale reflection of my face, hand pressed to my mouth. Peter Costello's name echoes through my head. It tangles with Tracy Ward's and Amy Keegan's. I think for a moment that there may be a chance that Neary didn't do it. That maybe the killer I'm hunting now is also Tracy Ward's killer. I take a breath. Shiver. No. Neary is guilty. No one else could have been involved in that murder. I blink hard, shut away the idea, and Eleanor Costello's smile widens in my mind.

CHAPTER 9

TOM QUINN WALKS into the case room, head bowed, a heavy black duffel clutched to his stomach like a shield. His feet scuff the carpet as if testing the solidity of the floor before he moves forward. As he moves, his eyes skirt the room: the desks, the team busy on phones and computers.

He's wearing a gray suit; the shirt collar is too tight on his neck, and rolls of stubbly skin sit over the top of the stiff material. He looks terrified. I hover at the coffee machine. I'm not sure caffeine will help him, but a stiff drink is not something I'm able to offer. At least prior to the interview.

"Would you like a coffee, Tom?"

I hear the shake in my voice and realize I'm frightened too.

He accepts the coffee, two sugars—a rural man's quota—with plenty of milk.

As he stirs the hot drink, I make a sweeping gesture over the room, noting, gratefully, that someone has thrown a cover over the case board.

"This is the team who're doing all they can to apprehend Amy's killer."

As I say the word "killer," the corner of Tom's left eye tightens briefly, as if he's expecting a blow to the side of the head. I'm moving through the office. Steve moves in parallel, on the other side of the office. He'll wait in the viewing room, recording, getting papers ready.

"Anyway," I say. "Thanks for coming in, Tom."

He pulls at his shirt collar. "Amy was like family to me, I want to help."

I nod, point him through the office. "I think the interview room is ready."

"Right, so," he says. I can see him emotionally picking himself up, dredging through his adrenaline reserves to get over the next two hours.

The tape is running. Tom sips at his coffee and settles his large frame into the plastic chair across from me. He glances around the room, stares at the mirrored window.

"Just like the TV," he says.

"They do get some things right."

He gives me a wary smile. "What is it ye want to ask me, Frankie?"

I smile back. Hold up a finger, then point to the rolling cassette. "Wednesday, second of November, two p.m. For the purposes of this interview, I, Detective Sheehan, am interviewing Mr. Tom Quinn. Work colleague of the victim's family."

I meet Tom's eyes. His face is solemn.

"Mr. Quinn, you have the right to a lawyer. You're not under arrest. However, it's important for you to realize that this is a murder investigation and therefore anything you say will be taken down, recorded, and could be used against you in a court of law. Do you understand?"

He sets his jaw. Clasps his hands. "Yes."

I get straight to it. "When was the last time you saw Amy?" It should be a comforting, easy question. A softball.

He runs a hand through his hair. "Oh, I don't know now. Could it be as far back as the summer?"

I give him a little more time. Leave a gap, wait for him to fill it.

"She came home sometimes from uni but, you know, didn't come down to the garage often," he adds.

"Eamon must have been so proud that his daughter was studying medicine?"

He blows air through his lips. "Christ. Yes. The sun couldn't shine brighter than Amy in her daddy's eyes. And, to be fair, she was very bright. But she barely had her foot in the door at some big company, and the recession came and took a big ol' bite out of her future." He shakes his head. "Didn't stop Amy, though. She kicked her pride into the gutter, ate up her failure, came home, and started over." He meets my eyes. "Takes guts, you know."

I do. "So she moved back home." Keeping him on track.

"Yeah. Moira was delighted, of course, and then last year she got a place as a mature student in UCD. They were made up. Then she got herself a wee flat in the city. It was hard, though. Money-wise for them, I think."

"Oh?"

"Amy wasn't the best with cash. She never seemed to have enough and Eamon never seemed to stop forking out." He frowns. "That sounds bad now. She was a lovely girl, though. Just lovely."

He nods, sniffs. Rubs his fist under his nose, then takes a slurp of the coffee. He takes a deep breath.

"I was as proud as any of them of that girl," he says.

I steer the topic away gently, like easing off a Band-Aid.

"On 31 October, can you remember your activities? Can you take me through your day?"

He grasps the topic, staring sightlessly at some point above my shoulder.

"I got up the usual at seven to open the garage. We'd a really full day, always the way when the weather changes, people get their tires checked and changed for winter and all that. Eamon and Moira weren't around. They do trays of goodies for Halloween. Toffee apples and other sweets for the kids. They headed to the shops to sort the stock out."

I smile, picturing the trays of apples at the annual bonfire, shining with thick toffee sauce topped with sprinkles. It was a highlight in my Halloween childhood memories.

He continues. "I went to check the bonfire after work about four, to see how damp it was, 'cos it'd been raining on and off for two days. I remember thinking, 'I'll need to help it along a bit to light.' I also like to check that the kindling is weighted down correctly, so I sometimes move a few of the tires about—that's so the wind coming in from the sea doesn't scatter the fire."

He looks up, guilt creases his brow. "Then I did head for a swift pint at the local, and sure, that took me up to eight."

Cards tight to chest.

I am nodding, encouraging.

"It was quite dark, you know." His voice cracks, and for a moment I panic, thinking that he may break down and cry. But he coughs, takes a drink, and goes on. "I checked that everything was all right with the bonfire. It seemed grand. We set out the canteens of hot chocolate and apples, as we've done for many a year. Lined up a few fireworks, and when folk started to arrive, I lit the first tire as normal and lifted it as far into the bonfire as my pitchfork could reach." He looks up at me. "Like I've done for well on thirty years, you know."

The image he paints is the image of my childhood. The moonless October night, the flaming hoop of the tire approaching the kindle.

One side of Tom Quinn's body illuminated against the flickering orange flames, and occasionally I can see a streak of black smoke ripple out over the tongues of fire. The tire is placed down, and it seems that, in no time at all, the entire thing is lit up, giving off waves of heat and showers of glittering sparks that rise into the dark night.

I clear my throat. "Tom, did Amy have any enemies that you know of? Someone who might've wanted to hurt her?"

He looks down at his hands. "None. She was a frail sort, Amy. But only really when it came to her own demons. She wasn't a pushover, to be sure. Respected, like."

"How about arguments? Disagreements?"

His hands work over each other on the table. He shakes his head.

"Anything. Even if it seems trivial. It might help us understand how this could have happened, Tom. Anything."

"A couple of weeks ago, I overheard them arguing. On the phone."

"Who?"

"Eamon and Amy."

"A fight?"

He runs a hand over his face. "Family stuff, mostly. She hadn't been home in a few weeks, and Eamon was on her case about owing her mam a visit. But Amy liked to say some provocative things when she was backed into a corner."

"Provocative things?"

"Suicidal thoughts, harming herself, and sometimes—" He breaks off, looks to the ceiling. Redness floods into his cheeks. He looks briefly up at me. "Sometimes things like who she was with. She knew how to push her dad's buttons. I don't think she could help herself."

"What else was said?"

He blows air out above him, shakes his head. "I don't know. Eamon, he was pretty upset afterward. Told me about it. She was going on about an affair she was having with some married man and that he loved her but the wife was one of her lecturers. She was off to some concert or other with him, a tribute band of a folk singer she liked, and needed money for it."

I glance at the window. "He didn't say who it was she was having the affair with? Did she give a name?"

He shakes his head. "Not that Eamon told me, no."

"Do *you* know who she could have been seeing?"

He smiles. "Sure lookit, my life rarely leaves the garage."

I keep pulling the thread, hungry for something on Peter Costello. "Can you remember anything else about that conversation?"

His eyebrows pull down; he shakes his head. "Only now, that the wife knew about it and didn't care."

"You said she was like a daughter to you." I reward him with a soft smile. "The last few times you saw her, did she seem happy?"

"Happy?"

"Yes. Happy. Content. How did she seem to you?"

His bottom lip juts out. Thinking. "She seemed happy enough, yes. Maybe, a bit distant now."

"Distant?"

"You know yourself. Home from uni for a weekend, probably eager to get back to her life, like."

"How about friends? Locally. Or even boyfriends?"

"Well, now you have me, Frankie. I mean, it sounds like she had her hands pretty full in that department with this other fella, to me."

"No one ever visited, came to the house, picked her up?"

He looks down at his hands for a moment, then shakes his head. "I don't think so. Sorry. I'm not much use to you now, Frankie."

"That's grand, Tom. You're doing well."

The corners of his mouth begin to twitch. His eyes water. He glances round, a flash of panic on his face that he may cry in front of me. He coughs into his fist, blinks a few times, coughs again.

"Sorry about that," he says.

I reach across the desk; my finger hovers over the record button.

"Interview terminated at 2:25 P.M." I stop the tape.

He looks up at me. "Sorry."

I extend my hand. "That's okay, Tom. You've done your best."

He grips my fingers and squeezes them as if he is trying to bolster me, urge me on, set me to task.

"I hope you catch whoever did this. Eamon Keegan is a broken man, he needs this person caught."

Trepidation whips about in my stomach. I take a breath. Nod.

"We all do."

THE DOOR HAS barely closed on Tom Quinn when I turn to Steve.

"Run a check on Amy's finances. Bank statements, cards, credit check if you can wing it. Where did her money come from? Was she in debt?"

He leans back into the seat. "Is he a suspect?"

I touch my fingers to my lips. "No. It's not in him. Lying, maybe, but not murder. No. He implied that Amy might have had some money troubles. There could be a motive there. And where there's a motive—"

"There's a murderer," Steve finishes.

I fish for my cigs in my pocket, then start for the coffee machine.

Steve follows me. "The dad, Eamon, admitted speaking to her on the eighteenth."

I feel a lurch in my chest. It hits the back of my throat. Mentally, I cross my fingers. Hope that it corroborates what Tom Quinn has just told me.

"And?"

"They had an argument. About her not coming home enough that escalated into her telling him that she was having an affair with a married man."

I let the air out of my lungs. I nod. "Tom said as much. Helen?"

She looks up from her station. "I'm just working through the CCTV on Peter's whereabouts," she says quickly.

"Can you take over on the Black Widow site? Username TeeganRed. I've made a start, but I think we're going to need more engagement with the other users on the site."

"Engagement?" She grasps her notebook.

"Have a look. You'll get the idea. Any bites, let me know immediately. Steve will get you the passwords; any problems go to him."

As a case gains momentum, the concept of working nine to five becomes just that: a concept. With the appearance of Amy Keegan's body and the horror of that video, the pressure to uncover all evidence, investigate each footprint of crime as soon as possible, mounts. Each day that passes causes valuable clues to be lost to the mouth of time: DNA samples disintegrate; bodies decompose; statements vary, are revisited; events are reimagined.

But somehow it's quiet and dark again. Somehow another day has dragged to a close and my body is beginning to break under the demand of sleep. I decide to decompress, take some notes back to the flat, catch an hour or two of rest and wash the residue of the Ward case from my face, my eyes.

Baz has offered to drive me home and is waiting in the street, engine running, white clouds of choking vapor smoking out from the exhaust.

I slide into the passenger seat as I finish a call. Baz meets my eyes. "Priscilla Fagan again?"

I nod. "She's set up a website and a Facebook page. She's doing a better job looking for him than we are, it seems."

He rubs a hand over his jaw. "Strange."

I clip my seat belt across my chest. "Not very. She feels guilty. Or rather her brother's guilt."

"You think?"

I shrug. "She must know it doesn't look good."

Baz leans forward, starts the car. "Jesus. Poor woman."

I gaze out the window at the wet concrete walls lining the Liffey. "I know."

Since giving her statement, Mrs. Fagan has phoned almost daily as to the whereabouts of her brother. She believes we should be mounting a missing-person investigation. "Where's the media coverage for my brother?" she demands. "Why isn't anyone concerned for him?" She has threatened to contact the local radio station. I'm not sure how she thinks this may get us on her side, but strangely it does, only not for the reasons she imagines.

I want her to make a press statement. If she was as close to her brother as she claims, it may encourage him to come forward. Conscience may be missing in some of us, but shame is always there. Newspaper coverage on the Costello killing has been barely more than a blip in the national press. Eleanor's profile was clinical and impersonal and has slipped the public consciousness completely.

Amy Keegan's face, however, smiles out from front pages. The Hollywood horror of the discovery of her remains is too delicious for the press not to swoop down on, then pick over every print-selling detail.

Mrs. Fagan's concern seems urgent. Genuine. It's now up on two months since she last saw him. She hadn't worried so much up until his wife was discovered dead, but now she insists it's unlike him. Something in the way she hounds us prompts me to think she knows what we're about and is waiting for us to tell her he's a prime suspect. No doubt she has her defense of her brother already worked out in her head.

Letting my head fall back against the headrest, I sigh. "What a day."

"You wanna grab a drink?" he asks.

There is more than a little hope in his voice, and I realize he doesn't want to drink alone. Amy Keegan's public death has got to him after all.

CHAPTER 10

THE SHEETS ARE bundled between my knees, knotted around my feet. There is an ache glowing around my shoulder blade that tells me I've not moved in the night. I've slept, and not just slept but really zonked out. "Clear conscience" was what my mother used to say. It turns out that alcohol is a good replacement when your conscience is a little murkier than clear.

Sweat is cooling across the back of my neck, alcohol seeping from my pores. It was late at the pub last night. We solved the world's problems, Baz and I, then stumbled back and passed out. I can hear his snores coming through the wall. He collapsed onto the sofa, his eyes half closed, and within moments he was asleep. His last groggy words barely intelligible: "We'll catch this sick fucker."

I picture the case board at work. It's filling up, building around one name. All leads come back to her. It's too bad she can't speak, but I'm not sure Eleanor Costello would spill her secrets even if she could.

The image of their pristine house draws itself into my head. Clean, fresh skirting boards. The absolute lack of clutter, no shoes lying under the coffee table. The sofa didn't hold any shape of the backsides that must have sunk into it on a daily basis, despite the fact that they were feather and down. I think of my own sofa, how it looks when I unfurl my stiff body from its insides in the morning, how the cushions are crushed into the corners.

Everything about Eleanor Costello is suggesting control, on an obsessive level. The art books, which we now know are Peter's, if they had been hers, if they had been read, would have been slotted away in alphabetical order on some shining shelf somewhere. Visitors would not have been invited to open them; they wouldn't see the excessive note taking in the margins, the yellow-rimmed stain where the open pages were branded with a morning cup of tea.

I can't shake the feeling that Eleanor, although a victim, is pulling strings behind the theater of her death.

I move to the window of my flat. My head pounds with the after-effects of alcohol. It's latish. Eight. My fingers are warming around a mug of hot tea. Grafton Street is a milling crowd of commuters, chunky sweaters, orange-tipped scarves and bobble hats in all shades of deep green, navy, and maroon. The sun is cracking open a bright day, and from how people are ducking their heads I can guess there's a nip in the air.

Baz wakes suddenly, his feet withdrawing quickly from the sofa, his body propelling itself into a sitting position. Immediately, he drops his head between his knees and grips his temples.

"What the fuck were we drinking last night? Cyanide?"

I laugh. "That would be the third bottle of Merlot."

He doesn't look up, but jabs an index finger into the air. "Ah. That would be the one." He grabs his head. "Jesus."

I carry the tea to him, place it on the coffee table. "Here."

He glances up to thank me, then frowns, noticing that I'm dressed for work already. "What time is it?"

I pick up my briefcase. "Just gone eight. I didn't want to wake you. We're both better off with clear heads, and we needed to sleep off the hangover. I'm going in to work on the Black Widow site."

He groans. "Give me a minute. I'll be right there."

I pause, hesitate. He won't like what I'm about to ask him. "Actually . . ."

He looks up again. Another frown. "What is it?"

I pass him the name of Eleanor's therapist. "Would you talk to him? See if he can tell us anything. Maybe give us her notes?"

His eyes are pleading. "Ah, no. Are you serious? I'm in a delicate condition here."

Baz hates shrinks; his mother sent him to one all the way through his puberty for no reason other than her belief that it was good for her boys to be in touch with their feelings. Baz said he came out with more problems than he went in with, and he's pretty sure he gave the shrink some.

"You can deal," I say. I walk to the door.

"I can't. I really can't. Why do they have to talk the way they do? The pauses?" He throws his hands up. "What are they doing? Everyone knows not to fill the silence with your own airtime. Hate it."

"Come on. Think of it as some sort of weird retribution. In that this time it'll be you asking the awkward questions and you leaving the protracted silences."

He sighs. "Fuck. Sometimes I hate this job."

"Great! He's expecting you by midday, so take your time. Have lots of coffee."

I give him a smile and step outside the flat, blinking into the morning light.

STEVE HAS UNLOCKED an e-mail account in one of the hidden files on Amy Keegan's computer. I stare down at the back of his head.

"Have you ever used the sites on the Dark Web, Steve?"

He throws me a confused look. "Of course. I work in law enforcement, Chief. I'm not having anyone nose through my search history."

I laugh. "It's that bad, eh?"

"Unashamedly boring but no one's business but mine. The Dark Web's the only true platform of free speech left in the world, in my opinion." He reaches out, takes a glug of something fizzy and orange. A waft of warm fruit rises over his shoulder.

I nod at the screen. "And this kind of thing? You ever visit these kinds of sites?"

He returns his attention to the laptop, his head shaking. "Nope. But each to their own."

We are in Amy's e-mail account. In a folder titled "Wishlist." There are about thirty e-mails from her, saved in the folder, dating back through almost a whole year.

"What's the date of the first one?"

He clicks it open. "Twenty-seventh of December 2010." Something grabs his attention in the contents. "Whoa!"

The e-mail is addressed to a TrustMe57, which immediately raises the hairs on my neck. Amy sent the e-mail around seven p.m. It reads:

> Thanks for sending me your e-mail address. I have no one else to talk to and you seem to get it. Death is all I can think about. I fantasize about it. What it might feel like. It excites me but I'm too scared. I'm such a fucking coward. Lol. You could help me. I can tell you want to. If I've read you all wrong just say. It would be like me to get things backward. But you seem nice and understanding. I think I could do this with you.
>
> No hard feelings if you can't.

A

There is no reply, but at some point TrustMe57 must have answered, as the next e-mail, sent only a day later, reads:

> Wow. It's no problem at all. I can do that. God, I feel so
> low today, haven't managed to leave the flat and I don't
> think my meds work anymore. Please help me. This
> fantasy won't leave me. Your e-mail has been the best
> thing that's happened to me in months. It's like I'm
> already halfway there. Nirvana.
>
> A

Every e-mail we go through. Each one building in detail Amy's desire for a taste of death without actually dying. There is a break in their frequency after 4 January, but then by the beginning of May they are going again and heavier than before.

Steve is shaking his head. "Is this stuff for real? I mean, are there really chat rooms, places on the web, for people like this to connect? Whoever this guy is, he's fucked up beyond belief."

"Let's look at the deleted folder," I say. "See if we can find who she's replying to."

Steve opens it, but the folder is programmed to self-trash every two days and there is nothing but junk and spam.

He turns in his seat. "I could try and hunt out his IP address from this e-mail. The chances are less than small, but it's worth a shot. If we can get an IP, then it may help in trying to connect on the Black Widow site."

"We still can't be sure that he's even on the Black Widow site. Besides, his IP would be encrypted on the Dark Web."

We're at an impasse. The workload for this kind of task is so time-consuming, but short of getting down to it, we've little else. After a short silence, I give in.

"Go on then, but if you meet a brick wall at any time, move on to something more productive."

Paul pushes back from his desk, swivels his chair round. "I've got the press conference all set for Mrs. Fagan this afternoon," he says.

"Great. If Costello's hiding in some friend's flat or maybe another lover's house, then a press conference might encourage someone to drop us a line. Or at least propel our suspect into action. I'm wagering he's getting a little bored with sitting tight. Let's light a fire under his ass."

A sharp intake of breath hisses from around the office; it was a bad metaphor in light of Amy Keegan's passing. I hold up my hands. "Sorry."

Steve speaks up. "You're going to out him, aren't you? As prime suspect. At the press conference. Is that ethical?"

"Peter Costello left ethical behind when he tightened a rope around his wife's neck." I sigh. "It's not how it's usually done, and no, I'm not going to out him. I'm going to out Eleanor."

"Eleanor?"

"Yes, her death was greeted with barely a shake of a broadsheet. I'm just going to draw the camera lens toward her a little. I'll restate that her death is being treated as murder. I'll make the announcement directly after his sister's plea and finish by saying that we really would like to speak to Peter Costello in relation to her death."

Steve is nodding. "And let the media connect the dots for you?"

"Correct. The media can be a great weapon in these cases, Detective."

Helen is hovering over my shoulder. I can feel waves of nervous energy coming from her. When I turn, she holds out a sheaf of stiff paper, still warm from the printer.

"Chief. Steve set me to look into Amy Keegan's bank account. I think you might find this interesting."

"Thanks, Helen." I take the paper and she continues:

"Not a bad balance for a student. Especially a med student."

"That's almost ten grand." I scan through the pages. Look for the deposit. Look for the quarterly dump of money from the bank of Mam and Dad. Helen has highlighted two account numbers; both are standing orders delivering money into Amy's account. One monthly, the other weekly.

She smiles, reaches out, points to the one highlighted in yellow. "That's Daddy's account, a conservative eighty a week."

I put my finger to the other account. "Is this work? Or a grant?"

Her smile fades a little. "No. That's . . ." She hesitates, almost as if she's afraid to tell me. "That's Tom Quinn's account."

I stare down at the number. "Tom?" It can't be. I shake my head.

Helen clears her throat. "Should we get him in for questioning again?"

Thumping starts up in my ears. My breath sounds loud. Helen's voice twists and slides around my head, the words long and spiky.

"Chief?"

I press my fingers against my eyes and take a deep breath. "No. Not yet. We have to get through this conference. Find Costello."

Steve looks up from the computer. "But, Chief, if Tom Quinn was paying Amy for something, shouldn't we look into it?"

"Put a car on him. If he's got something to hide, we'll find it, but I've known Tom Quinn most of my life. He isn't a killer."

Steve picks up the phone to make the call. "Everyone's a killer with the right motive," he says, echoing our previous conversation.

"Just get to work, and, Helen, keep an eye on Amy's account. Let me know if and when that standing order is terminated."

I knead the bottom of my back. My entire body feels snarled up. The patch of tender skin aches over my temple, and the base of my neck throbs. It's not yet midday, and exhaustion is hanging from the corners of my body, weighing me down.

THE PRESS IS waiting. Most of the room are looking down, adjusting their screens, typing, sending off tweets—#EleanorCostello. Looking at my Twitter feed, I see that word is trickling out, spreading like blood blooming in water. My hope is that it reaches the front pages by tomorrow morning; numb as the public are now to murder, a murder where the husband is missing may spark enough interest to sell papers.

I can see Steve coming down the corridor, Priscilla Fagan behind him. Although her gait is sure and measured, she is grim-faced and pale, and I feel a momentary stirring of guilt in my gut at using her. But in reality, the Costellos don't have many blood relatives around to pledge for them, and the public are always moved to give us more information if a family member makes a plea.

In part, I want to see how Priscilla does. Despite her apparent concern for her errant brother, there's a chance that Priscilla Fagan may know where Costello is hiding. They were close; she is possibly the closest friend Peter has, outside of his wife and lover. At the back of the room, I catch sight of a familiar face. The neighbor Neil Doyle is white-skinned beneath the flickering fluorescence of the room. I watch him take a seat at the back and crane his neck to watch the action.

Jack comes up behind me.

"We're almost ready," he says. "I'll lead."

The cameras are set, microphones tested. I remain standing, alongside the gathering press audience. Jack leads Mrs. Fagan, Baz, and Steve across the front of the room. I slide into a seat. My job is to observe, study Priscilla's actions, wait for her to slip up. Give her brother away.

Jack waits until all have been seated, giving the opportunity for the press to get their equipment ready, poised. Mrs. Fagan sits, takes a sip of water from one of the glasses provided, clears her throat, then greets the waiting lenses with a high chin and a challenge in her eyes. If she weren't real, I would assume her a cartoon character of herself, in that she is the kind of person who is exactly who she seems. Solid through, in physique, morality, and sensitivity.

Jack leans in, picks up a piece of paper.

"Thanks for coming here today," he says into the microphone, his voice grave. "As some of you might be aware, a woman was discovered hanged in her home on 20 October 2011 in Bray, Wicklow. We believe that the woman's death had occurred the evening previous, initially presumed by her own hand. This woman was Dr. Eleanor Costello. We now know that this is a murder case. It is important to point out that at this stage we have a few leads that may give us a better picture of the manner of her death."

There are murmurs rippling through the room, surprise, excitement. My stomach is sick with revulsion; the journos are preparing their ground, imagining how they will tell her story, crawling all over the tragedy of her death. I remind myself that, in doing so, they will help us. Eleanor Costello needs front-page status in order to push her husband out of his hidey-hole.

Jack's voice rises and the room quiets. "In addition, we also discovered the remains of Amy Keegan on 31 October 2011, a young medical student from Clontarf who appears to have been known to Eleanor Costello's husband, Peter."

From the front row, a hand twitches like a cat's tail in the air. The owner does not wait to be instructed to speak.

"Are we dealing with a serial killer?"

This is the best we could have hoped for. My gut twists for Mrs. Fagan, who is lost in the case presented to her. We have deliberately kept her in the dark about a connection with Amy's murder, but I could tell as soon as Jack uttered Amy's name that she had made the same leap I did on that night with Eamon Keegan in Clontarf.

Jack does not answer the journo's question. We're not dealing with a serial killer as yet. There have not been enough victims; even murderers have criteria to meet.

He continues: "We appeal for anyone who may have noticed anything strange or saw Eleanor Costello or Amy Keegan in the run-up to their deaths to come forward. We would urgently like to speak to Peter Costello, Eleanor Costello's husband. We believe he might have information that would help us greatly in our investigations."

"Is the husband a suspect?" someone shouts.

Priscilla Fagan purses her lips in protest. She looks as if she'd like to drag the reporter outside and give him a hammering. But instead she picks up her water glass again and takes another sip. Steady.

"No. Peter Costello is not a suspect. But we believe he may have vital information that could help us with our investigation. We and his family"—he nods to Priscilla on his right—"are gravely worried about him and urge him to get in touch or come home."

There is a pause while the cameras of the room turn; microphones are held out, aggressive and demanding, in front of Priscilla Fagan. She holds her nerve.

There is not a single note of tremor in her voice when she speaks into the microphone.

"Peter. Whatever you've done or didn't do, come home. I am worried sick about you. You've left your prescription behind, and I know how you can't get by without it. Come home." She coughs into her hand, and when she looks up to the camera again, I can see the strain line the corners of her eyes. "Come home. I need you."

It feels genuine. So genuine that I have a fleeting moment of concern for Peter Costello.

CHAPTER 11

EVEN WITH ALL my attention centered on Amy, her death feels like a tributary of horror that's feeding some darker evil. Eleanor Costello's face haunts every thought I have; there's something not quite right about her puzzle. Her home doesn't fit, doesn't slot into a life. Even for someone who was obsessively tidy, it has a stale feeling lingering in its rooms. Unlived. Unloved.

Priscilla Fagan's appeal to the masses secured a front page this morning. Some of the papers ran shorter stories on Eleanor and her tragic past. Something, I know, she would have abhorred. Or at least sneered at. Maybe she would have pitied herself? She suffered bouts of self-pity and hatred, undoubtedly. Those emotions would have generated drive in her, but they would also be the emotions that caused great caverns of weakness and passivity to open up in her, resulting in binge-purge cycles and secret moments of despair. There is never a better reason to hate pity than when it lives inside you, controls you.

I step out of my car. I'm not sure what's brought me back here. Back to the Costello home. Two Gardaí are stationed at the front door.

I sign the log book, and they nod as I duck under the crime-scene tape, step inside. Even after the SOCOs have traipsed through the house, it looks tidy.

Usually, when I attend a crime scene at someone's home, I have a sense that I'm trespassing. I've the urge to tell my team to whisper, almost as if they're in a library. The ghosts of occupants' memories are soaked into the walls and floor of the abode, and we should be respectful of our invasion. But when I stepped over the threshold of the Costello household, I got none of that. People did not live here; they existed. Nothing of note could be felt from its bricks and mortar except a pervading feeling of sadness.

I can't imagine Peter and Eleanor lying on the sofa watching TV, legs meeting at the middle, folded at the knees, or maybe her head in his lap, his fingers tracing the elegant line of her jaw. It feels as if the guts of the house have been torn out, removed, discarded.

I carry on through the house. I can't bear to look into her bedroom again; it's late in the afternoon, and my imagination will easily resurrect her body hanging from the beam. Instead I make my way to the office. I search the drawers again, look behind and above the curtains. Peer out at the darkening sky.

"Can I get you anything, Chief?"

I nearly leap out of my skin. One of the guards stands in the hallway, hovering at the door.

Hand at my throat, I reply. "No. Thank you. Have there been any people asking questions? Nosing about?"

He shakes his head. "Not a sinner. People tend to get awful fond of their own business when there's a murder inquiry underfoot."

I smile. "Yes. Thank you. I'm just going to have a look around."

He salutes and leaves me to it.

My gaze settles on the Post-it. The password to the computer scrawled in round, stern letters on the yellow paper: "Chagall." I'm not sure what it is exactly that has captured me, but I can't resist plucking it away from the calendar and holding it up to my face. After a moment, it registers. Hurrying to the living room, I almost trip over the sofa in my haste to get to the coffee table. There I open up the Chagall book that I'd studied briefly the day Eleanor was found. I look from the note stuck to the tip of my index finger to the book and back again, several times.

The handwriting is different. Remarkably so. The *a* in the book curls around, elegant, old-fashioned. On the Post-it, the letter is a round fat circle with a sharp, short line drawn down its side. Could the computer be Eleanor's after all?

Placing the Post-it next to the scribbled notes in the margin of the book, I take a few photos with my phone and send them to Steve with the instruction that they are to go for handwriting analysis.

I move from the room and out the back door. The immediate space in the garden is concreted over, and hard-looking rusted metal furniture stands like a lonely family in the corner. The rest of the garden is run-down and bursting with the wrong kind of growth. I peer over the hedge. The garden of the neighbor, Mr. Neil Doyle, is immaculate.

I turn to reenter the house when a voice greets me from behind. Fear gathers in my muscles. Neil Doyle approaches me from the rear of the garden. I take a breath. Reassess.

I can barely hear my own voice, just make my mouth form the words.

"You startled me." My heart is hammering. *Bam. Bam. Bam. Bam. Bam.* "Detective Sheehan. We met a couple of weeks ago. I'm working the Costello case."

He points at a connecting gate in the hedgerow that separates the properties. It's hidden well in the darkness of the swollen shrubbery. "Sorry. I saw you looking and wanted to know if there'd been any luck getting in touch with Peter?"

Anger stirs in me. How have we missed this link between the properties?

The neighbor continues, voice a whisper. "Fuck. I mean, excuse me. I never swear, just, you know. Fuck. He murdered her then?"

"We are doing our best to find out who's responsible for Eleanor's death. Mr. Costello is an important witness."

I tilt my head. "Do you have time for a few questions?" I ask him. My voice has just the right note of pleading. *It would be helping us out so much*, he hears.

He smiles, then answers: "Sure."

"Thanks. Mr. Doyle, right?"

"That's right. Neil Doyle." He turns, directs me with an open palm. "Shall we?"

I step inside.

THE WIND IS whipping rain in great streaks across Abbey Street. I shiver and hurry, head down, toward our watering hole, where Clancy is waiting, armed with a strong pint and a sharp tongue for a case update.

Crowds of theatergoers gather beneath broken umbrellas, waiting for the first night of *Richard III*. I have to step off the pavement to pass the queues, sending my feet straight into the cold, wet puddles that line Dublin's side streets. By the time I arrive outside the pub, my hair is soaked and stuck to my skull, the ends curling round my chin. My feet are soggy and cold, and water is running down the inside of my jacket, sending icy rivulets shivering down my back.

I nod to Enda and go to find Clancy and Baz in our usual spot.

"The state of ye," Clancy says. Concern is in his eyes even if his mouth can't express it.

"Charmer," is all I say.

I sit and stomp my wet feet beneath the table in a weak attempt to chase the chill from my bones.

"Here. Will ye sit there, for Christ's sake?" He gets up from his seat. Offering me the prime spot, next to the fire.

I don't need to be asked twice. Grinning at Baz, I hurry to claim the coveted position. The fire immediately spreads a warm glow against my back, and I can almost imagine the steam rising from my clothes.

"How come she gets the good spot?" Baz complains.

Clancy never relinquishes his seat. As the most senior of us, he is not shy of pulling rank and has always claimed the seat next to the fire when we go for a drink.

I stick my tongue out at Baz. We are children, siblings squabbling over the division of our dad's affections.

"Clearly, I've earned it," I say.

Baz raises his eyebrow: "You've definitely the soggiest brain."

Clancy groans. "For fuck's sake. You're a drink late, Frankie." He glances up at Enda, who deposits a rather full glass of inky red wine before me. "Another couple of whiskeys there, fella," he adds before the long, thin barman can escape.

I shrug out of my coat, hang it over the back of the chair. "Whiskey? It's one of those nights, is it?"

Baz throws the last of what smells like Jameson down his throat. Then comes the obligatory grimace and purse of the lips. His eyes seem to melt a little, his jaw relaxes.

"Sure, why not?"

"I returned to the Costello house this afternoon," I say.

Clancy's head snaps toward me. "Alone?"

I don't look at him. "I had a chat with the neighbor. Neil Doyle."

"Alone?" Clancy repeats.

A sip of wine. "It was fine. Relax."

"Christ alive, Frankie. Has the last year not taught you anything?"

"I'm a detective chief superintendent, Jack. What can I do if not walk into a crime scene? Besides, there were two Gardaí at the front. It was grand."

He grunts.

There is a brief silence. Baz leans on the edge of his seat. He wants to ask what it is I've discovered, wants me to share today's progress, but we both have to wait until Clancy has battened down his anger before we can continue.

Finally, he looks up from his drink. "Well, go on then, before we're all too bleary-eyed to make sense of it."

"Mr. Doyle is a bona fide creep. The guy is more than a little obsessed with his neighbors."

"Diary keeper?" Jack asks.

"Not that bad, but he seems to believe that Peter was the victim here." I give a short laugh. "The man spent most of the interview trying to look down my blouse. Complete dick. Probably believes that any woman who professes to have a life outside of the kitchen sink clearly is a nightmare to live with."

Jack holds up a hand. "Steady on there, Frankie. Let's say what we mean, please."

Baz laughs.

Jack takes a gulp of whiskey. "Be careful not to let prejudices cloud your judgment."

"Give me a break, Jack," I reply. "I can say the guy is a creep because he is, and ultimately there was a fair bit of misogynistic flair to his testimony, but"—I hold my hands out toward the fire—"what he said did make me think. We know that Eleanor Costello was able to take care of herself and that Peter Costello is not in rude health. There could be something to what he says. It's not easy to see or believe that a man of Peter's build, ill or not, would take a beating from a woman as slight as Eleanor was, but emotional manipulation is a strong weapon."

Baz frowns. "So what we're saying here is that Eleanor Costello may have been knocking her husband about?"

"Domestic violence against men does exist, and we can't deny that it would give Peter Costello a motive," I say.

"Being bounced around the house by the missus? Definitely not sure a judge would be sympathetic, though," Baz says.

Jack speaks up. "What exactly did this Neil bloke have to say?"

"I asked him why he thought their marriage was shaky. He said he thought Costello was knocked about by the wife. He claims that, over the years, he'd hear their arguments through the walls, and it was always her voice above his. He said that often the following day he'd spot Peter Costello and he'd have another limp, or if he didn't see Peter for a few days, he'd emerge with a hand bandaged up. Or one time he noticed a split lip, but the wife would always—and these are his words, not mine—'spring from the house the following day like a gazelle.' Not a bother on her."

"Right so," Jack says. "So we possibly have motive for Eleanor's killing. But what about the Keegan murder? And how can we corroborate what Doyle says if we can't find the husband?"

I wipe a trail of sweat from my forehead and shiver. "Christ. Am I supposed to do all the work?" A choking cough stops me short.

"You need to get home. Go to bed. You're sick," Jack orders.

Ignoring him, I take a sip of wine. "The other thing was that the handwriting on the note in the office is different to that in the books." I look to Baz, whose eyebrows shoot up.

"You're thinking that the laptop was hers?" he asks.

"I sent the samples to Steve, shouldn't be too long for the handwriting specialist to get back with the results."

Clancy takes another grumbling drink of his whiskey. His lips barely twitch as he swallows a large mouthful.

There's a long pause. Clancy and I wait for Baz to fill us in on his day. Finally, he looks up, surprised to find us both watching him.

"What?" he asks.

"Wow, old age is catching," I say. "You were working over the last couple of days? Remember? Have you anything to contribute?"

It turns out no. The stinking therapist that he went to see yesterday took one glance at Baz's badge, leaned back, and claimed he couldn't possibly admit that Eleanor Costello was his client.

"Patient fucking confidentiality," Baz finishes, a renewed hatred for the psychotherapy profession growing on his brow. "He even steepled his flaming fingers beneath his chin. The fucker."

I can see it clearly. An invisible battleground of control. I wonder now whether it would have been wiser to send Baz in under the guise of a patient.

"The prick," Clancy mutters. "We'll have to get a warrant."

In the meantime, the shrink, Dr. Burke, will have twenty-four hours to immerse himself in Eleanor Costello's file. Even the most honest of doctors wouldn't be able to help adding a word or two, removing a word or two, to make sure their notes look comprehensive. Evidence enhanced or subtracted. Ruined. I don't realize that I'm clenching my fists until I feel my nails bite into my palms.

Baz smacks his glass on the table.

"No matter. When the warrant comes in, I'll make sure I trawl through every part of his office." He gives us both a victorious grin.

He won't, though. He won't trawl through Burke's office. Warrants are very specific when it comes to medical files and institutions. Privacy and our rights to confidentiality get in the way of police work every day. People want to catch the bad guys, but they won't share jack shit about their lives in order for us to do it. Especially, it seems, Eleanor Costello.

The scar along my temple begins to throb; the wine dries the back of my mouth. I must look a state because Clancy is telling me again to get home, to get dry.

I grab my coat, not that I'm listening to him. I can feel the case stretching about inside my brain, unfolding its many branches, showing me flashes of the finished product, but I can't think. My eyes are scratchy and hot. My throat itches; my skin feels sore, sensitive.

"You need to stop babying me, Jack. You know there's nothing surer to piss me off."

"Go way to fuck. Babying you. I can see a fucking cold watering away in your eyes, and your sniffling is putting me off me whiskey. Just don't want whatever disgusting bug you're about to go sneezing over the pair of us. That'd be a grand thing, wouldn't it? All three of us leading this bloody case at home in bed."

I laugh. Clancy has never taken a day off sick in his life.

"Whatever bug I'm spreading is sure to be annihilated midair with that whiskey breath you're exhaling." I shrug into my coat, hug the damp wool tight to my chest, and wrap my scarf over my head. "See yis tomorrow."

ONE OF THE tiny branches has begun to brown. Its leaves are turning a curling gold around the edges, and dark brown spots are spreading at their center. It's such a stark contrast to the rest of the tree. I have to fight the urge to pick it off, to clip it away. I loosen the copper binding a little and hope that a good dowsing of water will revive it, that it will encourage new growth: a burst of smaller branches, smaller leaves.

CHAPTER 12

CLANCY, TO MY annoyance, was right. My head is spinning; the skin over my temple feels like it's been burned, branded in the middle of the night by a hot poker. I lift the thin strands of my hair away from my skull, just above my ear. The hair has only just started to regrow in between patches of angry pink skin. They said that it would calm down—the color—but they couldn't make promises about the pain. Some people find that stab wounds continue to throb for years after they're inflicted. What was unsaid was that they believed the pain was psychosomatic. If it's in my head, I'm impressed with the power of my own thoughts.

Checking the back of the paracetamol box, I allow myself a couple over the stated dose. And another coffee. There is a message on my phone. I can tell by the time it was left and the fact that it's an unknown number that it's my lawyer. Prosecution. Phoning to tell me when the Tracy Ward trial will continue.

The missed-call history shows that it's swiftly followed by four calls from my mother. Confirmation, if I needed it, about who has left the message. The family liaison officer keeps my family abreast of proceedings with the Ward case too. I am a victim. Lest I try to forget it.

Every few hours I get a text from my voicemail, telling me to listen to the message. Pushing. Each time my phone pings, I can feel my heart picking up, leaping. I should phone my mailbox. But some irrational part of me believes that if I delay listening to it, the content of the message may have time to change. History may have time to change, and I'll wake up one day to discover that actually this whole nightmare was imposed on someone else and that yes, I'm not mortal; I'm not easily struck down by the swipe of a knife or shackled by fear.

I should get in touch with my parents. I hold the coffee mug up to my mouth, enjoy the heat of the ceramic against my chin. My parents are used to my silences. My dad said that, as a toddler, I might have been supersensitive but that I wanted—no, needed—to walk by myself. No hand-holding. I came at right angles to life, slicing across whatever path my family tried to guide me toward. It's not that I was a rebel, more that I was aggressive in the values I believed I had. Zeal. That's what my dad used to say. Still says. As if it were some unusual, exotic quality.

I think of what I know of Eleanor's childhood home. The short letter that some concerned, well-meaning social worker sent to their superiors highlights how bad her home life must have been.

There is no record of any social welfare investigation into her past, and when I requested any reports pertaining to what happened to her parents, I was greeted with a big fat zero. It would seem that, as soon as Eleanor was old enough, she elected to go and stay with her aunt in Kilcullen. Any information around her parents she would have destroyed. She was a successful professional, and in her mind this was what she wanted to project to the world. For someone like Eleanor, anything less than perfect could be expunged.

Walking to the coffee table, I clear away used tissues and empty water bottles and open my work laptop. I flick through a few of the photographs I took of Eleanor's office—the contents of her drawers, filing cabinets—and her lab. Neatness. I've worked with scientists in the past; as exacting as their work is, they're some of the messiest people I know. They may argue over how one petri dish is half a millimeter too thick, but they will be happy to work from a desk that they share with last week's takeaway.

I can feel the frown aching across my forehead. Eleanor Costello purged anything undesirable from her life. As bulimics do. Maybe her need for control of this nature went outside the brutalizing of her own body.

Pulling my briefcase onto my knee, I remove Lorcan Murphy's card from it. I don't like asking these kinds of questions down the phone. You only get half an answer if you're not looking someone in the eye. But he may well be able to give me this one piece of Eleanor's personality. Could someone have cleared her office after her death? If that was the case, then who would have had access to it? Her husband? A colleague? Or maybe she treated her work space as she did every other aspect of her life—pinned down and under control.

I dial the number on the card, and as it rings, I glance up at the wall clock. Half past eight, well before nine. His lectures will not have begun yet, and sure enough he answers.

His voice is hesitant. "Hello. Lorcan Murphy speaking."

"Mr. Murphy! Hi. Detective Chief Superintendent Sheehan here."

There is silence on the other end of the line, then a mumble: "Go on in, I'll be there shortly.

"Sorry, Detective," he says down the phone. "I'm just about to go into my nine o'clock lecture." He is uncomfortable. His card was a gesture. He was not expecting me to phone, to get dragged in. I don't want to put him on his guard.

"It's only a quick question, if you don't mind." I sneeze into my hand. "Sorry. You did mention you were eager to help in any way you can."

"Yes, yes. Of course." He rushes the words, desperate to reassure that he will help.

"It's a bit of a random question, but I like to try and build a profile of victims. It helps us determine what type of person would want to harm them."

"That makes sense." More noise in the background. The sound of voices echoing down corridors. "What can I do for you?"

"I think we established that Eleanor was a particularly organized person."

He laughs. "Understatement."

I join in his laughter. "Yes. She seemed to like her life very much 'paint inside the lines.'"

I can hear him drawing air through his teeth. "Eh. I wouldn't necessarily agree with that."

"Oh?"

"Don't get me wrong, she was very organized, but she could be unpredictable. It was one of the reasons she was such a good lecturer. She'd have a class plan all laid out and then suddenly she'd have headed off down some rabbit hole of an obsession and dragged us all with her. The students loved it. No lecture the same."

"And outside of work?"

The tone of his voice lowers, shutters. "I can't really speak for when she was at home, but at functions and the like she could also be very unpredictable. There was more than one occasion when I had to help her into a taxi at the end of a night." He laughs, clearly recalling one such night.

"Her work desk, though. It's remarkably clear of junk, in light of how often and how long she worked there."

"Oh, yes." I picture him nodding. "Yes. I thought you might ask me about that. That you might wonder where the potted plant was on her desk and the like. She hated clutter. Had a huge thing about it.

Always saying that she didn't want junk, objects, ornaments, plants, following her around, carting them through life as if they were important. She never wanted anything around her for long enough that she became used to it. So she would . . . What was the phrase she used for it?" His tongue clicks, then: "Yes, 'life edit.' She'd announce a life edit. Clean everything that had nothing to do directly with her current work away from her desk. I was always amazed by it."

"Thanks for your help, Mr. Murphy."

He's pleased. Relieved. "No trouble at all."

I hang up.

BAZ IS WAITING in the office when I get in. I feel like week-old roadkill. A cool sweat has broken out over my body, making me tremble. I clap my gloved hands together and stomp my feet in an effort to warm myself after being outside. The actions are more effective than I'd like, and in the heat of the room I feel a swooping kind of flush creep swiftly from my feet through my body, where it makes my head feel swimmy. Baz has his hand beneath my elbow.

"Don't you hate it when Clancy's right?"

I manage a brief dry laugh before coughing erupts in my chest. I hold a finger up. "If you mention to him that I've a cold, you'll be the next death we'll be investigating."

He laughs. "Agree. But seriously, do you think you should be here?" He looks round at the rest of the team.

I straighten, battle with my body to get its sweating, listless self to fucking function. "We don't work in a nursery, Baz."

He holds his hands up. "Only trying to help."

"Well, for God's sake, keep your bloody voice down, or the next time one of the staff here decides they're a little freaking upset or stressed we'll have sick notes up to our ears and no staff to work with."

He salutes me. "Sure thing."

I drag myself to my office, where I sit in misery for a moment. The cliché, the bottle of whiskey in the middle drawer of my desk, is achingly tempting, but when I reach for it, I notice that Baz has followed me inside.

"What is it?"

"Interrupting your agony, am I? Go home."

"What is it?"

He slides a faxed report across the table to me.

"The handwriting is Eleanor's," he says. His finger is resting on the sample, the name "Chagall," from the Post-it. The round, fat letter *a*.

Baz runs through my thoughts, picking up strands, tying them together. "So the computer is likely hers."

I pull the laptop to me. With a firm tug the display comes away from the keyboard and becomes a tablet, the screen touch-sensitive, as Steve informed us weeks ago. A tablet would be easy for Eleanor to carry to and from work.

Each day facts slither away into darkness.

I look up. Sigh.

"What?"

"The laptop may be hers. But can she really have known what that program did? Maybe he put the Tor bundle on the computer so that he could access his fantasies. His own sister assumed as much. Eleanor wouldn't have use of the Dark Web."

"Why? Because she's a woman? I thought we talked about this last night." He pulls a face, eyebrows raised, challenging me.

"Well, yes. But I just can't see it."

He throws himself into the seat across from me. "You are aware of how sexist you sound right now? Toward your own sex, I might add."

"It doesn't fit."

"Her profile? You're putting yourself in her shoes, Frankie. Get out of her size sixes."

I'm too numb, too sick to reply. Could I have been steered wrong so early?

Baz is rubbing his left ear, a sign of stress. "Is it her profile? Let's go over it again, shall we?"

I glare at him. "Are you aware of how sexist *you* sound right now?" I sigh. "Baz," I go on, steadying my thoughts. "We found her hanging. In a way that implies she couldn't have been alone. She's the victim here. Don't forget that."

He holds up his hands. "And what about Amy Keegan? And where is Eleanor's husband? Effectively, he disappeared almost two months ago. Maybe our organized Eleanor got herself into some shit, maybe she's not only the victim but the guilty party too."

I shift in my seat. I'm uncomfortable with the thought. I turn it about in my head, try to make room for it among the rest of Eleanor Costello.

"But what about the Prussian blue? The pigment found on Eleanor's body and Amy's. An artist's paint. 'Purposeful application,' those were the words of the pathologist. Peter Costello is the art buff."

His shoulders fall. "I give up then."

I stand, go to the coffee machine in my office, and help myself. I pop another couple of paracetamol. "As I said, Eleanor can't be guilty, she was already dead at the time of Amy's murder, remember?"

"It doesn't mean she's innocent," Baz says.

"Really? Because when it comes to these murders, she is. She was the victim of one, she was dead for the other. I'm not sure I follow you."

"Do you really think we should exclude the Ward case from this?"

A coldness settles in my stomach.

"Hear me out, okay? I know, but when I think of the violence of Tracy's murder, knives. With Neary, there's already a question over his arrest. He says he came to check on her. He thought you were the intruder. Maybe we did act too quickly. His story could be true."

"Fuck. Of course he'd say that. What? You're doubting the evidence now? Evidence that you and Clancy compiled, remember?"

"I know, but maybe there is something in Neary's testimony?"

I round on him. "You've got Ivan Neary stepping out of the room that Tracy Ward had been murdered in, literally moments earlier. He was holding the murder weapon. He tried to kill me."

The air trips in my throat. A cough barks up from my lungs. A fresh wave of sweat rises and falls across my forehead. It takes me a few moments to quiet my body.

I know I'm not being fair. The same questions have been creeping into my head since Eleanor Costello's death. The same thoughts. Burrowing through my memory, making me doubt what happened.

"Sorry," I mumble.

He shrugs. "No. Look, I'm sorry. I'm not sure what I'm saying. I guess, there's a feeling of a bigger picture. A sense of something missing. I don't know."

I take up my pen, reclaim my seat. Brace myself behind the desk. "And is there? Do you think you missed something?"

A shadow passes over his face, but he shakes his head. "He was standing over you with that knife. I saw the look in his eyes. It wasn't fear, defensive or otherwise, it was rage. Pure rage."

CHAPTER 13

DESPAIR IS A detective who suspects a murderer has slipped the net. Almost one week has slid by since the press conference, sneering at our effort of slowing time and attempting to revive time lost. The influx of calls we had after Priscilla's plea has dribbled to a stop.

It might have been naive to paint Peter as the bad guy at the press conference. Somewhere along the line, the message the public received was skewed. The public decided they didn't want anything to do with a man like that, so any leads we wanted have dried up quickly.

The image of the case is smeared across the newspapers. And there in the midst of the fallout, next to a picture of Amy Keegan, is Eleanor Costello's wedding photo. Peter Costello's dark good looks suddenly become gothic. "Night of the Burning Dead," the headlines shout. "Killer Who Says It with Knives," another tells it how it isn't.

Everyone wants to peer in from the sidelines, but nobody wants to associate themselves with Peter Costello. After the conference, Mrs. Fagan was blistering with anger. Her husband had to hold her back from me as I tried to explain to her my reasoning. In her fury, though, she told me I was wrong. Peter was too ill to commit these crimes, she said. Hands shaking, she'd rooted about in her handbag and produced the set of prescriptions made out to her brother.

"There," she said, thrusting them at me. "That's the drugs he was on, antidepressants and painkillers. Much good they did him."

I thanked her and let her husband pull her away. I had to pause then for a moment in the midst of the swirl of people leaving the press room. An odd feeling of guilt seemed to have tagged itself onto the end of my breath. A wriggle of doubt that squirmed under my skin and asked whether I had gotten Peter Costello all wrong.

"Anything?" Jack barks.

We are weaving through the crowds along Dublin quays. Through the slicing cold, we've hit the lunchtime stagger. Workers march stony-faced, collars up and heads down, in search of a hot spot of lunch or maybe a bit of early Christmas shopping before final payday.

"About Peter Costello's prescriptions we have nothing new," I re-ply. "It's strange that she'd have his prescriptions."

"She says he couldn't trust that bitch with it." He glances sideways at me as we walk. "Her words, not mine."

"Do you think she was a bitch, though?"

"Maybe. I think it's fair to say we can't really rely on Priscilla Fa-gan for a character reference of her sister-in-law," he says with a single rumble of laughter. "Although I'd say it's nothing more than jealousy."

"You think?"

He looks at me again. "You don't?"

"Priscilla Fagan is the type of woman who, once she makes up her mind on something, I would think she's pretty unshakable, but I think for that reason she's not one to make up her mind easily."

"Eight years is a lot of reason when you believe your brother's wife only married him for his money."

"True."

We order a couple of takeaway coffees from a street vendor and head toward the car park. Settled in the driver's seat, I wrap my hands around the cup and soak the heat into my fingers. I take a sip, then fit it into the cup holder at my side.

"Neil Doyle was his reference," I say, half sharing, half thinking aloud.

"Come again?"

"The neighbor Neil Doyle. Peter Costello had put him down for a reference on his most recent work applications. The day of the press conference, he was there. I saw him. He had slipped in at the back of the room."

"Rubbernecking? Camera-hungry?"

I shake my head. "He does like to nose, but I think we may have actually found a friend of Peter's."

"You want to pay him another visit? Bring him in for official questioning?"

I put the car into reverse, ease gently out of the parking space, then speed up the ramp and out into the gray light of Dublin.

"No. I might put a tail on him. On the morning we found Eleanor, he mentioned that he was a consultant, but never really said what in. Now, if he was a financial consultant, great, that would make some sense, but otherwise, why on earth would Peter use him as a reference?"

Jack sits, one hand holding his coffee like a weapon before him, the other braced against the dashboard.

"Costello was hardly the popular lad in school, now, was he? A person wouldn't be happy about losing references if you were tied up in any way with the recession."

"Yes. But it turns out that Priscilla Fagan's summary of how Peter lost his job was in some part true, in that it was namely down to a poor investment he made in Eleanor's company."

Jack is nodding. "It might explain why she stayed with him so long through his unemployment."

"Well, it certainly doesn't seem to be down to love, now, does it?"

He takes a loud gulp of the coffee and swats a few invisible spots from his tie. "I think that's a given." He sighs. "Where are you going with this now, Frankie, because I'm beginning to feel like I've spotted a white rabbit and now I'm tumbling down a dark hole."

I pull a face at him. "Ha. Ha. Some good old-fashioned detective work. It may be a complete waste of time, but I'd like to know exactly what kind of glowing character reference Neil Doyle would give to a prospective employee. Doyle says only one company phoned him with regard to that reference."

"Doyle wouldn't have reason to give a glowing reference?"

I throw him a cynical look. "Oh, come on. Neil Doyle doesn't know his neighbors as well as he thinks he does."

Jack guffaws at that. "Clearly."

"You know what I mean. Not simply because of Eleanor Costello's death, just that he seemed to have little to say about their personalities, and he was never invited over for a drink or dinner. Which is odd in itself. Now that Eleanor is dead and Peter is missing, he's suddenly a character reference? And he was at the press conference, unable to look away. Either he's pathologically nosy or he knows where Peter is."

I pull up at our building, and we both step out of the car, face each other over the bonnet.

"You may be right. Let's see what this company has to say, if they respond to you."

"Never any harm in asking."

When I turn, I notice Steve at the door. His face urging us inside. I glance at Jack, then rush forward.

"What is it? Have we found him?"

Steve is walking, leading us back through the building to the case room. "No. But we've got something on Tom Quinn. Something big."

I follow Steve to the lifts.

"Tom?"

"I think you're going to have to bring him in again, Chief. Sorry."

Clancy shuffles into the lift next to us. "Tom Quinn? The Keegan employee?"

"Yes," I say. "What have you found?"

Clancy cuts across me. "I thought you said he was clean, Frankie?"

"He's been depositing money into Amy's account for the last year," I answer. The lift sinks to a stop, and I push out into the hallway.

"What? How long have you known that? Why didn't you bring him back in?" Clancy demands.

I stop outside the office door. "I didn't think it was enough to negate a lifetime of model citizenship, so I put a tail on him yesterday morning."

Clancy sags a little. "You can't tiptoe around a potential suspect because they share the same watering hole as your folks. Get him in for questioning. Stop messing about. It's fucking easier on the budget."

I press my lips together but nod.

He lifts the sleeve of his coat, glares at his watch. "I gotta go. Keep it under control, Detective."

He stalks off down the hall, leaving me glowering at his back.

FOLLOWING STEVE INTO the office, I remove my coat, straighten my blazer.

"What've they got?"

"At nine last night, he drove to Dublin city. He parked on Drury Street, and they followed him on foot to where he accessed an underground club in the basement of a bar. The club, called Rialú, has held BDSM nights for members for the last five years."

"BDSM? Sadomasochism?"

"That's right. Ordinarily, I'd say person's a right to whatever kicks he can get, you know? But in light of Amy's and Eleanor's lifestyle choices, this could be a link."

I let out a long sigh. Close my eyes. "Okay. Get him in. Let's draw a line under this. Tom Quinn is not our man."

"There's more," Steve interrupts. "Our plainclothes talked to one of the guys on the door." He rubs his fingers together, indicating that we've paid for this information. "The event last night was sponsored by an underground sadomasochism site called Black Widow."

He steps back, spreads his hands.

I feel the moment the blood drops from my face. The image of that baby rabbit stirs in my head, ears flat, heart flickering under brown fur.

I take a deep breath. "Thanks. You know what to do."

CHAPTER 14

TOM QUINN WAITS in the interview room. It's a rare thing that witnesses return so easily for a second interview, but Tom is old-school. He's got nothing to hide and stupidly trusts the system. I sort through the reports on my desk. Evidence is mounting, pointing fingers at him. I don't want it to be true. It's bad enough that my work has pulled back the film reel of my childhood and colored my memories with Amy's horrific death, but it seems too oppressive that such a familiar face could be capable of such evil.

The bouncer at Rialú confirmed that Tom is a regular. Examination of Tom's bank account shows that his payments to Amy equated to a third of his wages. Every month saw him dip into his overdraft. He had no savings. The connection to Black Widow has pitched the scales of justice down, laid a burden of guilt right at Tom's feet.

Baz taps on the door and steps in. "I think we're ready. You sure you don't want to do it?"

I stand. "Yes. I'm sure. I can't see beyond the Tom Quinn I know.

I can't see him as a viable suspect. Therefore, I can't get the answers we need."

"I've never known you to let sentimentality get in the way of work."

I sigh. "This is about giving Tom the best chance to clear himself. I may not go hard enough on him, and that's doing no one any favors."

He keeps his mouth shut but nods.

I gather up the reports. "You got everything you need?"

He pats a roll of paper tucked into his suit-jacket pocket. "Everything."

On the other side of the window, Tom Quinn is sitting bolt upright, his feet anchored against the legs of the chair, his face as gray as his suit. He doesn't look at the mirrored glass this time. He stares straight ahead, his mouth tucked in at the corners. I look for the killer in him but can't see it. When Baz enters the room, Tom looks up expectantly, and as if someone has flicked a switch, his shoulders droop, his chest sinks inwards.

"Detective." He reaches out a hand.

Baz shakes it. "Mr. Quinn. I'm Detective Harwood. Thanks for coming in."

Tom nods. "Of course, of course. Although I answered questions for Frankie the last time."

"The case is moving along and we've a few details we'd like you to clear up."

I see the muscles contract in Tom's throat, the Adam's apple dip beneath his shirt collar.

"Okay."

"We've already established that you knew Amy well?"

"As well as if she were my own flesh and blood."

"Did you get along?" Baz doesn't look at him when he asks the question, but when Tom doesn't answer immediately, he meets his witness's eyes.

"I don't know what you mean."

"Did you get along? Did you like her, loathe her, or have any disagreement?"

Tom tucks one foot under the other, folds a little more in the chair.

"Mr. Quinn?"

"We got along fine."

"When was the last time you saw her?"

Tom shakes his head. "The summer, I think."

"The summer? During the holidays?"

"I think so." More confident. "Yes."

Baz checks his notes. "She didn't come home then, during term time? No weekend breaks?"

Eyebrows go up. A smile. "Oh, no, hang on. I tell a lie. I left her back up to Dublin, must have been a month ago now. Eamon asked me to leave her up, he'd done his back in, tried to lift out a battery." He shakes his head, reliving the moment. "So's I took her back to uni."

"You left her at her flat then? Or on campus?"

"At one of the other students' houses, I think. It was in Sandyford. He looked a right posh one. A bit older, mind. Not sure Eamon would ha' agreed with it, now, but you know these young ones."

"Name?"

"Didn't get the name. She did tell me. I want to say Larry but can't be sure."

Baz makes a note, leans back. "Amy's bank statements show that you were paying her four hundred euro a month. Could you tell us about that?"

"She needed a few bob for uni, 'tis all. As I said, she was like family."

"Family?"

Tom's eyes slide to the table. "Yes."

"We think she was blackmailing you."

Silence.

"Mr. Quinn? Was Amy Keegan blackmailing you?"

Tom lifts his face. Pink blotches rise on his cheeks; the skin over his neck reddens. He looks at the window, as if he's seeing me through the glass; talking directly to me, his voice beseeches.

"It's not what you think."

"It's not blackmail?"

"No. I mean, yes and no. She . . . she wasn't always nice to me. She wasn't always a nice person."

Baz leaves space for him to continue. It takes a moment.

Tom loosens his tie, tugs at the neck of his collar. Finally, he looks up, pushes his graying hair back.

"She said she'd tell Eamon if I didn't pay her. He wouldn't understand. I'd lose my job." His eyes become desperate. "The Keegans, they're my family. I've no one else."

I put a hand on the window frame; the fear, the resentment in his voice, is almost motive enough.

"Why were you paying her, Mr. Quinn?" Baz presses on.

"She saw me, at a club I go to. It's not the norm. Not understood." He puts out the palm of his hand. "No one gets hurt, but it's a private thing."

"A sex club."

"Yes," he whispers. "She was there, but of course she could do no wrong in Eamon's eyes. Me, on the other hand. If Eamon knew I was into that kind of thing, he wouldn't be able to look at me again."

Baz removes a photo from the file at his elbow. "Is this the club?"

Tom glances at the photo, then pulls back. "Yes."

"Do you know a website called Black Widow?"

"Black Widow? No." A clear answer.

"Are you sure?"

"Yes." He pulls at the neck of his shirt again. "You won't say anything to Eamon, will you? He wouldn't understand. I can't lose my job."

Baz tucks the photo back into the file. "Mr. Quinn, did you murder Amy Keegan?"

Tom's mouth falls open. "What?"

"Did you murder Amy Keegan?"

"Me? I couldn't . . . I wouldn't. The Keegans—"

"Amy was blackmailing you. You must have thought about it? Getting rid of her would solve a lot of your problems. Those payments were slowly putting you in debt."

He's off the chair. It flies backward. He extends his arm, points at Baz. "You. You're sick. I couldn't do that. Not that. To anyone." He looks around for the door. "I'd like to go now."

"Mr. Quinn, please sit. Sometimes we have to ask questions that are . . . distasteful. I'm sorry if that came across a bit blunt. Please." Baz stands, moves around the desk, rights the chair, pats the seat. "Sit. I'll go sort your papers out."

Tom approaches the chair as if it were the edge of a cliff, but eventually he eases himself behind the table and watches Baz cautiously.

Baz smiles his thanks. "I won't be too long."

I'M ON HIM the moment he closes the door. "What was that?"

"There's a big stinking motive right here." He taps the manila folder in his hand.

"You didn't need to badger him so much."

Baz pauses. "I followed protocol and you know it."

I stop, close my eyes, and count to five slowly. "I'm sorry. You're right. You're right." Suddenly the room is too hot, too crowded. I pull my jacket off, throw it over a chair.

He sighs. "Do you want me to tell the Keegans?"

"No. I'll do it, but one thing." I hold out my phone to him.

He stares down at the screen, at the photo of Lorcan Murphy leaving campus with Eleanor Costello. "What?"

"Ask him if this was the man. The house he dropped Amy Keegan to in Sandyford."

Tiredness, exhaustion, waken in his eyes. He takes the phone.

I watch the interchange through the window, see Tom peer over the screen, watch his expression melt from doubt to certainty. He nods. Yes.

Baz closes the door. "I'll look into it. Not surprising they'd know each other. He lectured on the course she was studying."

I try to hide the plea in my voice. Try to steer my memories of Tom away from the case.

"I think we're on the wrong road with him, Baz. Let's put another set of eyes on him. See where it takes us. His arrest throws up more questions than answers. How would Tom Quinn get to Eleanor? Why would he kill her? Where's his motive in that?"

"For now, we've got a suspect for Amy's murder. That's all. We charge him or lose him."

"He wouldn't run."

Baz stares at his suspect. "You don't know that. We can't risk it. There's more to this club. The Black Widow site. We'll find it, but in the meantime, we have enough to charge him. Cases with burning are tough, Frankie. You know this, time of death, the killer's DNA all lost in the flames. We need a confession."

He hands me the phone. "I'll get the papers and charge him. Then we send Keith and the crime-scene lot to his house," he adds, then leaves the room.

By the time he's returned I've informed a distraught Eamon and Moira that they've lost yet another family member to this horror story. I hang up, cutting off Eamon's hollow anger and the ring of Moira's crying in the background.

Baz stands over Tom Quinn, pushes a printed version of his statement in front of him. Once Tom has signed, Baz will proceed with charging him for the murder of Amy Keegan.

Tom, who clearly doesn't know how soon his future will turn to shite, smiles his thanks at Baz.

"If you're happy with the statement, would you please sign and date it at the bottom of the form," Baz instructs.

Tom reaches for the pen, and my breath slows, stretching out time. I move closer to the window. His signature is awkward and slow, self-conscious loops with a swift stop at the end.

There's something in the way he holds the pen that's odd. A curve of the hand around the nib, the movement suggesting a backward lean of the letters. Baz reaches down when Tom writes the date and scoops up the precious statement. And then it hits me. I take a deep breath, a gasp, then rush into the room.

"Baz. Can I speak to you?"

"Hello, Frankie," Tom says, his voice an exhausted sigh.

I take the time to smile at him, then meet Baz's eyes. "Now."

Baz excuses himself and follows me from the room. He looks at me as if I've finally lost the plot.

"What is it?" he asks.

"He's left-handed."

"And?"

"The killer, in Amy's video, was right-handed. Tom Quinn didn't murder Amy Keegan."

CHAPTER 15

THE FAMILY LIAISON officer will visit tomorrow to take me through Tracy Ward's case again. She has suggested that we have the meeting at my family's house so that they too might be prepared for what will take place. It's an opportunity for me to reconnect with them, and I'm dreading it.

In the meantime, I've taken to bedding down on my sofa, working the Black Widow site, putting out feelers in other chat rooms, and staring at Amy Keegan's and Eleanor Costello's files, hoping that something, anything, new will reach out to me. More weeks have churned by, our witnesses and follow-ups as scarce as warm days. We are packed into a dark hole with not a chink of light to show us the way out.

Nothing has been said, but I can sense from Clancy that the commissioner is beginning to question whether the case warrants further resources. Meaning, of course, money. I sigh, tuck my feet beneath me, and check my phone. There've been no more silent calls. Steve remains vigilant on Cell Site, but nothing's come through on Peter Costello's phone.

I stare out across the mess of my flat. Dishes stacked in the sink. My coat still slung over the chair where I dropped it last night.

However, despite the chaos, the bonsai is shaping up. It's not as difficult as I imagined, stifling life in one area of the tree and encouraging it in another. Its foliage is a rich deep green that stands defiant against the freezing gray December skyline.

It's one of those days where the sun never really showed up behind the cloud and it felt dark before it even lightened. It's barely four, but the lamp at my elbow has been on since two this afternoon. The TV is flickering on mute. There is a weatherman waving his hand, fanlike, over Dublin, and with a flick of his fingers a snowflake icon appears. The temperature is predicted as below freezing over the next couple of nights, rising slightly by midafternoon. Wrapped up in a blanket as I am, I can't help but shiver.

I scroll through my contacts and dial Baz's number.

He picks up first ring. "Hello?"

"It's me. Anything?" He's been working slowly through Eleanor Costello's psych files, which by now we can assume that Burke has adjusted somewhat, if only to cover his own professional mistakes.

"I thought you were at your folks'?"

"Not until tomorrow."

"I can hear the joy in your voice." He laughs. "Family, huh?"

"You know yourself."

"Yeah." There is a shuffle of paper and I imagine that he's turning open Burke's notes. "So far, not much in the notes, as we suspected. It would be easier if we had his appointment diary so that we could ensure all the appointments are indeed accounted for here. It's so difficult to know whether he got rid of stuff."

I get up, uncurl my legs, and reach out of the sofa. Tucking the phone under my chin, I fill the kettle for tea.

"Can't you get the diary?"

"The warrant didn't cover it. The judge said he couldn't sign it off as it would compromise the confidentiality of other patients."

"You must have something that could help us."

"There's nothing about her fucking parents here, for starters. I mean, unless this shrink went to a different school of thought than the rest of them, that's gotta mean something. Mine never fucking shut up about my parents."

The corner of my mouth lifts into a smile. "Maybe you're more messed up than most people."

"Very funny. There's no mention of abuse in her childhood either."

"Well, that could be accurate. And if it's not, it's a lot to disclose to a person. She might not have felt able to tell him."

"You're probably right. I'm not a fan of this guy, that's all. I think he'll stick it to us every chance he gets."

"He'll have met his match in you then. Any other news?"

A sharp, short sigh comes down the line. "The final autopsies are through on both cases."

"Anything new?"

"Not that I can see. Could do with another pair of eyes, though."

"Anything on Lorcan Murphy?"

"Spoke to him directly. He remembered the night. Said some of the students who were underperforming were collecting course work. Amy was one. He gave me a few names. They checked out."

The kettle boils, clicks to a stop. Steam rises over my face.

"Right. I guess they were the same department."

"Like I said."

"I can almost see the gloat on your face."

"Brilliance is a burden, Sheehan, not a gift."

My lips twitch into a smile. "I wouldn't know."

He laughs. "Helen's come back with Peter's job prospects at the hands of Doyle."

"The company he was applying to for work?"

"Yes," he says. "And here's the shocker. He got an interview, but they said he never showed."

"A lack of focus on his part could indicate he had other things on his mind. Like killing his wife."

"Or that he *was* killing his wife. The interview was for 19 October."

"We need to find him."

"Lookit, I'm nearly done here. How's about I hunt down our dear Abigail and instead of a courier, dodgy as you like, I'll come over with both autopsy reports?"

Stirring the pot of tea, I carry it to the table. The local newsreader is looking grave, his mouth drawn downwards as he reports on something that's happening in the background.

In the corner of the TV there is a ticker that reads: "Live Events." There are blue lights parked all across Ha'penny Bridge; crowds of onlookers hold out their phones, snap at something in the water.

"Frankie?"

"Yeah, that sounds good. Do that." I hang up and reach for the remote. I've barely upped the volume on the TV when my mobile rings again.

"Sheehan," I answer.

"Frankie, it's Clancy."

I can see Clancy on the TV, a tall, gray-haired man striding away from the crowds, his hand cupped over the end of the phone. Gardaí are pushing people back from the edge of the bridge, putting up metal grilles to contain the gathering crowds. The tide is out, dragging the Liffey with it, showing up the green-stained walls of the concrete channel. To the left of the screen, there are two divers clambering up the steps that ascend from the river onto the street. Their heads are bent, dry suits gleaming with dark, filthy Liffey water.

"What's happening, Jack?"

"Another fucking body."

There is fear at the back of my throat, bitter, tart, sticky. A mouthful of tea, a pathetic tonic.

"Female?"

He turns around, appears to look over the bridge. "Impossible to be sure but, from clothing alone, appears male."

I need a while to process this. So much death. So much that we've failed on.

"It looks like suicide," Jack continues.

I'm surprised he can tell from where he's standing.

"What makes you say that?"

"His clothes, they look weighted down. The old 'stuff your pockets with rocks and drop yourself into a river' job."

"Right. You want me to come down?"

"Not yet. Keep your phone on, though. I'll wait for the coroner. If she suspects foul play—"

"I'll be there." I can hear the weakness in my own voice as I speak. A wave of depression washes over me, sinks its teeth into the back of my neck.

Baz arrives within a half hour. "Sorry, traffic was murder." He smirks at the joke.

"There's a body being pulled from the Liffey as we speak. Clancy may call," I say.

"Let's get down to it then." He sits and passes the reports to me. "You're definitely going to want to see these. I almost missed Eleanor's toxicology revelations due to the presence of Prussian blue on the skin postmortem, but this is bigger. A definite lead."

I open Eleanor's tox labs. The final result is a surprise but not completely. Systemic doses of the compound potassium hexacyanoferrate, or Prussian blue.

"This couldn't be from her arm?" I look up.

Baz shakes his head. "According to Abigail, there is no way the small amount that decorated the skin wound on Eleanor's arm could account for these results."

I flick to Amy's report, recalling what Abigail had told me about the paint in Amy's mouth. "There's nothing present in Amy's blood."

"We've got an MO of sorts, I think. The killer's trying to tell us something."

"Eleanor was ingesting the blue compound then? Intentionally? Regularly?"

"It seems so. I mean, it is or was so. The tests don't lie. It's anyone's guess why, though."

I go back, read through the full autopsy report again. The scars in the lower abdomen, which at first glance had seemed consistent with an appendectomy, had turned out to be old stab wounds. The recent fracture of the left wrist was explained as a closed fracture, the result of a severe crushing injury. She had suffered significant infection in one of the carpals, which had slowed healing.

The venous structure within the esophagus was distended, varicosities swelled all along its passage. A common finding with asphyxiation, but there was significant scar tissue found alongside. Scar tissue that had been allowed to build up over years, years of frequent convulsive contractions of the smooth muscle that confirmed Eleanor was bulimic.

Baz is lifting each page I study and leave down, slowly digesting the information after I've read it.

"Prussian blue. Our little friend just keeps coming back," he murmurs.

There's a graph at the base of the report, a study guide that shows common uses for the pigment, outlines how much would be expected to be found in the blood if the person had been a painter. Eleanor's blood shows three hundred milligrams approximately. Much more than a painter would expect to ingest just by using it.

Baz is flicking over his iPad; the screen is a white glow on his face. After a while he passes it to me.

"Check this out. Our friend Chagall was fond of that Prussian blue too."

I read through the article, soak up the information. Prussian blue is a deep, rich pigment used to create vibrant blues in painting. Involved in a revolution of sorts in the Japanese art scene, notably a print by Hokusai, *The Great Wave off Kanagawa*. The history of the pigment is layered with interesting anecdotes, from its accidental discovery through the mixture of blood iron and potash to the launch of the first telegraph of importance. I look up at Baz.

"It says here that it can be used to treat exposure to certain types of radiation?"

He shakes his head. "There's nothing in her medical history that would suggest she's been exposed to radiation, though." He taps the report. "Abigail's already run the tests."

"Spared no expense," I say drily.

"In fairness, she's done a pretty thorough job; they're not the usual tox reports. She simply noted a strange reaction on the bloods. Again at first she thought cyanide, but then, remembering Amy's results, she narrowed her search."

"Would there have been symptoms? Digesting this much of any chemical regularly can't be a good thing, surely?"

He blows air through his lips. "Agreed. But I can't see any side effects listed here."

"If it's drip-fed slowly, if the body is able to break it down, maybe you wouldn't notice anything?"

"Abigail reckons you'd have to swallow almost this amount a day for it to show up postmortem in these quantities. So whatever Eleanor Costello was up to, she would've known about the fact she'd ingested Prussian blue. This is deliberate."

Fury gathers in me. I am angry at myself for being unable to see the path this investigation is taking, angry at Eleanor Costello for being so fucking complicated. I fight the urge to throw the report, the file, across the room. Another cryptic factor to decipher. I'm angry at Eleanor, at Amy, at Tracy, at myself. I'm angry because we're rudderless.

"You okay?"

I run a hand through my hair. "Yeah. It's all so fucked up. It feels like we're piling mystery on top of mystery."

"I know. But we have a picture. It's not a clear one, but it's something."

I get up, flick the kettle back on.

"If I wasn't heading home for this bloody meeting tomorrow, I wouldn't be feeling so het up about it."

He looks up through his eyelashes. "You could make a day of it. If you're up to it, talk to Keegan, maybe a few of the neighbors?"

I put out two mugs, add tea bags, pour the steaming water. "I dunno. Eamon Keegan is very similar to Priscilla Fagan in that way. He won't want a visit unless we have new information—namely, the name of his daughter's killer."

Baz pulls out a large notepad from beneath the coffee table. Clicks his pen.

"May I?" he asks, and when I nod, he opens it up.

At the top he writes, "Sequence."

"We're saying that Peter Costello and Amy Keegan met online, on some unknown site on the Dark Web, possibly Black Widow?"

I place the mugs of tea between us and sit across from him, curl my legs beneath me on the floor. I nod in reply. "A work in progress, but for the moment that's what we're going on."

He makes bullet points as he speaks.

"Right. Priscilla hasn't seen her brother for, now, twelve weeks. He's been ill. She's tried to call but didn't appear to worry about him until his wife's death. His phone was in the same areas around Dublin frequently, along with Amy Keegan's. There is strong evidence that they were having an affair. Amy has an argument with her father on the phone where she confesses to having an affair with the husband of one of her lecturers. Two days later, Eleanor Costello is found hanged in her home. Still no sign of Peter.

"The killer then takes Amy to an unknown location, where he films and brutally murders her, streaming the entire thing live onto the internet. The killer takes Amy Keegan's body, in a vehicle not yet discovered, to her hometown of Clontarf—"

I hold up a hand. "He could live in Clontarf, remember. He may not have had to travel far. The house where he killed her could be anywhere."

Baz nods. "Okay. He waits until darkness to stake Amy's remains in the center of the town's annual Halloween bonfire. Hours later her body is discovered by her father's work colleague, Tom Quinn. So far so good?"

My eyes are closed. I'm listening. Listening for the answers that lie somewhere in the midst of the story. I nod and wave my hand. Continue.

"Interviews with both Priscilla Fagan and Tom Quinn corroborate the supposed sequence of events, however Priscilla insists on Peter's innocence. Costello's neighbor Neil Doyle has implied that Peter could get frustrated with his wife but also suggests that he may be a victim of abuse. Priscilla has a clear dislike of Eleanor Costello and may be sympathizing with her brother's frustrations with his wife.

"We know Peter Costello was likely depressed from his continued unemployment, and a daylight lamp in his office implies that this time of year was particularly difficult for him." He stops, sighs, turns over a page in his notepad.

Wrapping my hands around my tea, I fill in the remaining blanks.

"Peter is Irish-Italian, self-made in finance but unemployed for the past four years. No children; culturally, that may have significance and may be a further source of disappointment for him. To help bridge his time, he has become something of an amateur art historian and occasionally enjoyed painting. A well-known artist's pigment was placed by the killer on both bodies. The bristle of a paintbrush was found caught in a wound postmortem on Peter's deceased wife's left arm.

"According to his sister, he'd been suffering from ill health for at least a year. This appears to have weakened him sufficiently in that his neighbor also seemed to comment on it. He seems to have had little professional contact or done any networking over the last year, seeing that the only reference listed on his CV is his neighbor Neil Doyle." I take a sip from my mug, enjoy the strong bitter taste of the tea, then sigh. "And we still have no idea where he is."

My mobile flashes and vibrates across the coffee table toward us. I am almost grateful for the interruption.

"Hello, Sheehan."

"Frankie, it's Jack."

I straighten. "What's happening?"

"They've only pulled fucking Costello from the bloody Liffey," he says. Eloquent as ever.

CHAPTER 16

VICKY, MY NEURO consultant, waves the light in front of my eyes. First the left. Pause. Then the right. Pause. She clicks the penlight off, slots it into her pocket. Unconscious movements. Performed many times daily. Her index finger is upright before me. I fix my vision to it, follow the movement as she passes it in front of my face, drawing a crucifix in the air before me. A medical benediction.

"Prussian blue. Have you heard of it?"

"Prussian blue? Hmm. I dunno. Why do you ask?" She has turned, is making notes.

"An interest."

She looks up, her mouth pinched at one side. "An interest?" She shakes her head. Laughs.

"Oh, all right then. A case. Don't worry, I won't quote you," I say.

She stands, directs me to do likewise. She raises both my arms with her fingertips until they are straight, outstretched, shoulder level. I know this test. Have performed it many times. I close my eyes.

She pats me on the hand.

"Sit," she commands, and continues to fill in her notes. After a while, she signs her name to the bottom of my file.

"Firstly, you continue to show a clean slate. No indications of trauma or pathology. Your scar is healing nicely, although I know it still pains you. I can only say that it will get easier. The knife went through a minor cutaneous sensory nerve branch and it's regenerating, which may go to explain some of the burning sensations and tingling you've been feeling. Worst-case scenario, eighteen months. Otherwise, you're good."

I can't help the smile. Part happiness, part cynicism. My physicality is not the lasting problem.

"Thanks, Doc," I reply.

Eleanor Costello is knocking on the inside of my skull. Peter Costello was a mess. No phone was found with his body, not that he could have been making calls to me. He'd been in the water for near on two months. The fact that he's been missing almost as long corroborates Abigail's estimations. On the morning that his remains were found, there had been a spring tide, causing exceptionally low water levels in the Liffey. Costello's dark head had been spotted, bobbing about like a seaweed-clad buoy, by an early-morning walker.

Initially, the walker hadn't thought much of it, but as the water leveled, the ghostly shape of Peter's face flashed in the grim depths. And from there, the walker had contacted the guards. At first, like Eleanor's death, it appeared to be suicide.

There's no way of knowing whether Peter Costello was dead or alive when he hit the riverbed—forensics can only give us so much— but the opening call of the autopsy was murder. The injuries on his body indicated foul play. There were numerous stab wounds along his sides and the insides of his thighs. If he hadn't drowned, he would have bled to death.

In short, his remains were in a state but, to be honest, not in the state he should have been in for so long in the water. The cold start to the winter months was for once working in our favor.

Abigail pushed through some early tox reports. Time is not on our side, and with our sole suspect turning up bloated and months dead we have to bend time. Anything she could detect in Costello's blood that had to do with the compound Prussian blue, I wanted to know about as soon as possible.

"I'll deal with Finance later," I had said, to Clancy's openmouthed protest. "I can't risk missing something again, unless you want still to be figuring this out in a year from now, with our reputation torn to shreds in the press and a body count up round our ears."

He'd kept his mouth shut and walked away. Let me at it. And so I went at it. After it.

Abigail ran the tests, and there it was: no Prussian blue, but its associated poison, thallium.

Vicky answers my question finally. "We use Prussian blue mostly in the treatment of those who have been exposed to radioactive material. It's extremely effective. But there are other uses; in years gone by it was used as an antidote to a neural poison, a heavy metal called thallium. Not the most fashionable poison nowadays, although I'm not sure why, it would be highly effective."

"Why would you say that?" I step behind the screen in her office, step out of the role of patient, victim, and into my work clothes. Armor.

She laughs. "Are you sure I'm not on trial here?"

"I'm not sure I want to know about your other crimes, Doc, but on this one, you're safe."

"In that case, I'll oblige. To be frank, it's bloody difficult to diagnose. It's simply not on our radar. It should be, it's nicknamed 'the poisoner's poison.' But generally, it's effective because unlike some of the other"—she sighs—"preferred poisons, it's colorless, odorless, and you can make it slow-acting. Which generally means a culprit can have left the scene long before their victim succumbs to the effects. Presentation of symptoms can vary depending on a person's metabolism or their build, but it's a miserable death in any case."

"I see. It wouldn't have to be a deliberate poisoning, would it? I mean, could someone ingest it by accident?"

I come around the screen, adjust the collar of my coat, push my sleeves up. Regain control.

"Anything is possible. But in the amounts required to kill some-one"—she clicks a few keys on her computer, then turns to face me again—"I don't think so."

I push my luck. "Symptoms?"

She looks to the ceiling. "Oh, now you're testing me. Neurologi-cal, mostly. I think. Hair loss. It's been a long time since I studied it. Hang on." She reaches up, removes a thick medical tome from a shelf above her desk. Searches the index, then flicks through the pages. "Ah. Yes, alopecia. Here." She folds down the corner of the page and passes the book to me. "You can drop it back when you're done."

I tuck it under my arm. "Thanks."

I leave the medical center and head down the quays. The Liffey rolls by beside me. I brace myself against the cold December breeze and lean over the wall. The river moves thickly between the busy streets, the water brown, heavy with silt and grime. The current sucks and laps up against the concrete banks.

I let myself gaze down into the water. Imagine the chill that must have enveloped his body. Could a wife do this to her husband? Could Eleanor have done this to her husband?

Within the depths, he's stone-cold, skin flabby and bloated. His hair moves like seaweed, his head tugged left, then right, with the weight of water; his body leaning backward in the direction of the current, toward the sea, toward nothingness.

I can't help the wave of goose bumps that erupts along the base of my neck, travels down the length of my arms. The sensation has noth-ing to do with the cold. I can't keep the image of his passport picture out of my mind. He was handsome. Attractive. A perfect match for his wife. And now he's lying in a body bag, ravaged by the grimy Liffey waters.

There is a coffee shop that I used to go to years ago, when I first started out as a fresh-faced, honest-to-goodness Garda, where innocently I believed that, as long as I kept my nose and soul clean, I could stand by justice and watch her cut through badness like the proverbial hot knife. Right and wrong. Easy morals. But a compass does not only point in two directions. There are four poles. Two distinct and definite paths between north and south. The in-between—that's the world I live in.

I cross the river, walk away from the quays. On Lime Street, just up from what used to be Windmill Lane Studios, I find the café. The geography has changed since the last time I came up here. The studios have been sold, regenerated, remolded into something more enterprising in a midrecession Dublin, but there it is, the café. The fascia gray, aluminum. The type of café that doesn't bother with anything grander than plastic-backed chairs and shining easy-to-clean tablecloths but doesn't skimp on the coffee and doesn't ask you to sell your firstborn so that you can afford their takeaway.

It's late afternoon and it's comfortably occupied. Three or four individuals searching for answers in the contents of their cups. No one sits at the window, the high stools empty, punters unable to relax with their back to a room. I order a filter coffee, which the barista serves promptly from a pot already brewing. She informs me of their free refill option if I pay an extra thirty cents. The free option that you have to pay for. I suppress a smile and shake my head. No, thanks.

Sliding into a seat at the back, I open the page that Vicky had been reading from. Peter Costello would not have experienced symptoms of his thallium poisoning immediately. He might have had nausea, stomach cramping, diarrhea, even vomiting if doses were high enough, which at first glance they seem not to have been. Abigail is still unraveling how the poison affected his body.

His medical notes have been released, which was less trouble than we envisaged. His doctor seemed either to have great sympathy for Peter or to be fearful he might be found guilty of negligence. He released the notes without any to-do, barely glancing at the warrant.

Peter had been ill for almost a year. His GP appears to have checked for everything from Lyme disease to psychosomatic illnesses. In the end Peter was given a weak diagnosis of some diffuse autoimmune disorder coupled with chronic fatigue syndrome and irritable bowel syndrome. The man's hair had been falling out in chunks.

He'd suffered moments of weakness in both legs. There was one episode where he had fallen in the street, having lost all sensation in his foot. His ankle had been badly sprained by the incident, and he'd cut open his hand, enough for stitches, but still the GP stuck resolutely to his diagnosis.

It's safe to say that if he had been diagnosed, he would have had permanent defects from constant exposure to thallium. Possibly, he would have died from it eventually anyway. We are searching through the Costello house again, looking for where Peter Costello could have been exposed to such a deadly poison. But my feeling is that it was through his food and it's long since been disposed of.

There is guilt rotting in my chest, stinking up my insides, and unease is unfurling in my stomach. If Peter Costello has been in his watery grave for some time, who has been using his handset? Who is my caller, the breath in the darkness, the presence on the other end of the line? In my mind, Eleanor turns, glances back at me, smiles. And I know that smile now: She knows something. Has a secret. Had a secret. She was taking the ultimate control over her husband. Drip-feeding him poison. Weakening him.

I'm hoping that, somewhere in the Costello house, there's an explanation. A simple one that resets the scales. Takes me back to firmer ground where he's somehow the culprit we're after. But it can't be. The best I can hope for is that she poisoned him to protect herself. The

Prussian blue found in her gut is too much of a coincidence. Well, not a coincidence at all, as Abigail reminds me. Prussian blue is evidence that Peter Costello's wife tried to murder him or at least toyed with that idea.

I find the passage in the textbook. Titled "Decontamination." There. Prussian blue, or potassium hexacyanoferrate, is to be given as an antidote when thallium poisoning is suspected. It binds to the compound in the large intestine so that the toxin can be discharged from the body. At some point Eleanor must have feared she had ingested the poison too, or maybe she had done her reading. Thallium is very toxic; contact with the skin is enough to result in illness or death. Maybe at some point she decided she had been too close to her husband. Or maybe she experienced some of the symptoms he was going through.

Ultimately, she decided to take matters into her own hands, to regain a foothold in her personal life. What was it he had done to draw her eye to this? How far can one person push another? As far as a fractured wrist, apparently, or an affair with a younger woman.

When Baz phones, I'm not deflated by what he says; I've grown used to the idea that Eleanor might have wanted to punish or kill her husband. Thallium has been found in his deodorant, he tells me. Something she could rely on him using most days. An aerosol. Skin absorption. He couldn't have killed either his wife or his lover. He had been dead for longer than either of them. And this opens up the field.

I close my eyes. Think about the victims and what kind of person would want to kill them in this way. The killer will have known all of them. Not necessarily intimately. The acquaintance may be very superficial, a shop that they frequented or a restaurant or someone who watched them from the anonymity of the Dark Web.

I close the textbook and pick up my phone. I dial my family liaison officer, let her know I have to cancel our meeting with my family.

Back at the office, the whiteboard is filling up with information. I take the duster and clean the word "suspect" from beneath Peter

Costello's name. I'm angry that I allowed myself to believe in the stereotype. A man murders his wife, then kills his lover in rage, in jealousy, in an expression of power. I've seen it too many times, and it's why I should have realized that these murders don't fit the picture.

These deaths were planned and carried out by someone with no remorse, a cold hand. A small voice in the back of my mind whispers, *Someone like Eleanor.*

Baz stands beside me, pulls up a chair for me. I give him a weak smile.

"So, this is what square one looks like," he says, gazing at the case board.

"Pretty much," I say.

"It doesn't change the fact that Costello was a controlling fucker, does it? I mean, his wife's remains tell us that much. There are scars on her body too."

I sigh. "Neither does it change the fact that his wife was probably trying to kill him. Prussian blue is the antidote for thallium poisoning, and she was taking it regularly."

He blows air through his lips. Leans against the wall. "It seemed so likely that the pigment in her system was related to his love of painting."

"Here we have it. All the grays of an investigation," I say.

"And no phone?"

I shake my head. "Someone must have taken his handset, changed the SIM. We haven't had a sniff from it since Costello was found." I pull out my phone, check the screen for good measure; in the cold, comforting light of day I'm not intimidated by a silent phone call. "Nothing."

THE BONSAI TREE has shed its overlarge leaves; there is miniature lush foliage flourishing over the canopy. My shrink will be pleased. Textbook.

On the counter, Tracy Ward's file is resting beneath my bag. I move to the window, open it, and stare down on the dark street. I light up a cigarette. From the street lamps, orange circles of light project outwards into the blackness. The sky is clear of cloud, the lights of Dublin city not quite bright enough to obscure the cool twinkling of the stars or the steady white glow of the moon. I finish the cigarette quickly. Then turn, trace my hand over the stiff foliage of the bonsai, and head for bed.

My limbs and eyes are heavy. Months of chasing a ghost have exhausted me. Despite the horrors the last few days have brought, I believe I'll sleep tonight and my mind will open to all the fragments of terror I've witnessed over the past six months.

CHAPTER 17

BAZ JOGS TO catch up with me. I'm hurrying against the cold, the wind, and the time. This morning showed the first real frost of the winter. A hoarfrost. The university trees are still against the chill blue sky, their branches feathered white with bold, frigid spines. I lift the sleeve of my coat, feel the blast of air against my skin, and glance at my watch.

"We need to hurry. Otherwise we'll miss him," I say.

"I'll break my neck on this," Baz answers, picking his way along the edge of the path.

"There's always some collateral damage. Just hurry up," I say.

Lorcan Murphy is still following Eleanor's timetable; he is in the midst of a biochemistry lecture with year threes. There's only thirty minutes left before it finishes. That gives us approximately half an hour to chat, off the record, with the barista, before catching Murphy exiting the lecture.

I walk through the university doors and down the same hallways that Eleanor Costello walked or ran along each morning, although I can't quite imagine her ever being late for a lecture or a meeting. I see her taking sure, brisk steps ahead of me, the corners of her blazer flapping back over her hips as she walks, a file tucked under one arm, a briefcase in the other. I hesitate outside the coffee shop where I spoke to Mr. Murphy in the days after Eleanor's death. Baz arrives at my side.

Instinct tells me that Nicole Duarte—the barista—wouldn't cope well with a formal interview. She wanted to tell me something that day, but hesitated when she discovered Eleanor Costello had been murdered. With the right leverage, a desire to keep law on her side, she may talk. She is supporting a two-year-old daughter at home. Alone. A little digging about shows her claiming dole while working.

She has her back to us when we approach. Her hands are busy, stacking cups on the coffee machine in preparation for the eleven o'clock onslaught of students and staff in the next half hour.

"Hello again," I say.

She jumps, turns, her hand on her throat.

"Sorry, I didn't mean to startle you," I apologize.

She laughs, but I can tell she is unnerved already. "Detective! You're back."

Her eyes check over my shoulder, look beyond Baz, into the café, the hallway behind.

I laugh. Lighten the mood. "Just waiting for Lorcan to finish his lecture. We're early. Is it okay to have a coffee while we wait?"

Immediately, her slim shoulders drop. She smiles. "Sure. Americanos okay? Or cappuccinos?"

"Americanos are fine."

Nodding to Baz, I indicate that he should take a seat near the back of the café; then I turn back to Nicole Duarte.

"Gosh, it's quiet in here today." I make a show of looking around.

She shakes her head. "Not really, it's always quiet at this time. Between lectures. You get a few stragglers." She goes to the machine, flicks a switch, unscrews the coffee holder.

She glances back, smiles again. "Hangovers and the like, you know how students are. And Dr. Costello, actually. She was frequently late." She laughs. "Or living on the edge, she liked to say."

The ground shifts a little beneath me. I struggle to keep my tone light. Again, I find it odd that she brings up Eleanor so readily.

"Eleanor late? I wouldn't have thought it of someone like her."

She looks back at me, gives me a funny frown. "Eleanor? That was exactly like her. I mean, she was on time mostly, but at least once a week I'd hear her heels clipping down the hall. I'd have her coffee ready, she'd snatch it, laugh, and head on to deliver her lecture."

I pull back. Eleanor. She's a type A personality, high achiever. Determined. Perfectionist. I remember her childhood, the shoplifting, petty crime, and add risk taker to the list. I remember the contents of her laptop.

"Were there complaints?"

Nicole blows air through her lips. "Not one. Eleanor was one of the best lecturers this university has seen. Students would write from all over the country to sit in on them. She was very charismatic when lecturing. She lit up. Those students would have waited three hours for ten minutes of one of her lectures."

I lean in. "You've been to one?"

She looks down. Her cheeks color. "I listened. One of the students used to record them on a Dictaphone."

"Ah." I check my watch again. Fifteen minutes.

She places two cups under the shelf of the machine.

I place another couple of euro on the counter. "Here, have one for yourself as well. You can join us if you like. Tell us a little more about Eleanor."

She nods, meets my eyes, and I get the sense that she's wanted to talk all along. To talk about Eleanor.

"Take a seat, I'll bring them over."

"Thanks."

I turn, catch Baz's eye. He gives me a hard stare, which I ignore. This is not exactly aboveboard, shoehorning information from a potential witness without a tape running, without a formal interview, without the witness knowing what we're about. There's a strict protocol to follow. It's not right, but right now, it's not wrong either.

Nicole unties her apron, pockets the change I've given her, and fills a glass with water. Frugal. Good mother. She slides into a seat at the table, sitting on the edge of the chair, her knees pressed tightly together, her hands grasping the glass on her lap as if she's drawing strength from it.

She glances at my coffee, then meets my eyes. "Sorry, I'm not much of a coffee drinker."

I give her another reassuring smile. "I'm sure water is better for you anyway."

I take a sip of the coffee, then sit my cup gently back on the saucer. I stare purposefully out the window, down at the pitch where again teams of players are exercising in the crisp white grounds.

"They're determined!" I bring my attention back to Nicole. "I'll bet you're looking forward to the Christmas break?"

Her shoulders settle, and she places the water glass on the table, crosses her legs. "Oh, yes. I love Christmas. Gabe and I have a wonderful time."

"Gabe?"

She smiles. "Gabriella. My daughter." She produces a photo from her pocket.

I look down at it. A smiling toddler snug in her mother's arms. Pink-ribboned pigtails, round cheeks, shy smile.

"She looks like you," I say.

"Thanks."

"When are they finishing here? It must be soon?"

"Not until the twenty-second, but we don't come back until the eighth, so it all balances out. To be honest, I'm glad of the routine."

I nod. "I get that. Is there a staff party?"

"Was. Last week. They get earlier every year." She laughs. "I don't go often, though."

"It must have been strange this year. I mean, with Eleanor and all. Peter too."

"Peter?"

I raise an eyebrow. "Eleanor's husband."

Realization widens in her eyes. "Right. I never met him. I don't think, anyway. He may have called in, I wouldn't know, although I—" She stops herself, flushes. "No. Nothing."

Baz is glaring hard now. I can hear noise building down the hallway and know the lecture is finishing. I don't want Lorcan to see me talking with Nicole.

"Nicole, anything you know might be helpful."

She looks up, surprised. "I don't know—"

I hate myself for doing it, but I rest my hand over hers, squeeze lightly, and force as much sadness into my voice as possible.

"Nicole, please. You don't have to come to the station and give a formal statement if you don't want to, but we need more information to help us with Eleanor's death."

She looks down. The noise is working its way up the hall, and a few students step into the café, hover by the counter, staring up at the menu. Lorcan Murphy won't be far behind them.

There are tears thickening along the base of her eyes when she looks up.

"I don't want to lose my job."

Baz straightens and speaks for the first time. "A woman lost her life, Nicole. Help us find her killer."

A tear tips onto her cheek, and she pushes it away with her fingertips. "I was going to say that I think Mr. Murphy and Dr. Costello had a thing." She looks up, panic whitening her face. "I'm not sure. Only, he seemed to have a thing for her, I just don't know if she felt it back."

I nod to Baz, to check the hallway for Lorcan Murphy. He gets up, goes to the café entrance, and watches for Murphy's approach. I return my attention to Nicole.

"How do you know this? Did you see them together?"

She sniffs, shakes her head. "No. I . . . We kissed, at a work event. We had a few dates, cinema and the like. Nothing too extravagant. I like him. Liked. A lot. But he stopped calling. At the college finals dinner, I got pretty drunk and confronted him, he said he was sorry but he was in love with Eleanor and it wouldn't be fair to me to carry on."

She takes a deep breath, pulls her shoulders back, cleans her face with the back of her hand. "Wow. I sound pathetic, don't I?"

I squeeze her hand again. "Not at all. But you can't say for certain that they were involved?"

"They flirted a bit, but I couldn't see it as anything other than infatuation on his part. I don't know. I've never been very good at reading those kinds of signs."

Baz signals.

I sigh. "You and me both."

Baz smiles up the hallway, and I move Nicole's water glass to a nearby table.

I give her a final smile. "I think Lorcan's arrived."

Her face whitens again and she stands quickly, making her way back to the front of the café.

Baz is showing his badge, shaking hands. It's seconds before they are across the room.

CHAPTER 18

LORCAN GREETS ME with a handshake.

"Detective! What a nice surprise. I hope it's news on Eleanor's killer?"

I hold his stare for a second longer than is natural. It's sometimes remarkable how little it takes to unnerve a person. His smile falters.

"Mr. Murphy—"

"Please, it's Lor—"

"Mr. Murphy, I'm afraid I'm going to have to ask you to come in for a chat."

"Sorry?" He searches my face, then looks to Baz, then back again. "I can't," he says flatly.

"It's important that you come with us, Mr. Murphy."

"I've lectures all afternoon."

I retrieve my phone from my pocket, scroll through Eleanor's old calendar. "That's odd. I assumed you were free, from lectures at least. According to your timetable."

I hold out my phone so that he can see his schedule.

He sighs. "The lectures, they're private. One-to-one tuition. It's end of term. They wouldn't be on the timetable." He pulls his shoulders back as if he's decided something. "What's this about anyway? I mean, I said I would help, but I've told you everything I know."

"We need to talk to you about your relationship with Eleanor." I let the statement hang for a second but long enough to see his eyes widen, then add, "What she was like to work with, her professionalism. Absenteeism? Whether she was friendly."

He swallows. "But you know all that stuff, or if you don't, I'm happy to stop for a coffee now?"

I step aside. Give him room to move. "I'm afraid we need it all tied up. Official. On record. Really, you're one of our most reliable witnesses as to her personality. You worked with her for years as her assistant but, more than that, as her understudy on your PhD."

The lines on his brow soften; he closes his eyes briefly. Then, "Okay." He steps into the space I've made for him, and Baz joins his side, leading him through the university halls and out into the freezing December air.

BAZ BENDS HIS head, tugs at his hairline; his knuckles are mottled red and white.

"Keep your knickers on," I say.

"Murphy could make life very difficult for Nicole here. She could lose her job. You have to make him tell you himself. If you challenge him about his relationship with Eleanor like this, he'll know it came from Nicole."

"She knew that when she told me."

He puffs his lips. "Really? That's it? Have you no conscience? People like her are needless casualties in cases like this. She has a kid, for fuck's sake."

I raise my eyebrows at him. My hands are clean. Work in the gray.

Do what needs to be done with minimal damage. That's my duty of care. We either play with the lousy pieces we've got and lose, risking another death, or we cheat to win and catch this fucker. I know which one will help me sleep at night. We're all insomniacs with an unsolved case.

"Nicole Duarte knew what I was about. From the moment she first approached me, she's wanted to tell us that little nugget on Murphy. She's sweet and she means well, but she's human. Hurt. Jilted. On some level, she wants Murphy implicated."

His arms drop to his sides; his head tips back. "Christ. You don't know that. We're not all as emotionally screwed as you, Frankie."

I slam the case file shut. I don't need this bullshit every time I make a decision that makes his conscience whimper.

"Detective, this is a murder investigation. In case you've forgotten, a young woman, just a few years younger than you, has been slaughtered live on the internet for sickos to wank over. Another woman has been hanged, and our only suspect has been found dumped like a shopping trolley in the bloody Liffey. This is not Disney-fucking-land. There is no happy ending. There is, however, the occasional gift, if that's not too perverse a word, that's left behind for us to open. If you can walk away from that, fair fucks to you. But don't delude yourself. Don't think you are helping anyone by doing that. Because you're not."

I tuck the file under my arm and move to leave the office, but Baz blocks the way. Murphy is down the hall, sweating in the interview room. It's only been ten minutes since we brought him in, but ten minutes alone in a room can feel like an hour and I want him relaxed when we start.

"Frankie, wait." There is an apology hanging back in Baz's voice. "I didn't mean—"

"I don't give a shit what you meant. I've a job to do. If you can't help me with it, then get out of my way."

I brush past him.

"Frankie!" He wants to sit in on the interview. But selfishly, I can't stand the thought of it. I have enough demons sitting on my shoulders; I don't need a six-foot-tall angel of conscience looking over me too.

"I still haven't received your written report on the shrink. I'll expect it when I get back," I demand.

LORCAN MURPHY IS crying. Fat, messy tears that slip down the sicles of his nose and drop onto the desk. He mops them up quickly with his sleeve.

"Sorry, Detective," he mumbles. "This whole shit has got me, like, broken or something."

There is redness growing along his cheekbones. Embarrassment for crying. Embarrassment for being a man and crying. Fear or grief for his work colleague. That's what he insists Eleanor was. I've not told him what Nicole has said. Witnesses and suspects alike are best squeezed fresh. If they are given any context to work with, suddenly all their answers are colored with either offense or defense.

I reach out, take his glass. "Let me get you some water."

He glances up, and another droplet falls onto the desk. "Thank you."

Once in the viewing room, I hand the glass to Steve, who fills it from a water dispenser in the corner. I watch Murphy, arms folded.

Tom Quinn had identified Lorcan as a friend of Amy's. He could fit the profile. He's intelligent with a sort of schoolboy charm. He's the right age. Lives alone. There is something lacking in the way he presents himself. He scrubs the tears from his face. Tips his head back, sniffs. It could all be a performance. He must know that I'm watching him.

He turns, checks the corners of the room, clocks the camera high on the wall, over his right shoulder. Momentarily, he appears worried, surprised. This is the reaction most people have when they see that they are being observed; the next is looking at the mirrored window

I'm standing behind. And right on cue, Lorcan Murphy turns his head and looks guiltily into my eyes.

"Well?" Steve asks. "What do you think?"

I sigh. "He's a strong maybe. If what Nicole has said is true, he's as good as lied to us."

"He looks shifty to me."

"That's just it. Whoever our perp is, they're not visibly 'shifty.' They would be calm. In control. They would almost enjoy the attention and the knowledge that we had almost nothing on them."

"Blah! I don't go in for that kind of mumbo jumbo. He's performing. Look at him."

I do as instructed. Murphy has his head dropped down onto his arms. Hiding.

I turn away from the window. Take the glass from Steve. "Any sign of Baz?"

"He said he'd a report to write."

I can't help a thin smile. "Right."

Entering the room, I avoid Murphy's gaze. I sit across from him, then slide the glass of water over the desk. "Ready?"

He takes a long drink, then nods. I depress the record button and the cassette begins to roll.

"Tell us about your relationship with Eleanor."

"Relationship?"

I treat him to a half-smile. "Yes. When did you meet, and so on?"

He looks at the backs of his hands. "Oh, okay. Actually, we met quite a while before we started working together." He glances up, relaxes. "She was speaking at some charity thing. Encouraging big corporations to part with cash to get medicines to rural areas in India. She seemed fearless.

"Afterward, at the bar, my tutor introduced us. She was quite frightening close-up. I mean, obviously not in a physical sense. She was a stunning woman. I mean in the sense that she seemed so confident, so sure of herself, that she came across as quite stern." He laughs. "As I got to know her, though, I realized that this was just one of her many faces. Professionally, she wore a mask, but those of us who got to know her saw glimpses of her humor every now and then."

"Humor?"

"Yes. She had a wicked sense of humor. It wasn't obvious or frivolous. I guess I'd call it mischievous, but what made it so delicious was that you only glimpsed it if you knew her well enough. She was a mistress of subtext and innuendo so subtle it could be delivered in a priest's sermon and the congregation would be none the wiser."

In my mind's eye, Eleanor is running from me, her face tipped to the side in sunlight. The corners of her mouth raised with silent laughter.

He meets my eyes. "You look like her, you know. A little."

A little. He means not quite as beautiful. Not that she was beautiful when she was found, but before someone helped her to her death. Hanging is not one to preserve the looks.

I tilt my head. "So you worked with her for . . . ?" I let him finish.

"Almost four years."

"What's your PhD about?"

His head snaps up at the change in subject. "In everyday language: the management of *Staph aureus* against tumor cells through manipulation of temperature."

I raise my eyebrows. "You're curing cancer?"

He flushes. A delicate blush of pink to the tips of his ears. "Hardly. It sounds more progressive than it is, but in reality all science is brutish and clumsy. At the moment, I'm inoculating petri dishes with staph and examining what happens to them under different temperatures and in different environs."

"Environs?"

He shrugs, spreads his hands. "When exposed to blood, light, pigments. Believe it or not, even after so many years, it's early days."

I try not to jump on the word "pigments." "And?"

He sighs. "It's slow. It seems staph will grow unchecked in any manner of conditions."

"Not a good thing?"

"Basically, no. Unchecked, staph will take over, and for immuno-suppressed individuals it could kill, so presently not the best way to attack tumors. Preferably, we like to keep patients still breathing by the end of a course of treatment. We need control, visibility, and aggression." His face grows dark with determination. "An army is of no use if you can't check it and send it in the right direction."

"And that's why you need the pigments, to see where your army is traveling, so to speak?"

He nods. "You got it."

"How do you get a pigment to stain the right area? Will it not simply get into the bloodstream and light up everywhere?"

He holds up a finger. "We use a pigment that's already known to be taken up by cells exposed to radiation. Then you've got a substance that clings to treated regions. For a time, at least."

"That's impressive. Who would have thought that a simple pigment could do all that?"

"Prussian blue. It has been used for years by painters."

I lean closer but get off the pigment trail. "Explain to me how the tutor-student thing works with a PhD. It seems a very casual affair?"

"I write the stuff, do the work. She reads, gives suggestions, feeds back on the shape, references, and language. Although I'm not an easy student. I get distracted by the research too often. She steers me back, though."

"Steered," I correct.

"Sorry," he mumbles.

"You must have had a few late nights over the years. In the office together, bashing out a paper or some such."

He looks up. "No. Goodness. Eleanor, she always went home. Always. Five o'clock came and whoosh, beat the rush back to Bray."

"You never . . . ?"

He meets my eyes. "Never what?" Then sees my meaning.

"You were never involved then?"

"No." Emphatic.

"I'm only asking in order to build a picture, Mr. Murphy. Did you ever kiss Eleanor Costello in a romantic sense?"

"No." His hands are twisting on his lap beneath the table, I can see it in the movement of his shoulders.

"Did you want to?"

For a brief moment he looks genuinely haunted. "God forgive me. Yes."

I suppress a smile, hide my victory; then: "That must have been very difficult for you."

Fine, fair eyebrows draw down. "How so?"

"Working with"—I pause, dig up his own words—"such a stunning woman, but not being able to scratch that itch."

A flare of nostrils. "It wasn't like that."

"Wasn't it?"

"No."

"How was it then? Did you make a pass? Did she reject you? That must have stung, Lorcan?" I use his first name, soft-like.

He pulls back. "She was married," he says. Angry.

I hold his gaze. "Yes," I say. "Yes, she was."

I give him some time to collect himself, take a drink of water. He wipes his mouth with his fingertips. Pink splotches have risen on the pale planes of his face. I ease the foot off. I don't want to push him. No one wants to hit the cul-de-sac of a no-comment interview.

"Going back to your PhD. The pigment you used, what form is the pigment in when you use it?"

He waits a few seconds before answering. Cautious, wondering what corner I'll push him into now.

"Liquid," he replies. "But we make it up from powder."

"This pigment, Prussian blue, is also used as an antidote for thallium poisoning. Did you know that?"

He pulls himself up in the seat, looks around the room. I've surprised him. "What has this got to do with Eleanor?"

"The pigment that you're working with has been found on our murder victims—Eleanor Costello, Amy Keegan—and thallium was found in Peter Costello's blood. Do you know anything about that?"

His mouth is agape. He stutters, pushes back from the table. Hand outstretched, he shakes his finger at me.

"I know what you're trying to do here. Now that you can't blame Peter, you're going to try to pin this on me. I did not do this. I did not kill Eleanor or Peter."

"Calm down, Mr. Murphy. I'm asking you a simple question. Do you know how Prussian blue, a pigment that you're working with almost daily, got onto your tutor's dead body?"

"No." He goes to the door. "I don't need this. I've tried to help you, but I don't need this. Let me out."

I stand slowly, straighten my jacket, then approach him. He backs away from the door like a frightened animal, but there is liquid hatred glowing in his eyes. I open the door, then offer my hand.

"Helen will sign you out. Thank you for your time, Mr. Murphy."

He leaves, ignoring my hand, and I can't help the smile that pulls at the corner of my mouth.

Steve is out of the viewing room immediately.

"You let him go!"

"We don't have enough to hold him. Helen will put a tail on him. I want to see if he'll try to run."

Steve pushes a hand through the copper of his hair. "Jesus, you love chasing missing guys, don't you?"

I meet his eyes. "In my experience, they only run when they've something to hide."

LORCAN MURPHY'S FIRST move becomes clear the next morning. Clancy storms into my office and slaps the *Dublin Herald* down on the desk.

"The fucking rat," he says.

The headline reads, "Blue Murder," an entire section on the pigment Prussian blue, its colorful history, dark and favorable uses, and a renewed summary of our cases. The thrust of the article centers around the thallium story line, with the journo taking his readers back to the olden days when the heavy metal was used to kill silently.

"Murphy," I whisper. "He sold out."

"The fucking smartarse. Well, he's not as smart as he thinks, the fucker."

"He was pretty pissed when he left. This is his two fingers." I'm skim-reading. The article gives a summary of how our victims met their ends, how Costello had slowly been poisoned before his body was found in the Liffey. There is no mention about where the pigment was found on Eleanor's or Amy's body, but there in the text Lorcan Murphy has shat all over his innocence.

"Here," I say, pointing at the section. "This is what we wanted. I never told him that Eleanor had ingested the pigment. Here's the slip."

Clancy leans over my shoulder. "Well, he knows where he can stick his two fingers now. As I said before, Frankie, I'd almost feel sorry for this fucker. You gonna pull him in again?"

I shake my head. "No. Let him think he's gotten away with it this time. Instinct tells me we can learn more from him when he's out there than when he's in an interview room. When we bring him in, I need there to be no doubt."

In the article, there's a photo of Eleanor and Peter, taken on their wedding day. Fine blond hair cut in a sharp line along the jaw, softened across the forehead with a light fringe. Rose-pink lipstick, a gentle glow of blusher over the cheeks. In the photo, Eleanor leans in against her husband's right side. Their hands are gripped together, sandwiched between them at their hips. In Eleanor's right hand she holds the bouquet, a round posy of white roses. I imagine each bud studded with a pearl pin.

Peter is dark and handsome beside her. In her heels, she is a little taller than he, and with the proximity of their half-turned postures, she is looking down into his eyes. His hair is thick, inky black waves, the hairline almost identical to his sister's. His left leg is outstretched, his toe off the ground as if he has made to walk on and has been pulled back for the photograph. His face, unguarded, shows an awkward half-smile. Eleanor's is theatrical; her entire face is beaming.

CHAPTER 19

MID-DECEMBER AND NOAH Dillon kneels close to the banks of the Liffey as it tumbles through Newbridge in County Kildare. His father casts scented dummies into the water; then, with a swift hand command, sends his dogs in after them. They are large animals, built for water and working. They sweep by Noah and slide into the thick cold water.

Normally, Noah would watch. There is a thrill about the way the dogs lap up the dummy, turn in the fast water, then stroke back to the bank with ease, strong muscles powering and coats wet and gleaming. But this morning, Noah has found himself a task.

At the water's edge, where the river is shallow and ripples around straggling weeds and twisted roots, he sees the edge of a red bag, the strap of which is caught over a sunken tree branch. He's been trying to unhook it for what seems an age. He would have given up after the first couple of attempts as his hands are stiffening with the cold and the knees of his jeans are soaked through, but the zip of the bag is partially open and he thinks he can see the glint of something metal inside.

The dogs shake themselves off and his father casts the dummy far down the river again. Noah reaches out with his makeshift fishing rod. His tongue pushes against his cheek as he tries to reach the bag. The branch he's using snags on the bag, and he manages to drag it close enough that if he reached down on his tummy he could fish it out with his hand. He glances up. His dad won't like it if he gets his coat covered in mud. But his dad is busy, directing the dogs back to shore.

Quickly, Noah stretches out on the bank. He shoves his sleeve back, then reaches into the water. The bag rises with ease. He drops it on the bank behind him and tries to wipe his coat down.

"Noah! Your coat!" His dad looks over his shoulder. "What's that?"

"A bag."

His dad sighs. "I know it's a bag. Where'd you get it?"

Noah points into the water. "It was in there, I just pulled it out. I think there might be treasure inside."

His dad shakes his head. He doesn't believe there could be treasure.

"I saw it. Something silver."

Gary Dillon smiles down at his son. He tells his dogs to sit, to wait, then squats next to the bag.

"Treasure, is there? Well, now, that would be something."

Noah scoots to the side. Excited. His fingers drag the bag forward, tug at the zip, but Gary Dillon stops him.

"Let me, son."

There is an uneasy feeling developing in Gary Dillon's chest.

"Not all treasure is the good kind."

He unzips the bag and takes a peek inside. He's not sure what he was expecting but is somewhat relieved by what he finds.

"Lemme see!" Noah cries, and reaches over the lip of the bag to look.

The bag contains a set of keys—two on a key ring—and a mobile phone.

Noah is visibly disappointed. "I thought there'd be treasure."

Gary Dillon ruffles his son's hair, contemplates leaving the bag hanging on a nearby branch. Perhaps whoever lost it will come back looking for it. He reaches out to leave it on a tree; then, not sure why, thinks better of it. He hooks the leads onto his dogs and, taking his son by the hand, heads back to his van.

At home, he shows the bag to his wife, who agrees that he should drop it into the Garda station on his way to work tomorrow, being that some poor soul will be glad to have the keys back, even if the phone is ruined. When their young son is tucked in bed, they relax in front of the TV to watch the news updates on the Costello and Keegan murders.

ONCE IN A while the gods of justice appear to rouse themselves from their stupor to throw a desperate crime team a bone. Figuratively and sometimes literally. In this case, we have a phone and a set of keys. Or will have. Hot droplets of coffee run over my hands as I rush to get into the driver's seat. Baz is seated, waiting for me to head back to the office so that we can touch base with Helen and see whether TeeganRed is making any friends online. I pass him the tray of drinks and clip on my belt.

"Assume crash position," I tell him. "I've just had a very interesting call while waiting to be served. I'm either heading for the biggest let-down of this twisted case yet, or we've just been given a break."

Baz knows better than to say anything and simply raises an eyebrow, helping himself to a coffee.

THE OFFICER WHO greets me at the station in central Kildare was sensible enough to ask Gary Dillon if he'd mind staying put for the hour or so it would take for me to get there. When I arrive, I have the chance to hear how it was he noticed the bag, and he tells me that it was his son who located it. He phones his wife, and she agrees to take me to the spot where the bag was found, so that her husband can go to work. Things get better when she allows her son to show me exactly where he pulled the bag from the tangled roots at the water's edge.

I thank them, and once they've left, I have the pathway sealed off and instruct a forensics team to scour the area for any other scraps of evidence.

"It's a way out, isn't it?" Baz says on the way back to the car from the river.

"Meaning?"

I hear the rustle of his coat as he shrugs. "A way out. Distance-wise. From Dublin. From Bray, from Clontarf."

I step over a crumbling branch, pull my coat tighter against the damp air. "Yes."

"Might not be her phone. Could be anyone's."

"Yes." I set my jaw.

"And there's the water damage to think about."

I stride on. "It's Eleanor's phone, Baz. We've checked the keys, sent them to Dublin, they open her office at the uni. Stop cushioning me for a blow that won't come."

"I'm not. Just cautioning. I'm not sure dropping that phone in a bag of rice will make it work again, that's all."

I give out a bark of laughter. "At least the officer at the station had the sense to dry it out a bit. But you're underestimating modern-day science, Baz, just like this murdering cretin did."

I feel a warm glow in my chest. The dark shadow of evil that we are hunting almost succeeded in sliding away, almost got too far ahead, but now he's that much closer.

Our phone tech, Emer O'Neil, narrows sharp eyes on the mobile in front of her. She's another newbie, not just to the department but to her field. She looks fresh from the classroom, but there is a confidence in her stance, an ease in her movements that tells me she's completely in her element when it comes to the challenge I've presented her with. She picks up the evidence bag, slides the phone about inside it, wrinkles her thin nose.

Steve is champing at the bit behind her, his back pressed up against the window, his arms folded, sulking that I've called in another tech expert for the phone, but Helen is building up the profile with TeeganRed and I need him available to help her.

TeeganRed has yet to make a decent score in the chat room. It appears people who navigate the underbelly of the internet are an overcautious type. Who knew? Helen is planning on attempting to photoshop a few images she has obtained from elsewhere. Set out some bait so that TeeganRed can make some new friends.

"It's good for me to handle?" Emer asks. She pushes the wisps of her fringe back from her eyes.

"No prints. Too long in the water. It may have been there for over eight weeks."

She seems unfazed by the information. "Might take a while."

My eyes snap to Baz. His expression shocked.

"You mean you can get something from it?" I ask. I can't keep the excitement from my voice.

"I can't say definitely, but at the same time I can say, why not? Prolonged time in the water greatly reduces the quality of data, but"—she shrugs—"the chip is sealed with adhesive glue, so there's an element of watertightness. We can always desolder the chip, perform a full cleanse."

She lays the mobile facedown, pulls on gloves, then takes up a shining tool that looks like a high-tech toothpick, eases the back from the phone.

"Looking at this, my guess is that we can retrieve something at least. The SIM is intact, there's little corrosion, we could get a few hundred messages, e-mails, maybe even images."

I blink. "A few hundred."

She's looking down at the phone. "I know. It's not much, but that's all I'm willing to commit to."

Baz is shaking his head. "But it's been in water?"

Giving me an odd feeling of déjà vu, she echoes my words to him earlier, "Don't underestimate modern-day technology, Detective," and rewards him with a smile.

There is a wad of emotion in my throat. I could easily cry. Or laugh. We have a breakthrough. I reckon I can hear the tinkle of Eleanor Costello's laughter in the distance and see the gradual close of Amy Keegan's tired eyes. We are one step closer.

I am barely at my desk when Reception phones. After almost two weeks, Peter Costello's autopsy report is finally complete. I rush down to sign for it, tearing open the envelope as I come back through the case-building room, satisfying myself that it's the right file; then, tucking the folder under my arm, I head into my office and shut the door.

The amount of thallium in Peter Costello's blood is damning; although it did not kill him, it would have eventually. He must have been in severe pain. What's staggering is the length of time he had been exposed to the poison. Almost two years, as suggested by Abigail and corroborated when compared to his medical notes.

He first visited his doctor with complaints of nerve pain and rapid hair loss about nineteen months ago. There were old fractures too: his fingers, forearm (the ulna), the left temple or supraorbital bones. There're no matching reports in his medical files.

I rub the thinning scar at my temple; the skin is tender but no longer makes me wince. Whoever helped Peter to his death did so before Eleanor Costello was killed. So it's more than feasible that he was killed by his wife. It looks like he was in such a weakened state that Eleanor could have beaten him, but even a tall woman couldn't have weighted his body and dumped him in the Liffey alone.

A knock on the office door makes me jump.

I close the file and straighten. "Come in."

Baz steps into the room. "I know you've barely warmed your seat, but TeeganRed has received a private message. Helen's unsure how you wanted to play it."

I pass him Costello's report. "Cast your eyes over this, we'll need to run a team meeting at the end of the day."

"They'll love that," he says, taking the file. "Let me guess, Peter was the abused, not the abuser."

I tense. "Looks so."

He reads through the report summary, pauses for a moment as if deciding whether he should say something or not, reaching his decision rapidly.

"Frankie, I'm only saying this for your own good."

"Never a less inviting start to a conversation. Go on?" I challenge.

"You need to leave your own story behind. Not all men are bad."

"Oh, get over yourself. For fuck's sake. Who's making this about themselves now? Excuse me for pointing out the facts."

He leans on the other side of the desk. "Facts? Prejudice, more like. You're blinded by your own terror. Tracy Ward's case is stinking up your vision and you can't see what's right in front of you because all you can see is Tracy Ward's killer, your attacker, who happened to be male." He throws Costello's autopsy on the desk between us, jabs his finger straight down on it.

"This was done by someone who desires control. Someone who was precise enough but hard enough to administer poison and antidote in medically exact measurements over the course of two years so that they could control their victim. Someone who manipulated, verbally abused, even rejoiced in their victim straying so that the added guilt would enable them to wield further power.

"This abuser was not someone who was beaten or cowed by life, they were not driven by the fury of frustration or anger, they administered their torture with a happy and patient hand. They celebrated the control they had, reveled in the pain they caused. That is your abuser, and from the work we've done, I know which of the Costellos fits that profile more accurately, and it's not Peter."

During his speech my mouth has dried, sunken in with distaste. My ears are ringing. I struggle to swallow, then touch my tongue to my dried lips.

"You're right."

He throws his hands up. Turns his back. "Christ alive."

"Fuck, Harwood. What do you want me to say?" My voice is a whisper. "Don't you think I can see myself, Baz? I've become one of those women that I hate. But I can't unknow what I know. I can't unlearn the experience of feeling weaker, of being . . . of being a victim." I mumble the word. Bitter.

He faces me, surprised.

"But that aside." I point down on the file. "This killer. The one who ultimately killed Peter Costello, who killed Eleanor Costello and Amy Keegan. He's male and very dangerous. I'd put my life on it."

A ghost of a smile. He puts his hand on the door handle. "Well, for fuck's sake, don't go doing that. Not after last time."

"You're too funny sometimes, Harwood."

"I'm just a man. What do you expect?" He smiles, then leaves my office.

Once the door closes, I sit. Bring my mind back round to Tracy Ward. Stiffness draws over my shoulders, tugs my muscles tight. Tracy Ward. Fuck. Emotion is a hypocritical being; it seeks the truth but can't listen. Baz is right: Every time I think of Tracy, I feel a wrongness, a missed step somewhere along her case. The need I have to work this out is equaled only by the terror I have in discovering the wrong. Ivan Neary struck me. With a knife. I felt it. I feel it. I'm sure of it, but increasingly I'm not sure the source of my fear is Ivan Neary rather than someone else.

I take up my phone. Abigail answers on the second ring.

"Dr. James."

"Abigail, it's Frankie. Are you at Whitehall?"

"Yes. What is it?"

I nod into the phone. "Could you check a record for me?"

"I'm at my desk. Case number?"

"Three-zero-one. Tracy Ward."

The clack of a keyboard comes down the line. "That case is going to trial, Detective."

I grit my teeth. "Can you check whether there were nail clippings taken?"

"I didn't do the autopsy, but it would be standard. Hang on. Yes."

I can barely bring myself to ask, but here it is, the pebble in the shoe. "Could you retrieve them from the archive? On the right hand, there was a dark substance under the nails. The right hand. Blood, dirt?"

Abigail murmurs to wait. Then: "No. It was paint."

I swallow. "Was it analyzed? The type of paint? What shade?"

"Not at the autopsy, no. Just noted that it was paint."

"Could you retrieve the samples from the archive? If there was a pigment under the nails, run the same tests you've run with the Costello and Keegan cases."

A draw of breath. "Prussian blue?"

"Yes. I'll sign the paperwork this evening."

"Okay."

"How long for the results?"

"It's a chromatography test." She stops. "Once I retrieve the nail clippings from the archive, a couple of hours. Frankie? Are you all right?"

I close my eyes. "Thanks, Abigail."

CHAPTER 20

TrustMe57: Hello! How you feeling today?

TeeganRed: Same. Alone. Does no one else think about dying here?

TrustMe57: All the time. Although, the other way around usually. Lol.

TeeganRed: Other way around?

TrustMe57: In that I'm not the one dying!

TeeganRed: Okaaaaaaay. Maybe we should meet up? Lol. Although, I don't want to die exactly, but have this urge to experience it.

TrustMe57: It?

TeeganRed: What it feels like to die. Or get close to dying.

TrustMe57: Curiosity kills the cat.

TeeganRed: I hope not.

TrustMe57: DM.

Helen leans back into the chair, rests her fingers on her lap.

"He could be our guy?" I ask. "The username matches the e-mail address on Amy's computer."

"Technically, we don't know it's a guy, and we've been trying desperately to run a trace on his IP, but it's impossible. If he is the one, he's a freaking ghost. I've had to lay down serious bait to draw him out," she says.

"Bait? Steve, dare I ask?"

He looks sheepish. "We needed something more dramatic to get him to talk to us, Chief. There's been radio silence for weeks. We knocked up a few images." He clicks on a folder.

"Great artwork," I say, voice sharp with disgust.

He closes the file quickly. "It's the fucker's taste, okay, not mine."

I sigh. "Talk about getting your hands dirty." Pushing the images out of my mind, I fold my hands. "We're going to have to try to stage a meeting. With him."

Both Helen's and Steve's heads swing around in horror. "You're not serious?"

"We can't get him on here. There's no way to trace an IP on the Dark Web unless he gives more away. Are there any photos? Perhaps we could look at the background, videos that we could study?" They're shaking their heads.

Emer has been working quietly from a desk nearby. I'm aware that throughout our discussions she has stood slowly and made her way behind us to peer in at the computer. At first, I thought curiosity had summoned her from her workstation, but gradually she pushes between us, peels a latex glove from her hand, and scrolls back up the screen. At that moment the computer pings, announces a direct message. In it, there is one line:

You sound like someone who'd like to play dead. If so, e-mail: TrustMe57-at-minimail-dot-com.

"Interesting," Emer mutters.

I look down at her. "What is it?"

"You need to see this." She shoots back to her workstation. She's animated. Excited even. Driven.

She picks up a black device at the side of her computer. It looks almost like an external hard drive.

"The SIM card from the phone was good. Minimal damage, and with a quick dry I could retrieve quite a lot. I've yet to work on the chip."

She points to a notepad beside the computer, on which there is a phone number.

"This is Eleanor Costello's mobile number as taken from her bill. The phone company has confirmed that this SIM was issued with this phone."

"So the phone is definitely Eleanor's?"

"Without doubt," Emer says.

She points to the computer. The screen is filled with gibberish. Digital codes, a jumble of numbers and letters to my untrained eye.

Emer places her hand on the page-up button and the screen travels backward.

"The program is still retrieving and deciphering the data but—"

There. I see it. Words. Letters among the mess of dashes and boxes. I lean in.

"These are text messages?"

"And we've got e-mails. Here." She scrolls up.

> How's your charge? You've shown him who's boss? I
> really enjoyed our session yesterday. Again soon. Next
> time we'll try more of my games.
>
> X

The e-mail address is the same as on the Black Widow site. It's from TrustMe57. I look at Emer, see my own fever reflected in her eyes.

"It's him."

I tip my head back and breathe a silent thank-you to the heavens for whoever made that kid fish a bag out of the river a few days ago.

"Thank fuck for that," I whisper.

I nod at Emer. "Great work. I want all data lifted from that phone indexed and on my desk as soon as it's available, please."

Her eyes widen as if she wouldn't dare do anything else. I needn't have asked.

Helen is waving me over. "He's signed out of the chat room."

"He's waiting for a reply. This is make-or-break for him. He wants a victim that's all his. Reply. He won't relay what he wants directly to a stranger. You'll have to suggest it."

She gives me a blank stare.

"Jesus, Helen. Tell him that if by 'playing dead' he means BDSM, then you're in. Ask him if he wants to meet up." I sigh, thinking. "Tell him that you're not into time wasters, you had a partner before that said he was into it but wasn't really. You need more than a bit of spanking."

Helen and Steve glance at each other.

"As you said, it's the fucker's taste. Not mine."

I leave the office to meet with Clancy. I should be buoyant, happy; instead I am exhausted and tetchy. The curtain is half pulled back, but the room is still too dark to see the monster. In some ways it makes him all the more terrifying. He feels close. Too close.

He could be in the far reaches of the country, directing his fantasies onto the screen, but the immediacy of his replies makes it seem as if he's standing over my shoulder, whispering deadly threats in hot breaths down my neck. The reality is that he's likely local, maybe to the east coast, although Ireland is so small that it wouldn't be a stretch to imagine a murderer in Cork who came up to commit his crimes, only to return to a sterile environment far away from his playground.

This guy is arrogant, sure of himself, and will be enjoying every public scrabble my team and I go through in order to catch him. To his own mind, he is invincible. Master of his victims' fate. He will kill again, if he's not done so already.

Clancy is waiting by the car when I step outside.

"Well?"

"Well," I answer.

"For fuck's sake, Sheehan. What's the story?"

"We're on the trail again. Emer's doing some work on the phone." At that moment an e-mail comes through on my mobile. In the subject box is a brief message from Emer: "You're gonna want to look at this."

Clancy is waiting for me to elaborate. Tracy Ward's case waits for me. Her killer is being led from his cell, probably as we speak, head bent, and guided into an armored van, doors slamming, then speeding along Dublin's quays to the courthouse and the waiting buzz of the press and the judge's sentence.

The e-mail relays a text interchange between Eleanor and another user.

The first, sent 2 September at two p.m.: "I've been thinking about you all day."

Eleanor replies: "Sounds dull. I'm free at four."

The next text is sent over an hour later: "You've a choice of two weapons to play with this afternoon. Pain or asphyxiation?"

Eleanor's reply comes almost immediately: "Guess."

"Pain then."

"You know me. See you at yours."

"There might be fire. I'll be waiting."

I've held the phone between us, and Clancy is reading along with me. "Fuck. So she was fucking around too. Jesus, does no one stay loyal to their bloody partners anymore?"

I scroll down. "Wherever they met up might be where Amy's murder took place. If it's our guy."

"Well, I never," Clancy whispers, staring down at the screen of my phone. At the bottom of the e-mail, Emer has added a postscript that she has bolded. She ran the number through all involved in the case and came up with a match. Lorcan Murphy.

I smile.

"Where's his two fingers now, eh?" Clancy asks.

"Yes. You'd never guess he was the murdering kind."

Clancy starts up the car. "Rule number one," he chirps arrogantly. "We're all the murdering kind, given the right motivation."

We pull away into the afternoon traffic, head for court. I e-mail Emer, tell her to get a warrant on Murphy's house. Tell her to prepare the team, send a pair of eyes to the property, Helen and Baz to keep watch. Tomorrow morning we'll pick him up, seize his phone, his wallet, his car. Every millimeter of his existence is to be swabbed and cataloged. Justice has sat its narrow arse in our hands, and we can't let it slip through our grasp. Our job over the next few hours will be to connect Lorcan Murphy solidly to either Amy's, Eleanor's, or Peter's death.

I want to be here, stalking Lorcan Murphy's words for answers, but Tracy Ward's justice is waiting. I put my phone away and think of the hours ahead. Already I can hear the hum of anxiety in my ears. *Ivan Neary is guilty*, I tell myself. I tell myself this all the way to the courthouse.

CHAPTER 21

MY BROTHER'S GAZE never leaves mine as I take the stand. Worry has turned his eyes into small round beads. His mouth is tight, almost stern. He's angry. Possibly at me. My mother's hand rests over his, comforting.

Abigail was true to her word. One hour is all it took for her to find the clippings and analyze the paint found under Tracy Ward's nails. Initial tests show it's iron-based, a similar makeup to the blue used in the Costello and Keegan murders. The information has fastened like a tick in my head, and it's all I can do not to run from the court. It doesn't mean he's innocent. He attacked me. Self-defense? I squeeze my eyes shut, take a breath. Clancy is sitting at the back, his face pulled into lines of concern. For me or the case, I can't be sure.

I place my palm on the Book and raise my right hand.

"I do solemnly, sincerely, and truly declare that the evidence I shall give will be the truth, the whole truth, and nothing but the truth."

The Book is removed.

"Be seated," the judge commands.

I seek out Neary. He's tall but very thin. He's on hunger strike, proclaiming his innocence. An exercise in control, perhaps? A killer's trait. When the papers get a snap of his skeletal frame, it won't take long for sympathy to trickle down into the collective consciousness. He keeps his head low, but from where I'm sitting I see the moist glow across his forehead, over the top of his lip, the convulsive swallowing to wet an anxious throat. I see the signs of fear.

A warm prickle spreads in answer along my hairline. I pull my eyes away, face forward. I must waver because the judge's voice snaps through my thoughts.

"Detective Sheehan? Would you like to take a drink of water?"

Swallow. I shake my head. "No, thank you, Judge."

She raises an eyebrow. "Very well."

She looks to the prosecution, for whom I'm the principal witness. I know that my testimony is what's standing between Neary's freedom and Ward's justice.

"Your witness, Mr. Tanner. Stay between the lines, please," she warns.

Mike Tanner gets up from his seat, still looking at his notes. If it's possible, he appears more anxious than I do. His apparent nerves have the strange effect of easing mine. He stands before me, rests his hand on his stomach.

I cough, clear the stickiness from my throat.

"Detective Sheehan," he begins. "You have a very long and assured history working with the Gardaí?"

"Yes."

He presses his fingertips to his lips as if he might throw up. "Would you care to take us through your illustrious career?"

I frown.

He doesn't raise his eyes, waves a hand.

My breathing picks up. "I started out in investigative work, worked up through the ranks before being promoted to detective chief super two years ago. I now help manage the Bureau for Serious Crime. I report to the commissioner through the assistant commissioner Mr. Jack Clancy."

I pause, take a sip of water. "The bureau is a specialist department that deals with particular crime cases."

Finally, whatever seems to have been ailing Tanner appears to pass. He swallows, straightens, and manages a more definite smile in my direction.

"That's a lot of experience." He checks his notes. "On Saturday, 4 June 2011, can you remember where you were at ten p.m.?"

I try to ignore the march of goose bumps along my arms, the heat under my armpits, the dull pain like a toothache throbbing over the side of my head, down my neck.

"Yes." I touch my tongue to my lips. "I was responding to a distress call."

"Distress call?"

"An emergency. The call was serious in nature and had been patched through to me. It was a call from Tracy Ward's house."

"You were in your office when the call came in?"

"No. I was returning from a meeting with my superiors."

"So late?"

"We were working on a case. An attempted murder."

"Would you state for the court who was the victim of this attempted murder?"

Sheridan, the defense lawyer, speaks up. "Judge, I don't see what this has to do with the current case. Mr. Neary is not on trial for this other crime, so, respectfully, I object to the question."

The judge checks her notes, looks up at Tanner from above her glasses. "This related?"

"Yes, Judge."

"All right. You may answer the question, Detective Sheehan."

"The meeting was about an attack on a young woman named Rachel Cummins."

"Who did Ms. Cummins eventually identify as her assailant?"

"Once we had Mr. Neary in custody for Tracy Ward's murder, Cummins identified him as her attacker." I can't look up.

Tanner pushes me. "Is Mr. Neary in this court presently?"

"Yes."

"Would you identify Mr. Neary for the court, Detective?"

I press my eyes shut, then lift my head and look directly at him. "He's sitting in the front bench, white shirt, open button."

"Please let it be known to the court that the witness has identified Mr. Neary, the defendant."

The judge barks, "Notified."

"At the time of this meeting, you made some interesting observations about Ms. Cummins's injuries."

He passes a sheet of paper to me. It is a copy printed from my computer and details Ms. Cummins's injuries and a few shady guesses at the offender's profile from what Rachel had told us.

"Would you read them out to us, please, Detective?"

I clear my throat, lean in toward the microphone, and try to hold the paper steady.

"'Ms. Cummins suffered severe injury to her right carotid artery, which, if it had not been for her neighbor, would have undoubtedly resulted in her death. The offender had struck from behind, a blow that had stunned the victim but not knocked her out.

"'The offender then dragged her into the bedroom, where he proceeded to tie her arms to the headboard. He managed to get the left arm secured when Ms. Cummins came round and screamed. There was a struggle in which he tried to cut her throat. She kicked him hard enough to shake the knife from his hand, but not before he managed to nick the carotid.'"

I stop, take a drink of water. Heat rises to my cheeks and I long to press the cold glass to my skin. I continue to read my assessment of Neary's attack.

"'The offender escaped out the window, after he heard a neighbor come home. My understanding so far of the assailant is that he is likely male, strong, with unusual sexual drives that are aided by overpowering his victims.

"'Looking at the clumsy articulation of the crime, it's possible that this was his first attempt at murder. It is likely that the perp will try again with a different victim.'" The pages begin to tremble in my hand. "'Next time, he will plan it better. With better planning will come a greater arrogance and sense of control. The next victim may suffer mutilation before they are eventually killed.'"

Tanner has his head bowed during the reiteration of my notes. When I stop speaking, he nods. Then he reads a further snippet from my case notes on Rachel Cummins.

"In fact, you go on to say that the killer is 'likely intelligent, of at least average IQ, charming, possibly married, outwardly optimistic, manipulative, and will appear to function very well within the boundaries of society.'"

"Yes. That's right."

"Mr. Neary is a paramedic, IQ 98, was happily married, and is on the board of his local church, no less. Would you say he fits the bill?"

Sheridan stands. "Judge, this is not for the witness to decide."

"Calm down, Mr. Sheridan." She shoots a glare at Tanner. "You're driving a dangerous road here, Counsel. Life's too short for me to repeat myself. Another strike like that and you're out."

"Sorry, Judge."

Tanner walks back to his bench. "When you received the call to check out Tracy Ward's place, what did you do?"

I square my shoulders. Try to assume some command over my anxiety. I look to Clancy, steal strength from his presence. I can't let Tracy Ward down. A long sigh; then I take myself back to that night.

"I picked up the call. We were already on high alert because of Ms. Cummins's assault, and I suspected that her attacker would try again. I heard a call come over the radio and I phoned in. I was given the location and told that the woman had been cut off. I told the on-duty officer that I would take up the call and to let my team know. It was in a small cul-de-sac, in Drumcondra.

"When I arrived, the lights were off and I thought I might have the wrong address. As I was getting out of the car, the assistant commissioner Jack Clancy phoned, requesting that I wait for his backup before entering. I told him I would, but then I heard a shout that seemed to come from inside the house. It sounded threatening. I got out and went to the front door, but it was locked. The back door was open.

"I went through into the main hallway, the front door was at the end. It was empty but I could smell blood. I could see an open door farther on to my right, so I moved down the hallway. I knew that there was likely someone critically injured inside.

"There was a significant breeze blowing out through the open door and a glance inside showed me that the window was wide-open. I assumed the assailant had fled, but when I stepped into the room a dark figure lurched at me with a knife. I turned to run out of the front door, but I stumbled and started to fall. When I glanced upward, I saw Ivan Neary's face. The knife was in his hand. He struck me at the base of my neck, and then across my temple. When I came to, Jack Clancy, Detective Baz Harwood, and a uniformed officer had arrived. Tracy Ward was pronounced dead. Mr. Neary had been arrested."

A low banging starts up in my ears. The judge taps her pen on her notes. Each time the tip hits the paper, the sound echoes through my head. A woman leans forward, coughs into her hand; someone shifts in their seat, a rub of denim, a slow draw of warm air into a yawn.

"Detective?" Tanner is looking at me.

I force my nails into the palms of my hands, feel the bite of pain. "Sorry."

Tanner nods. "Thank you, Detective." Then he turns to the judge. "That will be all, Judge."

I study my clasped hands, try to get a grip. When I look up, Justin, my brother, is watching me.

He appears more concerned than ever, and his worry makes me momentarily confused until I see the defense lawyer gather his papers. I'm not finished. Merely through the warm-up.

Tanner returns to his seat.

The judge makes a note, then addresses the defense. "Your witness, Mr. Sheridan."

Sheridan stands.

I try not to look, try not to watch, but can't keep my eyes from Ivan Neary's. He stares at me, face pleading.

Sheridan's voice pulls me back. "Detective, is it true that you entered Tracy Ward's house alone?"

"Yes," I reply.

I can feel the breeze snaking down the hallway, feel it reach my skin. A cold summer wind, unlikely for June, coming from the open bedroom window. The sound of my breath, close, guarded, my arm raised, ready to defend.

"Detective?" Sheridan is waiting.

"Sorry, could you repeat the question?"

"Of course." He smiles. "Would you agree that there were no other witnesses present at the time of your attack?"

In my mind, I see Tracy's nails, as they were in the photo, paint caked beneath the tips. Then the short linear wound on the white skin of Eleanor's arm, the dark cavern of Amy Keegan's mouth. "Blue Murder," the papers had said.

The judge leans across the desk. "Detective, could you answer the question, please?"

I lick my lips. Clancy gives me a hard look.

"Y-yes," I stammer. "I was the only witness."

Sheridan continues. "Would *you* have attacked if you had come upon a killer? Defended yourself?"

"Speculation!" Tanner almost spits.

I jump in my seat; my hand bumps against the stand.

"The witness can't possibly predict what she would or wouldn't have done in that situation," he continues.

"Judge, I'm merely pointing out that Mr. Neary could have mistaken Detective Sheehan for the killer."

"Sustained," the judge says. "Counsel, there are rules to follow. Follow them."

"Apologies to the court." Sheridan answers smoothly, but his question has done its job, has allied itself with the doubts in my mind.

I would have attacked. Without doubt.

"Is it true that you lost consciousness soon after the intruder attacked you?"

"Yes, until my team arrived."

He smiles. "Ah, yes, your team." He meets my eyes. "Did your team make the arrest?"

The knife grates against my skull; there's a sharp grunt of Neary's breath as he strikes out, a cry of anger or fear? The smell of blood, so much blood, the warm path of it down my neck, the thick drip of it from my fingers. Not pain, a strange numbness, a heaviness along my arm, a dull throb across my neck, my head, and then I'm falling, Neary's face above me, knife shaking in his hand.

"Detective, are you all right?" The judge cuts across my thoughts. "Do you need a break?"

I reach out for the water; the glass clinks against my teeth.

"I'm fine."

Sheridan nods. Opens his mouth, closes it. He glances briefly at the judge; then: "Detective, considering your experience in murder investigations, do you believe Tracy Ward's killer was in that house when you were hit by Ivan Neary?"

Tanner stands. "Speculation!"

"Counsel, final warning," the judge replies.

But I hear my voice. Quiet, cracking, but sure:

"No."

TANNER IS PISSED. He storms off down the front steps, where he knows it will be impossible for me to follow due to the tsunami of media and paparazzi crowding the front of the courthouse. The press are waiting for his remarks. Ivan Neary is to be held overnight at least.

"This is a shit storm." Baz paces over and back in the courtroom lobby. He's looking into his phone, at Abigail's full analysis of the pigment under Tracy's nails. Prussian blue.

"Keep your voice down," I hiss.

A journo steps out from a corridor that leads to the bog. He crosses the lobby and leaves without a backward glance.

"Sorry," Baz mutters. "Let's get out of here."

He turns on his heel and sweeps out through the side of the building, where Clancy is waiting in the car. The entrance to the street is gated to prevent the press from bombarding witnesses, the innocent and the guilty alike.

Baz and I avoid the passenger seat and shuffle into the back. Clancy doesn't say anything. He pulls away, wheels spinning, then brakes suddenly when he reaches the gates.

Immediately, camera lenses reach out over the windshield. I lean up against the headrest to avoid the invasive snaps.

"Well, you've truly fucked us here, Frankie," Clancy barks, echoing Baz's frustrations.

I shake my head. "I didn't have time to tell you. You'd gone in by the time Abigail sent me the message."

"Well, here's a career tip for you, how about you fill your fucking team in on what you're thinking? You ordered the tests."

He sends a sliding glance at Baz.

"Don't look at me. I didn't know anything!" Baz shouts. "I've barely had time to eat and shit over the last few weeks working the cases we already have without digging up old ones."

"The tests aren't conclusive," I say. "But we can't ignore the connection between the cases, we can't let a man go down for a crime he may not have committed."

Clancy jerks the car through the traffic, punching the brakes and horn in equal measure against the Dublin crush.

"Well, we can't nail the fucker now. That's it. Innocent or not. We'll be laughed out of court."

I look out the window. I want to disappear.

Clancy continues. "He stabbed you, Frankie. Why would an innocent man attack a member of law enforcement at a crime scene? With the murder weapon, for fuck's sake. Fibers of his clothes were found all over Tracy Ward's body. Fingerprints! Everywhere! Not to mention the ID from Rachel Cummins."

"I'm not sure there were fingerprints everywhere," Baz mutters.

"Cummins identified him through an e-fit. She was shaken. Eager to put someone down," I add.

Clancy cracks open the window, pushes a cigarette between his lips, lights it.

"Fucking shambles," he says. He catches my eye in the rearview mirror, gives me a look of pure frustration. "You're a great detective, Frankie, but fuck, you've got lousy timing."

I turn, look out the window again. My voice sounds far away when I answer.

"That's the problem."

CHAPTER 22

SILENCE. TENSION. THESE are the great breeders of resentment. In the twenty minutes it takes for me to get back to the office, I've grown a substantial ball of fury in the pit of my stomach. Fury at myself. My fear, the paralyzing force that trails after every movement. I want to smack it down. Tell that bitch to shut her face so that I can think without a moderator.

At the office, Baz and I stand at the top of the room. Someone has placed a small plastic Christmas tree in the window, and a few stringy garlands drop down from the ceiling. Neither do much to lighten the atmosphere. The tension has followed us from the car and is now seeping out among the team.

We give a brief summary of the court proceedings, the brunt being that Neary will be released, that we may add Tracy Ward to our kill list. Anxiety vibrates through the heat of the office; worry hangs on every face. The sweat and tackle of an investigation relies on trust. They trusted the process, and we almost put the wrong bloke behind bars.

Pointing at the case board, I say: "Our priority now is to learn as much about Lorcan Murphy as we can. I want to know everything, from when he took his first pigeon-toed steps to which eye he opens first in the morning."

"So you're saying that Neary definitely didn't kill Tracy Ward?"

I share a resigned look with Baz. "No. We're saying that it's unlikely he killed Tracy Ward. Tracy Ward's case shares similarities with our current investigation."

Mumblings and sighs rise from the team, chatter erupts, heads shake, arms fold. Discontentment. No one likes a backward step.

Helen stands at the front, notebook in hand, pen poised. "This might be a stupid observation," she says.

"And what is that?"

"Well, isn't this a good thing? I mean, we don't want to convict the wrong man."

I think of what we've lost, how far ahead this killer is, further ahead than any of us comprehended.

I sigh. "No. We don't."

Her mouth opens to speak, she raises her pen, but I stop her with my hand.

"Get back on the e-mail trail. Look into a warrant on Murphy's number. I want up-to-date information on Cell Site, where his phone is hitting masts around the city. Blank spots that might show he's gone away for a weekend, or an evening. Get to know his habits, his movements. We'll need as much information as possible for when it comes time to interview."

"Okay, Chief," she says.

The team disperses and I go to my office. Tracy Ward's file lies open on my desk. I collect up the folder and head out. Clancy wants a postmortem on the case. In his words, he doesn't want to sound like "a fucking pleb" when he sees the commissioner in the morning. "At the end of the day, Frankie," he says, "there's no law without money, and the commissioner can tie up this case if he senses we've been careless with the credit card."

THE PUB IS busy; people mill around the bar. Clancy sits in the far corner, leaning back into his favorite deep chair. He's forgone his usual pint for coffee, never a good sign.

He looks up when I approach, a wry smile on his face.

"Sure lookit, if it's only your bona fide, two-for-the-price-of-one witness. Both prosecution *and* defense in a single unsuspecting package."

I sit, lay my reports on the table between us. The side of my head aches; the base of my neck aches. The reports contain statements from Tracy Ward's family. Words I could not make myself look at six months ago.

"She's the perfect victim for our perp," I remark, glancing back down at the papers.

Clancy sighs. "I want to go along with you on this. Fuck, no one wants to put the wrong guy down, but are you sure about this?"

I let out a long breath. "Yes."

He frowns. "We found that fucker running from the property with the knife in his hand." He points a finger into his palm. "In his fucking hand, Frankie. Still warm with your blood."

I rub the side of my head. "He said he heard Tracy's scream. Maybe he *did* investigate, scared off the real perp, and thought I was the killer." I sigh. "It was so dark in that house. I saw his shadow, he lurched, I turned to run, and . . ." I shrug.

Clancy leans against the seat, tips his head back, and closes his eyes. "Christ."

I take a mouthful of water. I need a clear head. After a while, Clancy straightens. There is worry circling his eyes.

"If Ivan Neary isn't guilty and this guy is still out there, he could come back for you, Frankie." He runs a hand over his face. "I've seen it before. You interrupted him and now you're threatening him again." He meets my eyes. "You got away."

A flutter of panics flaps in my stomach, but I pin it down. "A solid deduction, Clancy. Did anyone ever tell you, you'd make a great detective?"

He shakes his head. "We need to talk to Rachel Cummins again. At the very least, she needs to be warned. She's the only other surviving victim. What if he goes after her again?"

I swallow. "He won't."

"What makes you so sure?"

"Rachel was a shoddy failure. For him. She won. She got away after a clumsy attack. No. This killer is coming into his own now, there's no going back."

THE TEAM HAVE gathered like hounds on a blood trail. When I enter the room, Baz is pulling up a seat at the back of the group. The rest are seated, pens poised, around the case board. Lorcan Murphy holds the title of suspect.

News channels have already churned out the story that Ivan Neary has been released. That we've cocked up. Reporters are speculating over whether Tracy's body will be exhumed, reexamined for new evidence. Vultures.

I hate that we've been blindsided yet again, but I can't let fear leech away at this case. So much has already been wasted in the wake of my injuries. Guilt is not a friend of action. Eyes down, I need to keep on the scent and not lift my head until I spy the feet of the killer.

Lorcan Murphy's denial of his involvement with Eleanor Costello has started a new drive inside me. And I've decided the worm won't wriggle from the hook this time.

I stand at the front of the room and run through a summary of where we are in the investigation.

"As you know, we may need to add Tracy Ward to the investigation. Tracy was twenty-two years old and unmarried. She worked at a bar in Upper Leeson Street; it might be wise to keep her address and the location of her work in mind during geographic profiling.

"On 4 June 2011, Tracy endured a sustained violent attack; the cause of death was blood loss as a result of a cut throat. The connection with our other victims is the discovery of the pigment Prussian blue beneath her fingernails.

"Victim two: Peter Costello, forty-four years old, chronic heavy-metal toxicity, thallium for over nineteen months. Cause of death: likely drowning. Date of death is difficult to discern due to the cold water temperature in the Liffey, but if we go with visibility in Liffey and tidal flow, then any time between 9 and 12 October.

"Eleanor Costello was aware her husband had been missing. Thallium-laced deodorant found in the Costello household, along with confirmation of the poison in Peter Costello's blood and tissues, strongly suggest that Eleanor Costello was poisoning her husband.

"When viewed with the knowledge that Eleanor Costello was ingesting a thallium antidote, Prussian blue, on a regular basis, this theory becomes more certain. It also appears that Peter Costello had long-term signs of physical abuse, and, on speaking with his sister, he may also have suffered verbal and emotional abuse at the hands of his wife."

I pause. Digest. Then move on:

"Victim three: Eleanor Costello, thirty-nine years old, death by hanging. The mystery with Eleanor's death, among other things, is that she also displayed old wounds that could have been attributed to physical abuse. We now suspect that these wounds may have been inflicted as part of alternative sexual practices. This is something that we are hoping to draw out of Lorcan Murphy tomorrow.

"Victim four: Amy Keegan, twenty-nine years old. A vulnerable and troubled young woman who was desperately trying to keep her life in the living. We have now confirmed that she was Peter Costello's lover.

"An affair, which we know very little about. But in light of the websites that Amy Keegan had been visiting, namely a site called Black Widow, we believe it involved unusual fantasies, death-related fantasies, and extreme BDSM practices."

A gasp goes up as I say this. I'm amazed that they can still be shocked by the turns in this case.

"Amy Keegan was murdered live on the internet on 30 October, repeatedly stabbed until she eventually bled to death. Sometime afterward, likely the following day, her body was driven or taken to her hometown of Clontarf, where the killer attempted to get rid of her remains in the community's annual Halloween bonfire. We have to acknowledge that this killer may want to draw attention to his murders; Amy's brutal killing on the internet indicates a narcissistic nature."

I look out at the room. "Any questions? Comments?"

Nothing. The team return to their stations. Twenty or so people collecting information on Lorcan Murphy. I take a tremulous breath, then turn to Helen.

"Helen, can you look into why Rachel Cummins was so sure of the e-fit, maybe try her again with a set of photos including Murphy?"

Helen nods. "Yes, Chief."

"Good."

I move to Steve's desk. He's working through the Black Widow site, reaching out, making friends. His face is impassive, eyes focused on the screen, every now and then a flurry on the keyboard, replying to someone or starting a new thread. I'm not sure how he stomachs it.

"Steve? Can you assemble a team to pull in Lorcan Murphy tomorrow? Our best only, I want nothing to give us away until we're ready to go in."

He clicks over the screen, scrolls over an Excel sheet. "Yes. I've spoken to the officers already."

"Great. So this is how it will go . . ."

LORCAN MURPHY LIVES so close to Priscilla Fagan that they could be considered neighbors. The estate is red-bricked, quiet, dull. Driveways are occupied with steady, solid cars, nothing too showy. In the early-morning darkness, you can sense the slumbering residents inside the safe, warm houses. There are a few houses with lights on, families up early, making the most of the last shopping weekend before Christmas.

I switch off the engine and check my watch. It's seven a.m. There are lights on in the upstairs of Murphy's house; occasionally I see a shadow flash by the windows. I know that he's working today, that he leaves the house by seven thirty to make the twenty-minute commute to UCD. In his drive, there is a well-kept Renault Mégane; my mouth waters at the prospect of what evidence we may gather from it. Eventually, the lights flick off upstairs, and after a few seconds the front ground-floor light comes on.

Baz and Steve are stationed at the end of the street, near the surveillance van. I've parked near Murphy's house. The radio crackles and I pick it up.

"Sheehan."

"Are we set? Forensics will be here in a couple of minutes."

"Let's bring this worm in."

In my rearview, I see Baz and Steve step into the streetlight. I wait until they are almost at the house, then climb out of the driver's seat. The morning is dark and damp but surprisingly mild, with a light, warm breeze that does nothing to cool the sweat that's building across my forehead.

I nod to my colleagues and lead the way up the short pathway to

Murphy's door. Baz slips down the side of the garden, jumps the neighbor's wall to bypass the locked side gate to get to the rear of the house.

Lorcan Murphy won't have the chance to run out the back once we're upon him, but no one is taking any risks. The forensics van pulls onto the street, parks, and the team clamber out in a clamor of doors slamming, coughs, and chatter. I give them a moment to gather their gear, then raise my hand and push the doorbell.

There's a collective breath-hold, a few seconds of silence as we all listen for what may be happening inside. Finally, there are steps from inside and I remove the warrant from my pocket.

Lorcan Murphy pulls the door open. He's already dressed in a suit for the day, but on his feet are a pair of soft brown slippers. His face pales, creases, then frowns as he takes in my presence first; then his eyes lift to behind me, to the four SOCOs waiting to take his life apart.

"Mr. Murphy, I have a warrant to search these premises and any vehicles that you may own. Would you step outside the property, please?"

His mouth opens, closes, then opens again.

"Detective, what's going on?"

The SOCOs don't wait; they move by him, into the hallway, and spread out through the house.

Instinctively, Murphy moves aside.

"Would you mind if I put on some shoes first?" he asks.

I shake my head. "We'll get your shoes for you later."

"Later?"

"Lorcan Murphy, I am arresting you on suspicion of the murder of Eleanor Costello. You do not have to say anything, but it may harm your defense if you do not mention when questioned something which you later rely on in court. Anything you do say may be given in evidence."

"Detective? Seriously? I didn't kill Eleanor."

I nod to a nearby officer, who cuffs Murphy and takes him out to a waiting Garda car. Through the open door, the sky is lightening and some of the neighbors have stepped out of their warm homes to nose at the drama unfolding on their quiet, safe street.

I walk through the house, through the kitchen, where steam is still rising from the kettle. A tea bag waits in a mug for Murphy's morning cuppa. Freshly popped bread sits in the toaster. I move to the back door and flick the lock.

Baz steps in. "How'd he take it?"

"Shocked, stupefied, the usual."

"Proclaiming innocence?"

"Yep. Although, technically, they are all innocent until we can prove otherwise."

"We'll get him, Chief. He can't deny the connection between him and Eleanor, now that we have her phone. It's there in black and white." He looks me in the eye, senses how important it is to me after Neary.

"I know. Softly, softly."

The SOCOs are already carrying boxes of Murphy's possessions out of the house and stacking them into the van to be taken to the labs. Each box is a potential conviction, but each one costs. Costs the department, costs the government, costs the taxpayer.

"I'm not sure how I'm going to persuade the powers that be to sign off on all this."

"Let's see how he squares up to questioning, we've got a lot on him already. We simply need him to corroborate what we have."

I stare down at the waiting tea bag. "We need to find that other location. The blue room on Amy's video. If we can find that place . . ." I move away from the kitchen, push by the other officers, team members, forensic specialists.

Frantically, I start opening doors, peering into each room, checking the angle of light from the windows, the color of the walls. Checking linen cupboards for the blue floral pattern that adorned Amy Keegan's deathbed. I move up the stairs, Baz behind me.

There are three doors off the main landing, all open, all occupied by white suits; none matches the room where Amy Keegan was killed. Something sinks inside me.

CHAPTER 23

LORGAN MURPHY IS defiant. If looks could kill, we'd have him for murder on the spot. Anger shakes in his movements; his fingers grip the edge of the table as if they could snap it in two.

"Mr. Murphy, can I remind you that you've a right to legal representation?"

"I don't need a lawyer. I've done nothing wrong."

"Okay. In that case, we'll begin. You mentioned before that you used a particular type of pigment to aid in your research?"

"I didn't kill Eleanor."

"Could you answer the question?"

"Potassium hexacyanoferrate," he says sulkily. "Why have you brought me here? I'd nothing to do with Eleanor's death."

I wait.

"Is this about the papers? They came to me for the story. I only told them what I know."

"Yes, you did. Including that Eleanor had ingested the pigment."

"Did I?"

"I didn't give you that information, Mr. Murphy."

He shrugs. "It was an imaginative leap. I work in science."

"Okay. Dr. Costello would have had to get the blue pigment from somewhere. You use it in your studies. Would you know how she managed to access it?"

"It's not under any particular security, if that's what you mean. She could have accessed it at any time. She could have ordered it in herself, just like she could order a box of slides for the 'scopes if she wanted to."

"Right. In the week leading up to Thursday, 20 October, the day after Eleanor was murdered, can you take me through your activities?"

"Aside from work?"

"Aside and including."

He looks at his hands. I can almost see the wheels turning in his head. "I went to work, finished at four most days, then went to the uni gym and home between five and six p.m. On that Wednesday, I had a tutorial with Eleanor after work. We left just after five p.m."

I flick through my notes. Texts sent to and from Eleanor's phone two days prior to her murder were picked up from a mast outside the university at about five p.m. There was the text that promised a meet-up at Murphy's house, for two p.m. on the Tuesday, the day before she was murdered, and the reply from Eleanor's phone in Sandyford announcing her arrival.

"You go to the gym every evening?"

"Most. Unless something else comes up."

"So throughout that entire week you were in the university, working, and then at the gym until about six, apart from the Wednesday?"

He nods, then shakes his head. "No. Sorry. On Tuesday afternoon I went home early."

"Oh? Why was that?"

He shrugs. "I had problems with my boiler, a plumber was coming round. Fortune Heating, they're local to Sandyford. You can call them. Check."

"What time were they due?"

"They came around lunchtime."

"And you had no contact with Eleanor apart from at work for that entire week."

He shakes his head. "No."

We break for fifteen minutes. I arm myself with another cup of coffee while Baz fills me in on what they've found at Murphy's house. Eleanor's fingerprints have been found on bedroom-door handles, the nightstand, the headboard, the toilet, and in Murphy's car. Blood has been found on some of the bedsheets in the closet. The canine team have picked up cadaver scent in the car boot.

Steve has had no trouble accessing Murphy's computer, where, next to articles on microbiology, muscle building, and lecturing, there are files of pornographic material, some sourced back to the Black Widow site, screenshots from BDSM sites, victims tied up, knives to throat, cages, and submissive contracts. Nausea pushes up my throat. It takes all my resolve not to throw all our evidence at him, but somehow we need him to offer it, to trip himself up in his defense.

Steve looks up. "Can't we just show him the Amy video, put some pressure on him? Or hit him with what we've found in his car?"

"We want to get him to volunteer as much information as we can. Then we can challenge him with what we've got."

Steve pushes. "He's already admitted to being home on the Tuesday. There's a text interchange between them, arranging a meeting for that afternoon. It must mean something."

"It's circumstantial. Not enough for a conviction in court. We need to place him at one of the murder scenes. That's what we're aiming for." I straighten.

Returning to the interview room, I give Murphy a smile. I see doubt bloom in his eyes.

"You need more water?" I glance at his empty glass, then top it up from a jug in the middle of the table before he can answer.

He looks up at the clock. "I assume you've notified the university. They're short-staffed when it comes to microbiology lecturers," he says with some sharpness. "Is this going to take much longer?"

I give him a thin smile. "Hopefully not. Did Eleanor Costello ever socialize with any of her students?"

He sighs. "I told you that she took off home pretty much as soon as she finished her shifts."

"Yes, but she was freelance. Her lectures took up only a couple of hours when she was here, her research maybe more, but that still leaves plenty of freedom and free time to meet up with students."

"No."

"Would she have known many of them by name?"

"Of course. This is about Miss Keegan, isn't it?"

"Amy Keegan, yes. Did Eleanor know her?"

"On one of the lectures I sat in on, Miss Keegan approached her to ask for an extended deadline on a piece of course work as she had some personal issues that would delay its submission."

"Can you recall how long ago that was?"

He shrugs. "Ten months or so."

"Was it granted?"

"No. Eleanor always said that if you couldn't hack a medical degree, for any reason, you couldn't hack medicine. She didn't want to unleash a doc on the public that couldn't take the pressure."

Bitterness floods my mouth. "Did you think it was a fair decision?"

Again, he shrugs. "It wasn't my decision, ultimately it was hers, but yeah. Maybe."

"You know of the video that was found of Amy's death?"

"I know only what I've read in the newspapers, that's all."

I glance down at the notes Steve gave me. I sift through them slowly, taking my time. "Are you familiar with the work of detection dogs used by the Gardaí, Mr. Murphy?"

He pushes upright in his seat. "Not really."

"Our detection dogs can smell a great deal." I close my mouth, count to five in my head, let my words sink in. "A droplet of blood on clothing or bed linen, even if that clothing has been put through a hot wash. They can smell whether a dead body has been in your house, in your car, in the recent past. Or items taken from a dead body, a trophy, perhaps."

Color is running from his face; the skin at the corners of his mouth blanches.

"A trophy? I didn't do it. I swear it." He looks up suddenly, spreads his palms. "I don't know how that blood got there," he says. "Look, she was murdered in her house, right? Why would there be blood on my sheets from her death? And Amy? I couldn't . . . wouldn't do that to someone. You've got to believe me." He clasps his hands together, un-clasps them.

I look down at the desk. "We found the phone, Lorcan. Eleanor's. It's amazing what our forensic tech-heads can do nowadays. Did you know that it's possible to recover data from a waterlogged SIM?"

I give him a wide smile. "And the phone's memory? I was surprised to discover over five hundred saved messages on Eleanor's phone. And you know who some of those messages were from?"

His breathing is thin, thready with panic. He glances around the room, looking for escape.

Suddenly, he drops his head into his hands. He groans, then looks up at me through his fingers.

"I couldn't have killed Eleanor. I wasn't near her home, or mine, for that matter."

He runs his hands over his face, pulling his pale skin down so that the lower white orbs of his eyes flash at me. He tips back his head and lets out a long sigh.

"I think I'd like to speak to a lawyer."

GET HIM A lawyer," I bark at Steve when I step out into the office. "He says he has an alibi. Shagging one of his fucking students." I throw Murphy's statement onto Steve's desk.

"Christ," I fume.

"You called?" Baz looks up from his desk.

"Very funny," I say.

Helen approaches, waits for me to take a breath, her pen tapping against her leg.

"Something new on the Black Widow site?" I ask.

A brief shake of her head. "Chief, we've had a couple of calls from Moira Keegan about where we're at with Amy's case."

Moira Keegan, desperate for a line of hope. A fix of something, anything, that might sate her need for answers. And there it is, guilt tipping forward, running sharp jabs into the parts of me that should be hardened to this shit.

"Helen, I can't talk to her about the case. You know that. Get in touch with the Keegan family liaison officer."

"Yes, Chief."

"Anything on Rachel Cummins?"

She twists the tip of her pen around. "She's been quite down, especially since the trial. The doctor's put her on some meds, so she was pretty fuzzy. But she said that when she looked at the e-fit of Ivan Neary, she was exhausted. She wasn't sure she'd picked the right guy, but when you testified, she got more sure."

"See if she'll come in for questioning."

"Chief, she really wasn't herself."

"Just do it."

I turn to the coffee machine. "Fuck." I frown. "Why didn't Lorcan just tell us about his alibi sooner? Something feels off."

Baz glances up. "You've got a guilt hangover is all."

Doubt nibbles away at my conscience.

"If his alibi checks out, he can go. No bad." He pushes back from his chair. "I was thinking." He gives a half-smile. "This morning, Lorcan's arrest, it started the mice running round the wheel." He circles his finger at the side of his head. "The blue room. I was thinking about it. Where it could be."

"If this is the result of your thinking, you need to phone Mensa right now."

He sighs. "You said 'that place.' As in, another place altogether. Not Clontarf. Not Bray. Maybe not even Dublin. That's what you meant, right?"

"If there's a point to this interrogation, Baz, get to it."

He tucks a hand into his pocket. "You should be glad someone round here values your insight. Even if it's provided unwittingly."

I tip a sachet of sugar into my coffee. A cigarette is already in my hand.

Baz leans forward and clicks the track pad on his computer. The screen lights up, and Amy Keegan's terrified face fills the screen. I almost cover my eyes, the desire to protect myself from what's before me is that strong.

"Close your eyes," he says.

"I've seen it before. A little too late for shielding my sensibilities."

"No. Close your eyes. I need you to listen. Not see."

I do as he says, and shortly after, I hear the click of the track pad, then Amy Keegan's strangled breath as she attempts to drag air into her starved lungs. I am about to shake my head; then I hear it. Beyond the sounds of the room, beyond Amy's panicked breath and the creak of the bed, a church bell is ringing out the Angelus.

I open my eyes. Baz gives me a delighted grin. "Well?"

I give him a smile. "The Angelus is most commonly played in Roman Catholic churches; unfortunately, they seem to number quite a few in Ireland."

I shrug into my suit jacket.

Baz closes the laptop. "You not staying to harass little mister anymore?"

"Nope. No fun when there's a lawyer interrupting every few seconds. We have enough to hold him for twenty-four hours, let's hope that something solid turns up at his house so we can charge him. We should start with towns and villages known to our victims and of course our suspect, Murphy. Steve, phone me with anything significant. I'll be working from home tonight."

There is a gentle cough behind me. I turn, and Steve's standing, stiff-legged, behind me with a pale, stricken expression on his face. He holds out a sheet of paper.

"It might be that his alibi is stronger than you think."

"What is it?" I grasp the page.

It's still warm from the printer, and on it is the latest direct message from TrustMe57.

TeeganRed,

There comes a time when words need to become action.
It's time we meet. I have the perfect place.

TrustMe57

I turn, stare through the viewing window, to where Lorcan Murphy sits, head in the crook of his arms at the interview table.

Baz looks over my shoulder, reads the two lines of text, and swears under his breath. He turns, takes a few steps toward the window, then faces me again.

He points at the note. "This has just come in?"

Steve nods. "This minute."

I steady myself on the back of the chair. "Well, it can't be Lorcan Murphy then, can it?" I think of the blood in his car, on his sheets. The cadaver scent in the boot.

"Maybe the internet weirdo isn't our guy?" Baz says.

"Whoever he is, he's been e-mailing two of our vics. That's a connection we can't overlook."

"But Murphy?"

"He's in there somewhere too. Texting Eleanor Costello right up to her murder." One of the text messages writes itself into my mind: "You've a choice of two weapons . . . Pain or asphyxiation?"

Pulse thumping, breath tight. Patches of heat creep across my chest and up my neck. I close my eyes for a few seconds, shut out the buzz and tension in the office, the before and after of every decision. When I open my eyes, the room sharpens.

"We're close. Murphy's out of play until we have something that puts him at one of the murder scenes. Let's arrange a meet-up with this internet freak and see where it goes. If he's not directly involved in the murders, he has known the victims. We need to question him."

I turn, pick up my coat, and make for the door. I yank it open, then turn back.

"Steve, send me Nicole Duarte's number. I'd like to get her in for questioning. I want to know once and for all what she's dancing around."

CHAPTER 24

AN IRATE COMMUTER is leaning on the car horn. A string of swear words that would pink the cheeks of a mafioso rises through my flat window. Sun is streaking through the pane, happily scorching the top of the bonsai tree. I roll off the sofa, then scramble to capture my work pages before they scatter over the carpet.

I gather up the paper and move it to the coffee table, turn off the TV, and stretch the shape of the couch from my back. Moving to the window, I stare down at the static traffic below; there is a man leaning out of his window, his red fist balled and shaking at a bus that's edged out in front of him.

I shake my head and carry my slowly desiccating project into the kitchenette. The soil around the tree is gritty and dry; when I touch my fingertips to the leaves, they are so brittle that one brushes from its branch and drops off into my hand. Without the binding and pruning, some new branches have formed and shot outwards like gangly teenage limbs.

"Sorry, mate. You got a rough deal when I chose you from the garden center," I murmur. I run the tap and stand the pot in a small pool of water while I've breakfast.

The kettle bubbles to a boil and I stir up a sachet of granulated coffee. A text from Baz tells me there's little else on Murphy showing up at the house. He'll be released in two hours. In anticipation of his lawyer's arrival, he's reduced his answers to "No comment." I almost shrug. He has an alibi. If this were a battle, this would be the time to pull back, weigh up another line of attack. That's what we have to do.

Nicole Duarte. The barista. She's a way in. I lift the mug to my lips, drum my fingernails on the counter. Why did she want to tell me so much about Murphy anyway? At the time, it felt like she might have some urgency to help out the investigation, that her conscience or her jealousy of Murphy's relationship with Costello was pushing her to speak. My spine straightens. She knew. She knew Murphy liked some messed-up shit.

I pick up my mobile, rush to the file, and find Nicole's number. Pacing over and back across my flat, I finish my coffee while I wait for her to answer. It rings out to voicemail. I hang up and try again. And again. Finally, I call Baz.

"Yo!"

I sigh. "Yo?"

"Just trying a thing."

"Well, don't. You've not released him yet?"

"Murphy? No."

"Is the lawyer there?"

"Hold on." The sound of a door opening and Baz's loping gait, his feet hitting the floor, comes through the phone. "Not yet. But he refuses to speak until the lawyer arrives."

I think of the picture that Duarte showed me, her daughter, pink-ribboned pigtails and a gentle, shy smile.

Baz continues: "Murphy's alibi checked out. The student is male.

Nineteen. I've spoken to him. Murphy was with him all night and went straight into work from his gaff."

"There's blood in Lorcan's car, on his sheets, Eleanor's prints are all through his house, we have lurid messages from him on her phone and replies to his phone—"

"Shouldn't we wait for DNA to come through—"

"Do you really think he had nothing to do with it?"

He sighs. "I'm not saying that, only it seems like this other online nutter fits the profile better."

"Then why would Duarte come to us? She gave us that information on a plate."

Silence.

"I'll be there in ten minutes. Don't let him out yet. I won't be long."

ON THE WAY to the office I try Nicole's phone three more times, but each time I'm left with only the drone of her voicemail. I leave a short message, telling her to call me as soon as she can. My pulse picks up and I have to reassure myself that our prime suspect is safely tucked away in an interview room, where he can harm no one.

Only he's not. When I arrive, Lorcan Murphy has been released.

Clancy is standing at my desk. Hands on hips, a purple scowl on his face.

"Tell me you didn't do it."

"Sheehan, your time was up with him. You know the deal."

"I'd another half hour." I say the words slowly, pushing them out between gritted teeth.

"His lawyer beat you to it. There was no point in detaining him any longer. His alibi was verified." He approaches me. "Work faster," he orders. "Or by God, this fucking case will sink and that'll be the end of it."

I reach out, feel the support of my desk, lean into the wood. My knees give a pathetic wobble beneath me that I hope Clancy can't see. He mistakes my silence for contrition.

"Look, I know you're doing your best. But we'll soon be three months down the line and we've sweet fuck all. Money's tight." He has the grace to look ashamed as he says it.

It's what justice comes down to, after all. Who's got the money to order the right tests. Who's got the staff to throw at a scene. Justice costs.

I manage to pull myself upright.

"I've got another lead." I hold up my hands when his eyes snap onto mine. "Don't worry, it won't cost us a fucking penny apart from a tank of gas."

"Well, for Christ's sake, get on with it."

I DON'T GET ON with it. Not right away, at least. I've never taken a verbal smacking easily, and the rebel in me has dug her heels in. Besides, I need time to think about how I'm to get Nicole to talk. I drive to the café, my old haunt, and settle down to a table at the back. Baz slides into the seat across from me.

He looks about furtively. "We're on the clock, aren't we?"

"Yep." I wave the waitress over and order two coffees.

"Don't you think we should be getting on with it?"

I hold up a finger and dial the office.

"Steve, can you check out someone for me, please?"

"A background check?"

"Sort of. Nicole Duarte."

I hear keys striking the keyboard on the other end of the line.

"Could you also check if she gets child support payments from anyone?"

"Child support?"

"Yes."

"I'm on it."

"Oh, and Steve, maybe keep this on the QT, you know, Clancy doesn't need to know."

There's a small silence then. "Okay."

"Phone me with any problems."

"Helen wants a word," he replies.

"Helen?"

Helen's voice comes down the line. "Hi, Chief. I've got a list of churches for you but thought perhaps it would be best to start with Eleanor's hometown. There are two Catholic churches but only one with a bell tower. St. Dymphna's. I'll send through the address."

"Great. Thanks, Helen." I hang up.

Baz finishes his coffee. "So Nicole's not answering her phone?"

"No."

I shake my head. I'm waist deep, mired in a shit storm of lies. Sighing, I tuck the phone away. "I've a bad feeling about this. I need to talk to her."

"We could go to the university? Speak to her there?"

"It's the weekend, she won't be in. Fuck."

I push out of the seat, throw the rest of my coffee down my neck, and leave the cup on the table. "Come on, we're going to Kilcullen."

"Kilcullen?"

"Eleanor's aunt's house."

"You think the blue room might be there? It's hardly a quick spin in the car during Murphy's lunch break, is it?"

I move to the door. "As you say, it's looking likely that Murphy's not our man, but we need to find that room and this is all we've got for the moment. The aunt's house is close to where the phone was found. Maybe checking out Eleanor's past will help us get to know her a bit better. She's hiding something from us."

"Was hiding."

"Sorry?"

His face is lined in concern. "She's dead."

"Let's get on the road before Clancy decides we can't afford to drive and sends us on horseback."

BAZ IS STRETCHED out in the passenger seat. His head is tipped back against the headrest, mouth open. With every turn and bump of the road, his body rolls closer to the window, until eventually he is cradled up against the door like a child.

I glance down at the map I've brought up on my phone. The screen has seized, a gray message box telling me that my GPS can't find my location.

"Christ," I mutter. Slowing down, I take in my surroundings and try to remember the last turn I took, the last time my phone gave me an instruction. Eleanor grew up in Kilcullen. We should only be a couple of miles away, but the road is giving away nothing. It's narrow, crowded with trees that obscure the landscape beyond.

I pull over, tight into the ditch, to sort my phone out, but now the signal is lost and I'm unable to bring up the map.

Baz jolts awake, stretches. "We're here?"

I stab the phone a few times with my finger. "No. Lost."

"Lost, how? Surely not possible in this country, sure you could nearly walk to each end of it?"

He gives me a sleepy smile but I'm not in the mood for humor and scowl at him.

"My GPS has stopped and now I've lost reception." I punch the screen a few more times, refresh the maps, but the signal is fucked.

"Here. Keep driving." He stretches out his hand, flicks his fingers in on his palm.

I pass the phone to him, start up the engine, and pull jerkily away from the ditch.

From the corner of my eye, I see him frowning down at the screen. "Jesus, your phone is outdated."

He slides his finger across the screen, then points ahead through the windscreen. "There's a roundabout up ahead. First exit."

In the distance, among the browns and greens of the countryside, the shape of the town is stretched out in rooftops and power lines. Nestled in the center is an impressive bell tower.

Baz leans forward in his seat, gazes out at the tall stone tower that reaches upward from a short, squat church. His eyes swing round to mine.

"You think that's it?"

"Anything's possible," I mutter under my breath.

"Let's hope it's anything then," he breathes.

My foot leans down on the pedal. The car cuts through the roads and the town grows before us.

Eleanor's aunt's home is on a tidy little estate right on the outskirts of the town, but more importantly, we have a warrant to search it.

A frisson of adrenaline skitters through my veins. I set my eyes on the church ahead.

"Call in the crime-scene investigators. We'll deal with Clancy once we find this room," I demand.

For once, Baz doesn't argue.

ELEANOR'S TEEN HOME in Kilcullen, the house she shared with her late aunt, is among a row of terraced houses, mimicked by another row on the opposite side of the street. I glance down at the address in my hand: 45 Howth Row. The number is mounted on a plaque and framed by thick ivy. The garden is small; giant swells of hard-wearing plants reach up the low wall that separates the property from its neighbor. The gate scratches across the drive when I push it open. I let my hand linger on the bolt, feeling the cracking black paint scratch beneath my palm.

I imagine Eleanor Costello's hand where mine is, try to picture her movements up the short drive to her home. Would she have moved slowly, confidently, sure in her actions? Unashamed. Or did she keep her head down? Furtive. Shrinking at the grate of the gate across the gravel. Would there be someone with her? Or was that someone already waiting for her inside?

Baz passes me an envelope. "The key."

I empty it into my hand. "Come on." I stride up the drive. The neighbors' cars are absent, although two doors down I see a rounded hatchback in a drive. The curtains twitch, and a woman's face appears in the front window, then disappears almost as quickly. I smile.

I twist the key in the lock and the door groans, then shudders open, the wood swollen from the wet Irish winters. Inside, we both take a moment to put on some gloves; then I reach for a light switch. It's a bright day outside, but the house is north-facing and the hallway gloomy and chill.

I reach out, rest my hand on the wall. It's papered, deep blue floral patterns with a plain blue border.

"Maybe it's a running theme," Baz murmurs, hope rising softly on his face.

A draft reaches in from behind the front door, runs around the collar of my coat like a cold finger. I turn, make my way slowly down the hallway. I am aware of a purposeful softness in the roll of my feet on the tiles, as if by limiting noise I can creep up on the past, catch our killer before he has time to kill Amy Keegan. The first room is a living room, a dull peach. I glance back at Baz, who has pushed open another door on the opposite side of the hall.

He shakes his head. "The bathroom."

The kitchen and dining room are visible at the end of the house, open plan with gray-white light spanning through the doorway.

I brace myself. Then reach out to touch the final door in the hall-way. Amy Keegan's cries muffled through the oak veneer, a desperate scuffle of footsteps and the rattle of plastic. I shake my head, clear the ghosts of the case from my mind, and push down the handle. The door swings inwards. My eyes blink, squint against the light. This side of the house is almost full south, and the setting sun blasts orange through the net curtain and across the bed before gathering in the dresser mir-ror in a burning glory. My body sags against the door frame. Baz groans behind me.

There is a clatter of noise coming up the drive and a rap on the front door.

"CSI!" a man calls.

I take a deep breath. "Yes."

I turn away from the room. Pale pink.

"Gav Streeting. Lead crime-scene officer, Naas Gardaí. Where should we set up, Chief?"

I glance at Baz, whose face is suddenly full of doubt.

"Clancy would never have signed off on this."

I smile at Gav Streeting. "Give us a moment."

He frowns but nods, then turns to his team, makes a twirling mo-tion with his index finger, and obediently they turn and filter out of the hallway.

Baz follows me into the kitchen.

Sliding in behind the kitchen table, I drop my head in my hands for a few seconds.

When I look up, Baz is leaning up against the sink, the corners of his mouth pointed and tight.

"So?" he asks.

Back against the hard wooden rungs of the kitchen chair, I glance around the small kitchen, which still looks as if it is kept by an aged aunt. The two houses are at such odds with each other, from the clin-ical, fresh order of the Costello house to this dark, lived-in town house.

It is hard to imagine Eleanor creasing her tailored trousers on the seat I am sitting in.

I get up, go to the doorway.

"Streeting?" I call down the hallway. Immediately, the investigator appears in the doorway.

I wave him inside. "Carry on. Full sweep, please."

He nods and turns on his heel to collect his team.

I push down the hallway, out of the house, where the Kildare skies are now gray and a soft drizzle swirls in the cold air.

"Sheehan!" Baz calls out from behind, but I'm already clambering into the car.

Slamming the door, I plunge the key into the ignition. He throws himself into the passenger seat, but before he can say anything, I speed away from Kilcullen.

"Clancy will have our heads."

"He won't say anything."

He snorts.

I throw him a sideways glance. "Why do you think he worked so hard to get me back on board, Harwood?" I laugh. "I'm no better than many of my subordinates." My hands tighten on the steering wheel.

When he doesn't say anything, I give another short laugh. "Don't rush to contradict me."

"No doubt your giant ego can take it."

"He pulled me back in because he knows I'll make the tough choices. The choices that he wants to make but can't because he's the one who has to report to the commissioner. The fact is, the Kilcullen house"—I jerk my thumb toward the rearview window—"may give us the final clue. We don't have the money to search it, but we can't risk not finding it. The phone was dumped in the Liffey not ten miles from here," I remind him again.

He sighs, looks out the window. "You're right. Just could do without a tongue-lashing from Clancy this afternoon, 'tis all."

I laugh again, but inside my guts are twisting. There's a good chance that Clancy will send me packing, return me to sick leave, despite my assurances to Baz, even though he'll know I did the only thing I could do.

THE LIFT SINKS and the doors slide open. The tops of my arms ache from driving the narrow country roads, Baz whinging in my ear all the way, wanting me to go for a drink, anything to take the sting out of our failure. But I've shored up enough exhaustion to keep my adrenaline in check and I'm longing to crash out.

I push my bag, the case folders, victims' lives and deaths, into my free arm and go to unlock the flat, but it's already open. The door moves, creaks as if sucked inwards by a stray breeze. I freeze, lay the bags, the folders, down carefully and stare in through the crack in the door. I try to remember when I left this morning. The hours, days, nights, all meld together in a haze of interviews and crime scenes.

I was rushing, couldn't be late. Did I lock the door? I can't remember.

I step to the side, push the door wide. Wait. Then reach in. Turn the light on. Dishes in the sink, clothes over the back of the chair, my coffee mug sitting on the windowsill. It looks like home. I step inside, scan the room. Nothing seems out of place. I move to the bedroom, flick the switch. Nothing. Bedcovers thrown back, wardrobe open, hanger on the door. Each drawer, each window, I check lifts more tension from my shoulders.

I return to the door, gather up my bag, the notes from the hallway, then go back inside and lock the door. Take the time to slide the bolt at the bottom. I pour a glass of wine, sit down on the sofa, try to relax. After a while, I move to the window. From this vantage point I can watch the angles and corners of the flat, all the nooks and crannies where fear wants to hide.

CHAPTER 25

RACHEL CUMMINS WAS found in her bathtub this evening. Wrists open to the elbow, the water still warm even though she'd been dead for almost an hour. The wound on the right arm was jagged, repeated efforts from where the already injured left hand had been disabled.

The rain is beating against my building. Spatters shoot through the narrow slit of my flat window. Cigarette smoke clouds up in front of me, then filters out into the angry night. The wind lifts the hair from my forehead, sends a shiver shaking through my body. I fold my arms. My reflection grimaces before me in the window, and the insides of my flat project out into the darkness. An unopened bottle of wine sits on the coffee table. I lift my mug to my mouth, taste sour coffee, and swallow.

I pull on the cigarette, watch the smoke pour out against the glass, billow, then shunt upward to the open window. The coroner was quick to confirm it as suicide. A note had been found describing how Rachel couldn't live with her guilt and fear. Is this what I should have done? Let my guilt drive a blade down my arms? I might not have put Ivan

Neary away, but I led Rachel to believe that he was the one. I push the stub of the cigarette into the soil of the bonsai pot.

I remember her nerves, her anxious, skittish movements. Her eyes never stilled on mine once but slid from floor to me, then floor again. Her hands moved rhythmically over each other in a constant dance of worry. She would have said anything to get away from that case.

Was that what it was worth? A life for six months of Ivan Neary's innocence? I push another cigarette between my lips, squint as I light it, and blow out the smoke in a straight line toward the ceiling.

The phone buzzes on the kitchen counter. I jump; then, rolling my shoulders, reach for it and return to the window.

"Sheehan."

"Hey, Frankie, it's Helen."

I pull up at the use of my name.

"Sorry to phone you, I know you're probably trying to wrap your head around what's happened to Rachel Cummins."

I take another drag of the cigarette. "What is it?"

"I thought you might want to talk." I can hear her picking her words. "Rachel Cummins did what she did. People have to take responsibility for their own actions."

I gaze at my reflection on the dark window. "Sure. Was there something else?"

Silence breathes down the line. "Moira Keegan. She called again."

"I told you, unless she's new information for us, the next time I speak to her will be to tell her we've got the fuck who murdered her daughter."

"She says she only wants to check in with you. I thought in light of Rachel—"

"Christ, Helen, who are you? My fucking conscience? Fine, I'll phone her. Happy?"

"She's actually on the other line. Waiting."

Of course she is. Helen, nothing if not efficient. I look beyond myself, out the window. Black, black night. A white moon buried somewhere behind dark cloud. The violent rush of rain has passed and is now a soothing patter over the city.

"Put her through."

"Frankie. It's Moira Keegan here."

Moira's voice is tied up with so much unspoken grief that I can't bear it.

"Moira. Sorry I've not had a chance to get back to you, especially after Tom—"

"I wondered if you'd had any leads?" Straight to it, no small talk. The business of murder makes strangers of us all.

I hold back the sigh building in my throat. "I'm afraid I can't re-veal too much, Moira. How's Eamon doing?" I frown at the inanity of the question.

"Sure, you know yourself. Thrown himself into work again. Tom's only climbing the walls to get shot of him." A pause; then: "I think he feels a bit guilty, you know."

And just like that, the detective in me sits up. "Guilty? Tom?"

"No. Eamon. They argued sometimes, you know." She drops her voice to a whisper. "That time she told him about the affair. Sure, what could he have known?"

I nod. Relax. "Yes."

"The funeral was last week," she states.

Shame sweeps up my neck. "Sorry I couldn't make it."

"We kept it small. Family. A few friends, but it was nice. Amy would've liked it; we had her sandwiches out, the chocolate she liked, one of the local bands set up in the house, played music from her fa-vorite singer. You know, nice."

I remember Tom Quinn's interview, Amy's plans to go to a concert with Peter Costello.

"Her favorite singer?"

"Oh, yes. Joni Mitchell."

"Parking lots and paradises?"

"That's the one, yes."

I like that song. I say so. And that seems to be enough for Moira.

"You'll let us know, won't you, when you've any news?"

"As soon as I can, Moira."

When I hang up, I pour a glass of wine, pull the window closed. Seal myself away from the city, cut a siren off midscream. I drop the phone onto the sofa, then notice that there is a voicemail message waiting. Baz is likely drowning his sorrows somewhere and wanting me to join him. I click through to check his number against the list of missed calls, but the message was left in the minutes I was talking to Moira Keegan.

There is no number. I press the phone to my ear and wait for it to talk me through to the messages. Finally, there is a loud beep and the message plays. Raw silence comes down the line. I press the phone harder against the side of my head. It's as if the caller is leaning up against me, listening, waiting for me to speak. Unease. A shiver. I strain to hear a rasp of breath, the scratch of a finger fumbling over the phone, but there is nothing but a strange, hollow quiet.

I go to hang up when I hear a sharp intake of breath. I tense. Listen. Then the caller whispers one word into my ear: *"Cunt."*

The line goes dead. I am frozen. A dark mixture of shame and terror creeps over my face. I swallow, touch the heat of my ear, and look down at the screen. The message has finished. I drop the phone, let it thud to the carpet.

After a moment, I get up, check the door, push over the bolt. Then, backing away, I sit into the sofa and take a steadying drink of wine. My eyes are fixed on the floor where the phone lies. When the screen lights up again, I jump. Edging closer, I see a text on the screen.

With shaking fingers, I take the phone into my hand. It's a message from Baz. He's in the pub, down the street. I pocket the phone, turn, grab my coat, and leave the flat.

———

BAZ PUSHES HIS index finger into his ear and presses the phone against his head. He frowns. When he looks at me, his expression is a mixture of confusion and concern. He pushes the mobile back toward me as if it were a grenade without a pin.

"Christ. I thought the calls had stopped."

I look down at my wine. "There's not been a single hit on a mast since Amy's murder. We all thought they were a hoax, someone who'd managed to get hold of Peter's old handset, to taunt me. Steve has got a location already. It came from a mast on Duke Street. We've checked through CCTV, see if we could catch someone on a phone. Nothing."

"Duke Street? That's off Grafton Street, isn't it? Frankie, that's right beside you."

"You don't need to tell me where I live."

I think of the flat, the open door, the feeling of another presence in my home.

Baz is studying my face. "What?"

"I'm not sure someone hasn't been in the flat. When I got home yesterday evening, the door was open."

His eyes darken. Flash. Anger. He takes a gulp of his pint.

Laughter erupts from a table behind us, an office party or a group of friends, thin paper crowns and tinsel tiaras crooked on their heads, broken Christmas crackers at elbows.

"A break-in?" Baz asks.

"Nothing was taken, nothing to suggest a burglary."

He nods. "Murphy was released. You think he might have chanced an unwelcome visit?"

"Dunno. I'm not sure I didn't just forget to lock the door." I chew down on my lip. "I was in a rush in the morning. Maybe I pulled the door over too quickly, it didn't slam, and I didn't check."

"It could be the killer."

I look down at my fingers, spread like a starfish around the base of my glass. I'm afraid to move them, afraid they will shake.

Baz leans in. "Your phone, there's always voice-recognition technology."

"And who would we compare the sample to? Besides, a one-syllable word would be near impossible to get a match on even if we had a suspect in custody."

"What if he's after you?"

"He's not." I can't let that thought in. "He's taunting me."

"You don't know that."

"You're right, I don't. But I know enough about murderers. He's frustrated. Frustrated that he's not managed to tell us how thick we are and how clever he is."

"You think he wants to get caught?"

"Maybe." I shrug. "Mostly, he wants acknowledgment."

"Frankie, there are people out there that you've pissed off. Some of them might want to hurt you: Murphy, Ivan Neary," he says.

I raise the glass to my lips, breathe out through my nose.

"Maybe I should speak to him. To Neary."

He slides his hand over mine, and the action is so swift that I can't help but jerk away.

"Sorry," I murmur.

"You're not the big bad in this crime, Frankie. You're not the murdering scumbag."

"I know. But neither is Ivan Neary."

He nods. "I guess maybe a visit is warranted. He is a witness."

"It's more than that. We're both victims, both carrying different scars from this case. I was going to give him a wide berth, but, after Rachel Cummins, the least I can do is drop in. I don't know, it seems like I owe him that much."

I settle back into my seat. "I'm thinking of going back to the Kilcullen house."

Baz straightens. Hopeful. "They found something?"

"No. This evening, I was speaking with Moira Keegan on the phone. She mentioned something about Amy, that she was a fan of Joni Mitchell."

"And?"

I reach out, open the photos of Eleanor Costello's childhood house on my phone, scroll to the set I took of the living room in Kilcullen. Settling on one, I turn the phone round to face Baz.

"This one. Here."

"What am I looking at?"

"The CD rack. Three down. It's her album."

He tips his head at me. "Who on earth uses CDs anymore? Can't seem to cast off the nineties, no matter what you do. Frankie, is this really worth another trip down there? I think I even have a copy of Joni Mitchell somewhere. Or I would have, if I bothered with CDs."

I take the phone back. "I thought it was worth a shot."

"If the CSI didn't find anything, I'm not sure your CD will bring a killer to justice."

I gaze out the window at the black night. More laughter and shouts from the party behind, a stumbling start at a song, off-beat clapping, and a crippling version of what could be Bing Crosby's "White Christmas."

I sigh, look back to Baz. "I don't know. Something is telling me to go back there. Maybe I'm frustrated that I never seem to get to know her."

"Eleanor?"

"She's the key. Where're the knife marks? Where's the cutting? It was the killer's hard-on, but apart from old wounds and a pathetic slice on her forearm, there's not much on her body that matches the type of injury on Amy's and Tracy's bodies."

"Peter was stabbed."

"Yes, but where were the teasing slices, the wounding cuts to torture and terrify, designed to draw out death, not deliver it? With Peter the wounds were sudden. Injuries to bring a man to his knees, a surprise attack. When I looked at the X-rays of his chest, out of the seven stab wounds, five had gone through ribs. These were forceful, angry blows."

Baz pours another glass of wine. Holds the bottle up. "You want?"

I nod and he fills my glass.

A sip; then I keep with my train of thought. "Peter's injuries were not consistent with our perp's other victims."

Baz settles back down into the armchair. "Do you think a woman would have the strength to do that? To stab through bone? Eleanor?"

"Yes. If her victim was already weakened with illness and unable to fight back. But what if it was a joint effort? Between Eleanor and someone else. A fantasy, a kill for both of them."

I am in full profile mode now. I see Eleanor's wedding photograph again in my mind's eye. Such poise and control. Her husband not ready, never ready. That smile. Knowing too much. It would be her downfall.

"Eventually, the killer would have had to get rid of Eleanor; she knew too much or maybe he believed she had become too powerful. In a strange way, he respected her, loved her even. Serial killers often make trophies of some women, elevate them to wife status, and often these women are spared the same fate as the killer's victims. But Eleanor was not to be persuaded into the submissive role. She had to go."

I make a mental note to talk to Murphy again. If he and Eleanor were in a relationship, it may be that he lent her his car. As his alibi has checked out, it would explain the cadaver scent in the boot. A scent that didn't belong to Eleanor but to her murdered husband.

"Excuse me," I say to Baz.

I know Abigail will still be in the office. When she answers, her voice is scratchy with tiredness.

"Dr. James here."

"Abigail, it's Frankie. Any updates on the blood from Murphy's car?"

"We're almost there," she says.

"I know it's late, but could you run through all sequences tonight: Eleanor, Peter, and Amy?"

There's a pause. "I've a lot of paperwork to do."

"I know. I'm sorry. It's a lot to ask, but we could really do with some clarity here."

A sigh. "Clancy has loosened the purse strings, has he? All right, sure. In the next few hours?"

"Thanks. I'm on my mobile."

When I hang up, Baz gulps down a mouthful of Pinotage. "You're too good at this job sometimes, Frankie. But even if that theory is true, we'll still be no closer to nailing it to this guy. We're running out of time."

"I know," I say in frustration. "I know!"

"Lookit, you were right with what you said before, there's one person who says he saw the killer. Clancy won't be happy about prodding a wasps' nest in case it lights the tinder on a libel case but—"

"Neary?"

He nods.

I sag against the chair; panic patters up my throat.

"Forget Kilcullen. We've been already," he says. "Get Eleanor out of your head. She's dead. The killer isn't and could be moving in on his next victim any moment. Neary might have the lead we need."

"I'll see him first thing."

"You want me to go? Wait in the car, in case he threatens you?"

I give him a tight look, try not to think about the tsunami of memories a visit to Neary will trigger. "Are you having me on? If he gets a gander at anything but my mug, he'll take my nose off with the door, he'll slam it so hard."

The party are moving, bundling toward the door, arms over shoulders, high heels twisting on the carpet.

Baz stretches. "Can I crash at yours?"

And I know he's offering so that I don't have to be alone.

I get up. "The couch is yours."

When we get into the flat, Baz kicks off his shoes and stretches out on the sofa. His legs drop over the end; his head is overly high on the armrest. But he closes his eyes and waves off my offer of a pillow. "No need. I'm as good as asleep."

"Night," I say.

I get to my room and stretch out on the bed. When I wake the next morning, it's early; the sound of traffic thickening on the streets below tells me it's close to six. I scramble for my phone, still in my pocket from last night.

Abigail's message came through at four a.m. Eleanor's blood on Lorcan Murphy's sheets, but the results of the DNA profile found in the boot of Murphy's car were decisive: Peter Costello.

CHAPTER 26

IT TAKES ME almost a full fifteen minutes before I can meet Ivan Neary's eyes. He greeted me at the door of his house, escorted me to the living room, and presented me with a glass of water, and I've somehow avoided looking at him.

Tension builds across my chest, but I make myself do it: raise my head, strap down the nervous smile that is threatening to pull across my face, and look at him.

His head is bent, hands cupping the tops of his knees. His fingers pressed into his jeans.

"Mr. Neary. I'm sorry."

"Don't."

Mouth dusty-dry. My teeth work across my bottom lip. "Okay."

He's soft-featured, not in a pathetic kind of way, but he has the kind of face that you know will age into deep benevolent creases around youthful blue eyes. It makes it all the more difficult to look at the pain pulling at the corners of his mouth and the flare of his nostrils.

"What're you here for?"

His question unlocks me.

"Oh." I cough into my hand. "Can I just say thank you for meeting me."

"What else could I do?"

"You're a free man. There was nothing that could stop you from saying no."

He sneers. The soft lines deepen. "Free? You think I'm free? I've had to move fucking house. My wife has left me."

He takes up a newspaper, glances at the cover, then throws it at me. "You call that free?" A trembling finger wags at the front page.

The headline reads, "Man Arrested for Ward Murder Released. Murderer Connected to At Least Three Other Deaths."

He turns away. "How can they be allowed to print that shite?"

"I'm sorry."

"I don't want your fucking apologies."

"Mr. Neary. I know you don't want to talk about it but—"

"I've been doing nothing but talk about it for the last seven months, Detective Sheehan."

I look up.

He stops, reclaims his seat. Rocks back and forth. Clasps his hands. Unclasps them. Cups the tops of his knees again.

"I'm angry, yeah, but I've my share of guilt." He extends a shaking finger at the floor where the newspaper lies. "It's that head-fucking I can't stand. Lying pigs."

He takes a breath, holds it. Swallows. It looks almost as if he is pushing down a great weight deep into his abdomen.

"I've never hit a single person in my bloody life. You won't believe that, I'm sure. With the work that you do, like. But 'tis true. I'm fifty-three and always the first to turn my back on a scuffle. Even as a kid."

His head shakes. "To use that knife. To feel *your* body give under it. I get night terrors thinking about it. And the smell. That hot smell of blood. I can taste it."

Sweat is beading across my hairline. It itches. I sit on my hands. Take long drags of air into my body. Tell my brain to get with the fucking program. Words. Just words.

His eyes meet mine, and I swear he can see the terror I'm hiding.

"I'm sorry too," he says.

A silence stretches out between us and I am there. Returned in a moment to the scene of Tracy Ward's murder. There is thumping in my ears and a terrible, throbbing inevitability as I hear the scuff of stone under my feet. I'm creeping around the back of the house. It's dark but I daren't turn on my torch. The screaming has stopped and I want to rush inside but I'm sure I see a shadow shift in the blackness ahead of me. My brain, all-knowing in hindsight, fills in the darkness with Ivan Neary's silhouette.

The side wall of the house is cold on my back. I blink hard a few times, persuading my eyes to adjust to the lack of light. I draw short quiet breaths in through my nose. I hear a man's voice shouting out, something violent, threatening. A warning. The back door is wide-open and there isn't a chink of light inside. I step up, into the house, and immediately the bitter, cloying smell of fresh blood hits the back of my throat.

Ivan coughs into his hand and I snap back into the room. He's ready.

"I didn't even hear you pull up. That road out there. Always so busy, to be fair. 'Twas the same in the old place. It's a wonder I heard poor Tracy at all. She was a quiet sort. Barely even watching the telly, and the way the walls are between our houses, you know sometimes I could hear the hum of her dinner spinning round the microwave in the evening."

He shakes his head. "I heard the scream, like I said before, and I came around the back, up the garden, and saw that there weren't any lights on. And I know it's strange, but I knew something wasn't right from that moment. I came up the yard and in the door, which was open a little way. I was scared but at the same time knew that she was in trouble, so I didn't bother looking about too much. I thought I could hear something up the hall, like.

"I shouted out that I had a weapon and then heard a scuffle from the bedroom. I figure that's when he went through the window. She was laid out on the bed. Blood was still—" He swallows, points to his neck. He takes a few seconds, then continues.

"The knife was on the ground. It was dreadful. Awful. I didn't know what to do. I should have pressed against her neck or something, but I couldn't make myself. I checked her wrist. I couldn't find a pulse. That's when I heard a noise in the hallway. I didn't even think.

"I picked up the knife and hid to the side of the doorway. It was so dark. I felt sick. The knife was still warm. But I thought he was coming back, you know. When you came around the corner, I struck out. I was suddenly furious. You turned to get away but I thought you were him. And I was so angry at what you'd done."

"The killer had done."

"Yes. The killer." He sighs. Rolls his shoulders, then sags onto his hands again. "I was a madman. Blind. Determined. Terrified."

The silence rises again between us, and my final image of Tracy Ward returns. The smell. The horror. The blur of my vision as my head falls back over Clancy's arm, looking at the inverted scene and Tracy's neck open, her head tipped over the edge of the bed, eyes white and staring at me.

I swallow, give Neary a hard look. "You knew I would come here?"

"I thought you might. It's what I would have done."

"Did you see anything of the killer? Anything? A glimpse as he went out the window?"

He shakes his head. "Nothing." But then he frowns, as if he re-members something after all.

"What is it?"

"Only, the houses. The windows are very dated. In my house, at least. Wooden. Sash."

"They open, though?"

"Just. You have to get close. Shuffle them upward. The wood swells in damp weather, you see. You'd have to know how to do it. There's a knack."

My mind offers me photos. Photos of the inside of Tracy's room. Feminine, if not a little cluttered. The window, sash. Open. The curtain gaping on one side.

"He'd been in there. Before. Or Tracy slept with the window open?"

"No." His voice is sure. Strong.

I study his face. "She didn't have the window open?"

His head is shaking from side to side. "It might have been June, but it's still June in Ireland. It was so cold that night. They were harping on about it breaking some record on the news. Near freezing, it was."

I remember. The surprise of the cold when I stepped out of the office that night. More details from the case stir in my mind. There had been no sign of forced entry. A killer who knew his victim was part of the story now, and should be part of Tracy's.

"You don't know of any personal connections between the Costellos and Tracy, do you?"

"Aren't you supposed to be the detective?" He leans back into the chair. "No. Ever since my solicitor told me about the link between the murders, I've been wracking my brain trying to put them together, but they were worlds apart: Tracy's world and that Costello lady at least. To me anyway."

He's forward in his chair again. Staring at his hands.

The killer is the only one who completes that link. I push out of the seat and Neary's head tips up slowly.

I extend my hand and he shakes it lightly. He doesn't stand.

"Thanks, Mr. Neary."

"He'll kill again, this fella. If you don't get him fast."

My lips harden against my teeth. "I know."

WHEN I OPEN the office door, there is a brief show of glances; faces lift quickly from their desks, then dip back behind computers. The fear in my gut that Clancy has boxed up the investigation begins to subside. My gaze flicks to the case board. It's intact. Nothing removed. I search the room for Clancy. He's not here, but he has been. I can feel the resultant tension in the room. No one wants to tell me he's about to declare the case cold.

I shut the door and walk steadily to the board, pick up a pen and reach to a space right above Eleanor Costello's name. I write, "Victim one: Tracy Ward," and fill in her details, adding "Known to killer" afterward.

Steve hovers behind me; his pale face is a white shadow on the sheen of Eleanor Costello's photograph.

I remain staring up at Tracy's name. "What is it, Steve?"

"Good news and bad news," he says. "I managed to get Murphy to answer a few questions over the phone. Without much persuasion he told me that Eleanor Costello borrowed his car for two days, 8 and 9 October, to go to a work conference in Cork. We have tollbooth photos of his car passing through the M50 toll on those days. The photos clearly show a female driver in the car, no other passenger. I contacted the conference that she was to attend, but she never showed."

Hope stirs again in my chest. "So she definitely used his car to move the body, and throughout the day at least, she was heading south on the M50."

He nods, passes me a sheet of paper. "The other thing was that there's a press release due in a few hours. To be signed by the commissioner."

"A press release? Let me guess. An announcement about winding down?"

He clears his throat. "I'm sorry."

"Where's Clancy now?"

"Chief, he's pretty pissed at the little stunt you played in Kilcullen, especially as CSI didn't find anything."

I turn, take the press release from him. Crumple it up in my hands. Drop it on the floor.

"That 'little stunt' was necessary. It wouldn't do if it got out that we'd failed to investigate one of Eleanor Costello's hidey-holes, now, would it?"

"Chief, I agree with you. I feel like we're so close to this fucker I can smell his ass crack."

I look over his shoulder, survey the office. "Any more on the chat room?"

"Helen has been stepping up the honey trail, but our man's not biting."

"I don't like this."

"I know. It's almost like he's busy with something else, because he was certainly keen before. Myself and Emer have been tracing TrustMe57's history of commentary on the forum. Looking at his activity rates over the last year. And it's all peaks and troughs. Things heat up for a while on his end, then go quiet. We put the dates together with the estimated times of death for all our victims."

My mouth dries. "And?"

"He definitely switched off for a while when the murders happened."

"Peter Costello's?"

"Yep."

My heart picks up. "And now?"

"He's been completely silent over the last few days. His account remains inactive, no matter what we do. Short of giving him an online lap dance to engage him, we've tried everything, and he's not playing."

Coldness drops through my body.

"He has another victim," I whisper.

Steve sighs. "I mean, our theory's not foolproof, but it looks that way, yes."

Nicole Duarte's smiling face appears in my mind's eye. "Nicole."

"Nicole?"

"Yes. The coffee girl at the university. I keep trying her number, but it's going straight to voicemail. I think she's involved in this somehow. She's hinted at knowing Eleanor and Murphy intimately. And everyone in that little club takes part in a kill-or-be-killed philosophy. I'm worried for her."

I turn to leave.

"Wait!" Steve calls out. "Clancy wants to talk to you. The press!"

"Tell him I've work to do!" I shout back at the door.

I text Baz, let him know to meet me at the university. Lorcan Murphy can at least help us find Nicole Duarte. I think of her youthful complexion, the photo of her daughter. My feet pick up the pace, and before I know it, I'm running down the steps toward the car park.

When I reach the car, my stomach plummets. Baz is waiting, stony-faced and staring at his shoes. His entire being hangs like that of a scolded schoolchild. Clancy is grim-faced beside him. I slow to a walk, then stop in front of them.

"Jack," I say by way of a greeting.

His eyes slide away. "It's over, Sheehan."

"I've got a lead. The barista. Nicole Duarte, she's a possible target, she's been missing for days."

He looks up. "You're chasing shadows. How about taking leads on the victims that we know are dead, Sheehan. Is there not enough of them? You went to Neary's."

I pull my spine straight. "It was all right. He was expecting me."

Clancy runs his hand through his hair. Baz takes a step back, as if he can protect himself from hearing what's coming.

"It doesn't fucking matter what he was expecting. What if the press had got a shot of that? What if he goes to the papers?"

"He wanted to help."

"If he's giving a new statement, then he needs to come to us." He looks me in the eye. A challenge.

I blow air through my lips. "You fucking know he won't do that." I take a step closer and I see Baz's head snap up. Caution. "Jack, the window, it's one of those old fob latches."

He raises an eyebrow. "The window? What fucking window, Frankie? Have you lost it completely?"

"Tracy Ward's. Her bedroom window. It's not easy to open if you're not familiar with the mechanism. There was a knack to how it's opened."

His shoulders shift beneath his jacket, but I can see the intrigue glint in his eyes. It takes him a few moments, but he catches on. "Tracy knew him then?"

"It would explain why there was no forced entry. She let him in, and when he needed to run, he was used to handling the tricky window."

He seems to be coming around, but suddenly he shakes his head. "No. It's too late, Frankie. If it was solely up to me, then—"

My fingernails bite into the heat of my palm. "Don't give me that bollocks, Jack."

"Sheehan!"

"No, fuck it. Fuck you. Why did you put me on this case if I wasn't going to be able to see it through?"

"There's no more money in the tin, Frankie!" he's yelling. His voice booms around the dark underground car park. "The case is not the only thing to be shut down."

"What are you talking about?"

"I'm out." He sighs. Then tries to smile. "I'm retiring, end of next month."

"Retiring or being forced into an armchair?"

He shrugs. "Does it matter?"

"It's because of me, isn't it?"

"Get over yourself, Sheehan. The way I remember it, I was the one who snapped the handcuffs onto Neary's wrists and pushed him head-first into the back of the wagon. You were out cold."

"You're being fed to the press then?"

"Hardly. I'm not a fucking victim, Sheehan. I put an innocent man behind bars."

I force down the ball of anxiety that's rolling up my throat.

"I'm sorry, Jack. I am. I could be told to pack up my office next, and where are our victims then? I can't let anything get in my way. I need this to end right." I meet his eyes. "You know that."

I take a deep breath, feel the tension creep away from my shoulders. I picture Nicole Duarte. "You knew that when you brought me in on this case. I won't give up."

"It wasn't supposed to be like this."

He means that it wasn't supposed to be tied up in the mess of Tracy Ward's death.

I set my jaw. "Well, it is."

He leaves me hanging for a full ten seconds, then meets my eyes. "I can delay the paperwork for twenty-four hours. At. The. Most."

I smile. "Come on, Jack. We're on Ireland time here, nothing gets done in twenty-four hours."

His mouth thins. "Twenty-four hours, Sheehan, but first go relieve the guards at the Costello house. Clear the tape and seal it up for the lawyers. At least look as if you're playing ball."

Clancy grumbles something about his pension plan as he strides to his own car, a washed-out silver Mondeo.

I smile. Catch Baz's eye. He's already opening the car door.

CHAPTER 27

A **SLEETING RAIN SMEARS** over the windshield. I turn up the heating in the car, feel the blast of it on my face. Slowly, the fog lifts from the window. Baz is squinting through it. He's wondering, no doubt, why we're headed out the N11 and not out the Bray road to relieve the Gardaí at the Costello house, as Clancy demanded. After a moment, he shakes his head. Lays it back on the seat. A sign for the university sleeks past.

"Lorcan Murphy again?"

"He owes us. He's muddied and he knows it."

"He's not going to incriminate himself, Frankie. Not now. We've shown him our cards and he's royal-flushed our asses."

"I still can't reach Nicole Duarte."

"The coffee girl?"

"Yes, the coffee girl. And Lorcan's onetime date. A girl who was probably pretty jealous of Eleanor Costello."

"Or Eleanor of her."

"You could be right."

"She's young. Vibrant. Single. And Eleanor's playboy had a thing with her once."

Slush is gathering along the roadside; cars are rolling by, drivers slowing ahead. I move out, overtake them. Turning onto the Belfield road, I follow the signs to the university, go up the drive, and park in front of the distinctive building.

The halls are clammy, the hot breath of hundreds of students in from the frigid air steaming up the walls. We push up through the mass of people toward the biology labs and lecture hall upstairs. I check my watch: It's almost one.

Alibi or no, I can't ignore the evidence we've gathered against Murphy or the fact that he has repeatedly failed to give us essential information that could have cut our investigation in half. Eleanor's blood on his sheets, the phone messages, his lying, his deceit, his relationship with Nicole.

When I turn the corner of the café, I'm not surprised to find someone else handing hot chocolates and coffees over the counter.

Baz states the obvious. "Nicole's not here."

I approach the barista. She's plump. Older. Flustered. Students wait, tight-faced and angry in a line extending out through the seating area.

"There's a queue," she barks, as if I could miss it.

"Where's Nicole?"

She turns, jiggles a metal jug under a steamer. Twists the air on for a moment, then off. Without looking up, she shouts, "Who are you?"

"Detective Chief Superintendent Sheehan. Where's Nicole?"

Abruptly, she flicks the machine off, turns. She slides her hands down the sides of her apron. "Aren't youse the ones that should be answering that question?"

"What do you mean?"

"Sure, yis are supposed to be looking for her. Her mammy put in the report days ago."

"Report?"

"Jesus, no wonder the country's in the state it's in. I dunno where Nicole is. She's been missing for days. No one knows." She shakes her head, then turns back to the machine.

I glance back at Baz. He's already on the phone, telling the office to search for the report. Bring him feedback. The pulse is ticking away over my temples; I rub the sensitive skin.

"Do you have her mother's address? Her number?"

She slaps a milky coffee down in front of a waiting student. For a moment he looks set to object but then thinks better of it. He takes up the mug and slinks off into the café.

"Do you want me to get out there and start looking for her meself? Lazy fucks."

"Please. Nicole could be in danger. Help me find her."

"Well, then, you'd best speak with the dean, so. He'll have her ma's number. Up one floor there and at the end of corridor."

"Thanks."

Baz stalks off down the corridor.

Joe Clifford is the dean. Even though my team have been in and out of his university almost as often as his students, I've yet to speak to him. When we reach his office, the door is wide-open and Clifford is clicking through his computer with one hand, a steaming cup of tea in the other. When he spots us in the doorway, his face is an expression of soft-lined welcome.

"What can I do for you?"

"Mr. Clifford, I'm Detective Sheehan and this is Detective Harwood."

His mouth eases out of a smile. He looks mildly terrified. "Not another murder?"

"No. I was hoping you have a home contact number for a member of staff."

"Normally, the utilities manager holds all those records, but I should be able to get something on the file here. What's her name?"

"We appreciate that, Mr. Clifford. Nicole Duarte. She works in the café."

He scrolls down through a file of staff records; the screen freezes for a moment and he swears. "As you can see, we've not updated our system in a while. Life"—he blushes—"or rather death has got in the way of normal service in some ways. We've had a few staff shortages in our admin team, folks nervous about this killing business."

He pauses. "How's your investigation into Dr. Costello's death going?"

"It's moving along."

"I would have thought you'd got everything you need by now?"

"All except the killer."

"Sorry. I wish I could be more help." He leans back from his computer, taps the screen. "There we are. Nicole Duarte. Her mother's number."

I type it into my phone. "Thank you."

We walk back down the corridor, damp soles squeaking on the tiles. A woman steps out of a door; a heavy stack of paper leans forward in her arms. A few sheets slide from the top of the pile as she attempts to close the door behind her. I pick them up. Replace them. She smiles her thanks, then walks off. When I straighten, I notice the sign outside the door: "Behavioral Sciences: Dr. Jeremy Burke."

I glance up at Baz. His eyes are fixed to it too.

"The therapist you talked to, right? Eleanor's therapist?" I ask.

"Looks the same. Same name. Surname," Baz says.

"Coincidence?"

"You know how I feel about those." He reaches out to grab the door handle, but I stop him.

"No. Go. Find Murphy. I'll see how this one plays out. Your report didn't flag up anything abnormal."

He points at the door. "He never mentioned he worked here, though."

"Murphy's a loose end. We're up against the clock. You've already spoken to this guy, let me try."

"Murphy's a lawyered-up loose end."

I push a hand through my hair; my fingers brush the sensitive spot at my temple. "I don't give a shit. Get to him."

Baz turns, heads off down the hall. I wait until he disappears round the corner and down the stairs; then I lift my hand and knock.

"Come in," comes a male voice. I push the door open. A man is standing at a printer in the corner of the room. The printer is spewing out sheets. The man is collecting pages from an already printed pile, dividing them in three and stapling them together. He looks up quickly from his task when I enter, stapler hovering over the corner of a fresh print.

"Sorry, I can't stop. Lecture notes. What can I help you with?"

"I'm Detective Frankie Sheehan, I'm looking for Dr. Jeremy Burke?"

He pushes the stapler and lays the paper down, quickly retrieving another set of notes to do the same.

"I'm afraid Dr. Burke's away. He's taken an extended holiday over Christmas." He pauses, tips his head back to the ceiling. "I think China or something. Oriental. Unusual." He returns to the printer.

I move a little farther into the room. Peruse the walls. There are plaques over the desk, declaring Burke's heavyweight qualifications for human psychology, behavioral sciences, and cognitive behavioral therapies. I get a flashback to my training years, our first day of criminal psychology and my lecturer makes a joke about how the only people who study psychology are the only people who need it.

There are no pictures on the desk, of family or the doc himself. But on the wall above the printer there is a large Chagall print. The first page in Peter Costello's art book. The same image that was in the downstairs toilet of the Costello house.

I lift my phone and take a picture of it.

The man stops in his task. "Are you allowed to do that?"

I lower my phone. "I just love that painting is all," I chirp, not attempting to hide the lie.

Removing my card, I pass it to him.

"Have Burke call me as soon as he gets back, please."

He tries to return it. "I'm not his secretary, only his understudy."

I give him a tight smile. "Great. You'll be talking to him when he gets back, so you can let him know then."

I STOP ABRUPTLY OUTSIDE the microbiology labs, where Baz is waiting. I frown at him. "What are you doing out here?"

"He said he'd be with me shortly."

I glare at him. "Jeez, if he told you to run off a cliff, would you do it?"

"Ha. Ha. You're hilarious. I'm trying to keep him on our side. He doesn't have to answer our questions."

I put my hand on the door. "People often value their reputations more than their integrity, Baz. He'll answer our questions because he wants to get shot of this mess."

When I walk into the lab, the white-coated students, who are gathered round a workbench at the front of the room, stop listening to their tutor to stare at us.

"Mr. Murphy." I give him a cold smile. Feign confidence. I could be thrown off what's left of this case just for approaching him without his lawyer present.

His face drops and then there is anger in his eyes.

"Write this up," he barks at his students. "I'll be back in no more than five minutes." He stalks by me, snapping off a pair of latex gloves and dropping them in a bin on the way out the door.

I swallow. Baz grimaces and leads me out. "Let me," he whispers.

Murphy turns and walks about ten strides away from the lab door. "What the hell are you doing? I asked you to wait."

Baz holds up his palms. "Lorcan, please. The case is choked up.

It's dead and all we wanna do is follow through on a lead. But we can't do that without your help."

Murphy can't help stepping forward; his neck strains; spittle gathers at the corner of his mouth.

"Your utter incompetence hasn't got anything to do with me. You've dragged my reputation through the mud. How dare you come back here."

"Nicole is missing," Baz states.

Murphy blinks, draws back. "What?"

"We've been trying to reach her for days," he says. "Please, just answer a couple of questions."

"You—" He glances about. "You think this guy has Nicole?"

The shoulders lift beneath Baz's thick woolen coat.

Lorcan looks down. "I know what you found round my house and that. It doesn't look good." He shakes his head. "But that was what we did. It's a turn-on, a sex thing. That's all."

"To cut someone?" I ask.

Murphy bristles and Baz glares at me.

"Eleanor liked to cut herself. You have to be into it to understand." He looks around. "Fuck. If this gets out, no one will work with me. Do you know that? You will have fucked up my career for good. Eleanor was dominant, I was submissive. You see? She liked to cut *me*. She liked to cut herself when we were . . . you know . . . It was her thing. Pain."

"Sure it was. And you were a helpless victim? Why don't you tell us about your relationship with Nicole?"

Murphy's lip quivers with restrained anger. He pushes the edges of his white coat aside; his fingers work down the buttons on his shirt. Opening them. It's my turn to be nervous. What the hell is he doing?

"Actually, yes, I was a victim," he says between clenched teeth.

When he lifts the side of his shirt he points down his left side. From the bottom of his rib cage to the top of his waist, there are numerous puckered scars. Some appear as if from shallow injuries; others look more traumatic.

I look away. I can't bring myself to meet his eyes without screaming at him.

Baz peers at the scars. "Eleanor did this?"

He tugs his shirt closed, his fingers marching up the buttons, fastening them. "Yes."

"Why didn't you tell us sooner?"

A scowl, a flash of triumph lights his eyes. "Because, Detective, it's none of your fucking business."

My teeth bite down on my anger. A sting of pain at the back of my tongue. "People are dead, Lorcan."

His lips draw tight. "Look, I had my interests, Eleanor had hers. They were nothing to do with me."

Baz leans in. "What interests?"

Lorcan shrugs. "She arranged for Amy and Peter to get together. Peter was the only real innocent in the entire fucked-up ring. It was an obsession. She spent years orchestrating her husband's downfall. She'd tell me that she could beat him, torture him. I didn't doubt it. She was a manipulative tour de force."

"That's one way of describing it," I murmur.

"You wouldn't get it. The control, the planning it takes to pull off what Eleanor could pull off. The affair was just another way to keep him down. Peter sought refuge in Amy, not knowing that Eleanor was pulling the strings so that she could use his guilt against him."

My ears are banging, the blood thumping around my head. My fingers curl into my palm; the muscles all along my arm tighten, shorten, ready to strike Lorcan Murphy down.

He's gazing at the floor now, a soft half-smile dreaming on his lips. Remembering. Finally, he sighs, looks up, meets my eyes. Hard clash.

"You could've told us this weeks ago, Mr. Murphy," I say, teeth pressed together.

He tilts his head. "I could've. Yes."

"You are aware that I could arrest you for obstructing the course of justice?"

"I'm not sure I wouldn't enjoy that, Detective." The smile breaks across his face.

Baz puts a hand on mine. Restrains.

"Nicole, Mr. Murphy," I manage.

"I don't know where Nicole is. I never had a relationship with her. We had a few dates and a kiss or two, but we didn't share the same . . . tastes, shall we say?"

"Thanks for your time again, Mr. Murphy."

"Is that all?"

"Thanks," Baz says.

"Next time you show up to question me without my lawyer present, I won't even wait for a hello before I'm on the phone to your superiors!" he shouts down the hallway.

Baz comes up behind me. "You could've at least tried to be nice."

I keep walking. "To that? Nice is wasted on men like him."

"He was angry. Pushing buttons."

"He's no right to be fucking angry. It's not my fault Costello's blood was found in his vehicle, Eleanor's on his sheets. It's not my fault that he didn't tell us about their sick little sexual rituals before we arrested him. He's kept his secrets regardless of what it's cost our case. The guy's a fucking coward."

"Frankie!"

I stop.

He runs a hand over his face. "Sorry. But this is our job. Not his."

I turn heel and leave the university. Out into the cold air, my fingers are already dialing Nicole Duarte's ma.

"Hello?"

"Mrs. Duarte?"

"Yes, who is this?"

"Mrs. Duarte, this is Detective Frankie Sheehan. Has your daughter been in touch with you?"

There's a nervous swelling in my stomach.

"Detective, I reported my daughter missing days ago." Her words are spoken with a thick Spanish accent.

"I know, I'm sorry. And the team are working on it." I wince. "But has she tried to call, or managed to contact you?"

I can hear the sharp intake of breath, of impatience and anger, on the other side of the line. "Do you think I'd be wasting your time, Detective, if she had? The way you seem happy to waste mine? Her daughter asks for her every day. It's coming up to Christmas, she should be with her mama. Where you looking? How you looking that you have to ask me if I've seen her?"

A rush of students exit the building. Laughter and banter swell out into the cold afternoon in soft clouds of vapor. I put my hand over the mouthpiece and move farther round the building.

"I'm sorry, Mrs. Duarte. Really I am. But I only got news of Nicole going missing recently and am running to catch up on what I can."

"Well, run faster, Detective, because in case you didn't realize, she has a young daughter here. A young girl that's missing her mama."

"Mrs. Duarte, did Nicole ever mention anyone called Lorcan Murphy?"

"Nicole is a very closed person. She'd given birth before she told me she'd been pregnant. She doesn't share that kind of thing with me."

I nod into the phone. "I see."

BAZ IS LEANING up against the door and smoking. "Well? What did Dr. Burke have to say for himself?"

"Nothing," I answer, clicking the car open. "He wasn't there. Gone away."

He straightens. "Away, huh?"

"Apparently." I get into the driver's seat and wait for Baz to fold his long limbs into the car. "But there was a Chagall print in his office that matches the one we found in the Costello house. Did anything ever come up from those prints we dusted from that picture?"

"We?"

"Jesus! Okay, you?"

"Nothing, but then we don't have Burke's prints on record."

"We might be able to lift some from his notes on Eleanor. The ones he gave you?"

Baz grimaces. "We should be so lucky."

I sigh. "We have to be. Call the office. Get Helen to phone his clinic, see when he gets back."

Baz takes out his phone, makes the call to Helen.

CHAPTER 28

CLANCY HAS BEEN absent all morning. I suspect he's leaving me to it, looking the other way while I break all sorts of protocol. But he doesn't have to worry. I've run up the road and into the ditch—there's nowhere else to go. The thin line of investigation has been whittled down to "he said, she saids." Circumstantial evidence.

I move to Helen's desk. She has the Black Widow site open on one screen and is working on reports with the other. Totting up her work over the past few months so that the summary can be stacked away in a "Case Unsolved" box.

"Anything?" I ask her. "On the Black Widow site?"

"Maybe. I've been hanging out around the greetings board. Newbies, like me, are more likely to share. There's been a new administrator of the website appointed. It seems that the original site founder has been found dead. I trawled through the historical posts—well, as far as I could before the site automatically deletes for security. But it seems the founder was female and was murdered over two months ago. She was known as the Black Widow."

"Eleanor?"

"I'm almost certain."

I lean over her desk. Peer into the screen. Scan down the posts. "Who's taken over?"

"They've not announced it yet. But I reckon it's our man. TrustMe57. There's been a ballot."

"How democratic."

"That's what I thought."

A painful flutter of hope bats in my chest. I squeeze Helen's shoulder.

"Good work. Hey, did you phone that doc?"

"Dr. Burke? Sorry, it was late. I left a message on their machine, though."

"Thanks."

I head to my office to gather my notes and bag. I don't want to be there when the investigation board is taken down. Failure is already dragging at my heels, I can't cope with the impending despair at the death of this case. I can't watch our investigation grind to a stop while Nicole Duarte is still missing.

Her case will remain in Missing Persons, who will sit on it until it becomes a murder, and then, when the investigation's as cold as Eleanor Costello's bones in the ground, we'll have to start the whole thing again. I collapse into the chair and swing round, watch the gray light of the morning on the frosted window.

I type out a quick text to Baz and am about to hit send when his name flashes up on my screen.

"Hey," I answer.

"Hey," he replies. He sounds breathless.

"You all right?"

"Fine," he says. He doesn't sound fine. "Listen, sorry I haven't been in this morning. It was a bit of a late one last night."

"Drowning sorrows without me? I thought you were a friend?"

"I went to Murphy's house. He wasn't there."

I shrug, even though I know he can't see me. "So? He probably went out to find a new toy to play with."

"His car was gone. I waited all night for him to return. Had a feeling, you know?"

"Best not to tell anyone about those," I answer.

"I'm serious, Frankie. I think he's run. Or he's hiding something. So, I went to the university this morning. He's not shown up. Bear in mind that after his beloved tutor was murdered, he turned up to work immediately afterward. I spoke to the dean; he says he's not known Lorcan Murphy to be a no-show in the time he's been working at the uni."

"Where is he?"

"That's it, no one knows."

"Nicole," I breathe.

Baz swears. "Look, maybe Jack will give us an extension on this. This has to be something?"

"Clancy has said his piece. Unless we have a body or a firm suspect, we move on this afternoon." I shake my head. Sigh. "Murphy is allowed to disappear, Baz. He's not a suspect."

"Yet." His voice stabs out the word.

"We have a few hours, keep working on Duarte. We need to find her. My guess is, we find her, we find Murphy."

"Right, I'll get in touch with Duarte's local Garda station. See if I can retrace her steps."

I chew down on my lip. "We might be looking for a body," I say.

"You think she's dead?"

"It would fit his MO. I know Steve is monitoring the site for another snuff movie. And I think he's right."

I can feel Baz's anger down the line. "Fuck it."

"Yeah. See you later. Get in touch if anything comes up," I say. I hang up, rub the tender spot on my temple. Our twenty-four hours is almost up.

IT'S PISSING DOWN when I get to Bray, a drip of a day and no sign in the dirty sky of it letting up. People are pushing down the promenade, hoods up and clenched to their chins against the drizzle. The sea is a slate of dark gray, small white waves curling lazily on the brown sand. The smell of seaweed hangs beneath the dampness, and the air is cold enough to draw my fingers up my sleeves.

I step onto the Costello drive and make my way toward the house. It looks lonely and quiet. The garden has grown up along the driveway, and long brown grasses bend over the fence. Two Gardaí, one female, one male, are hunched under the porch, the door behind open but covered in black plastic; yellow tape crisscrosses the entrance.

I've never kept uniforms on a scene this long. Normally, we've a scene pinned down, scooped out, in a couple of days. The longest stretch, three weeks. But this case has crashed forward, spitting out victims once clamped between the jaws of Eleanor Costello, and I couldn't help keep my guard up, keeping that scene mine until the end. Now we've run dry, that effort to preserve seems somewhat futile.

I nod at the guards. "How's it goin'?"

"Afternoon, Chief."

I pull up my sleeve, check the time. Where has the morning gone? The hand has moved by midday.

"Afternoon," I answer. "All quiet?"

The woman stands, knocks some wall moss from her backside. "Quiet. Apart from the neighbor, not much. No press or journos about at all."

Even the media has moved on.

"Well," I say. "You can head back now."

The man straightens, adjusts his stab vest. "But we're on till three."

"Get back to your station. You'll be on till three somewhere else. I'm cleaning up here."

"Right so," he replies. Not one bit happy that he has to spend the rest of his shift actually working rather than sitting on his arse, smoking fags.

"See ya, Chief," the woman says. She walks down the drive, gets into their vehicle, and starts the engine.

They pull away slowly and I'm left staring at the onetime family home of the Costellos. A house that's a keeper of dark secrets and witness to years of pain both physical and psychological. The black plastic rattles in the sea breeze; a stray end of yellow tape flaps out over the side of the porch like a torn flag.

I begin tearing the plastic from the doorway. Inside, the house smells of the sea and the outdoors; none of the musky scents of family living linger in the hallway. The doors to the rooms are open, and even though the house is still fully furnished, my footsteps echo on the wooden floor when I walk across the living room. The Chagall book is still under the coffee table. I reach down, straighten it, bring the corner of the book in line with the others, the way Eleanor Costello would have liked it.

I move round the house, drawing the curtains and pulling down blinds. I'm sure the solicitors will waste no time in getting to the house, but the case will have left a sourness in many. Mrs. Fagan was like a tree felled after the news of her brother; who knows how long it will take before she can set foot in her brother's home again?

I move to the main bedroom, draw the long curtains there too, not wanting the daylight hours to bleach the carpet, but I don't linger. The image of someone forcing a rope around Eleanor's throat and yanking her off the ground in her own bedroom is like a movie replaying in my head. Like one of those terrible dreams where someone is after you and, although you sense you know them, your brain refuses to fill in the blank of their face.

When I've been through the house, I step back out on the porch and pull the front door, letting the latch snap shut.

I grasp the yellow tape and begin to wind it around my wrist, following its path out through the garden around the posts the forensics team set up on that first morning more than two months ago.

"You're wrapping up then?" A voice behind me makes me freeze. I turn. It's the neighbor. Neil Doyle.

"Yes."

He shakes his head, a glimmer of a smile twitching at the side of his mouth.

"What?" I ask. How on earth anyone could find humor in the situation is beyond me, let alone someone who lived next door to the victims for the guts of a decade.

"It's just so like Eleanor is all. A mystery. A glorious mystery. Always secrets."

I roll the tape up around my arm and ball it into my pocket. "It seems we might never know all her secrets." I shouldn't comment, but I can't help myself.

"She always said that it was growing up in a small village. Nothing like a tight-knit community of curtain twitchers to teach you how to hide stuff, she used to say."

"She said that?"

"Oh, yeah. She was so private, I'm only sure that she wouldn't ever have given me the time of day, only I guess she needed me to watch the house on the occasions she and her husband were away."

I feel all the moisture evaporate from my mouth. "Away? Together?"

He shakes his head, then nods. "Sometimes, but no. Rarely together. It was more her thing. She had a lot of work trips, but she visited Kildare, kept her aunt's house in check, aired it and the like. These old houses, they don't do well if they're not lived in, and she always said she couldn't bear the thought of a tenant in her childhood home, sleeping in her bed or using the stuff she shared with her aunt. You know she had a very troubled upbringing before she moved there?"

I nod.

"Well, it was special to her and, of course, she still had a social life there."

"She had many friends in Kilcullen?"

He shrugged. "I assume so. She often spoke of having a few too many when she went home, so I just reckoned she was out with friends. Shame. It wasn't really reflected at her funeral. People are funny, you know, when the word 'suicide' is bandied about. Or 'murder,' for that matter."

"Yes. Murder rarely brings out the talkative side in people."

"Ah, well, I suppose it's going to Peter's sister now, is it?"

And he's back on the gossip hunt.

"I couldn't say."

"He had no other family, did he? And Eleanor, I don't think she had anyone else?"

"You'll have to ask their lawyers that, I'm afraid. I'm sure you'll find out soon enough. Thanks, Mr. Doyle."

He puts his hand to his forehead, gives a smart salute. "Good luck to you."

I continue on, clearing up the tape, then collect the metal poles round the garden that sectioned off the areas the team had wanted to investigate.

I pack the lot into the back of my car and send a text to Clancy: "House cleared for probate." I sit for a moment at the steering wheel, thinking about Neil Doyle's final summary of Eleanor and her husband. His assessment of her life in Kilcullen, that it was a getaway for her and occasionally her husband, makes my decision. I turn on the engine and head north toward Dublin, knowing that when the turn comes I'll take the Naas Road away from the city and head for Kilcullen once more.

———

WHEN I STEP inside Eleanor's Kilcullen house, I need a little time to think about what it is I'm searching for. I move slowly toward the kitchen. Signs of Lorcan? That anyone had been here apart from Eleanor? I step out of the kitchen, away from the stale damp smell that clings to the walls and into a crowded garden.

It's only three in the afternoon, but already it's darkening, the December sky closing down the year. The rain has stopped, but the air is damp and cold in my chest. The back garden is narrow; a thin concrete pathway leads to an aging garden shed. There are grand, big rhododendron bushes swallowing up most of the space, residual from her aunt's gardening days, no doubt.

Turning, I step back into the house. The drive to get to the bottom of this case is like a persistent itch somewhere under my skin that I can't quite reach. I move upstairs to the rooms, check the lighting again, the glow of daylight coming through the window.

In Amy's video, there was sunshine. I recall the angle at which the sunlight had lain across Amy's feet before reaching her eyes. None of the windows here catch the light that way. The house is old-fashioned, small stingy windows facing east and north. All the same, I use my penknife, lift back the corners of the wallpaper, check the walls for the telltale blue that highlighted the room in the video. But beneath the wallpaper there is only rose-colored paint and patchy plaster. I make my way back down the stairs and into the living room.

The stack of CDs next to the TV and stereo is arranged in alphabetical order. I trace down and find the Joni Mitchell. The CD box is broken and the top cover comes away in my hand. I lift the CD out, look it over, as if I might find answers etched into the shimmering back. My own wobbling reflection looks back at me.

Turning the stereo on, I push the disk into the player and sit down cross-legged on the floor. The fast swinging tune of "Big Yellow Taxi" strums out of the speakers, and suddenly I have tears in my eyes. Tears of frustration and sadness for Amy Keegan. I remember her round youthful face and feel a twinge of sorrow for not getting to know her better. I think of her father and the years of worry and love that he's now drowning in. Rubbing my eyes, I lean back against a nearby chair.

When I open my eyes again, my backside is numb and my neck aches from where my head has tipped over the seat of the chair. I must have fallen asleep. The afternoon has stolen away. The house is quiet; the music stopped long ago and the room is full of dark shadows. A mean bloom of streetlight comes through the window. I sit for a moment; defeat clings to my shoulders. There's a text message from Baz: "Nothing new. Where are you?"

I check the time the message came through. Almost two hours ago. I give him a call, but there's no answer. I type out a quick text and hit send: "In Kilcullen. Eleanor's aunt's house. Heading back soon." I push up from the floor and make my way out of the house. The evening is cool; the scent of damp, rotting foliage and mud carries on the light breeze from the green close by.

I am making my way to my car when I see him. Chin tucked down, hands deep in his pockets, his gaze fixed on the ground ahead of him. The man from Burke's office at the uni. At first I think I'm seeing things, but instinctively I step off the pavement and get into my car before he has the chance to recognize me. He strides past. Stops on the edge of the pavement, checks the road, then jogs across the street. He's tall, a triangular build. Something says "yoga" in the way he moves—a carefulness of foot, the length of his neck.

I watch as he removes a key from his pocket, then dips quickly into a house. A work colleague *and* a neighbor of Eleanor Costello. He may not know anything, may well be as prickly as when I met him at the university. But the link is enough to make me step back out of the car and into the biting December night.

CHAPTER 29

PAUSE ON THE porch, take in mouthfuls of damp winter air, try to silence the banging in my ears. Beyond the noise of my breath, my heart, are the gentle sounds of the village traffic, the occasional bleat of a car horn. I raise my hand and lift the knocker. The rap of brass echoes down the dark street. There's a scratch of footsteps, the soft thump of feet on stairs, and then he is there, smiling in the halo of the porch light. Eyes dark. Hair the wilder side of conservative curls round his ears.

When I don't speak, his face takes on a good-humored look of confusion, as if he is somehow tickled by my inability to move. Then he recognizes me. Places me. I see it dawning on him as a veil might drop from a dark window.

"Good evening, I'm Detective Sheehan," I say.

He smiles. "I remember." He tips his head; worry corners his eyes. "Is there something wrong?"

"You were a neighbor of Eleanor Costello." I point across the street.

He looks over my shoulder, frowns at the house, looks back at me. "Yes. Yes, such a tragedy."

"Your name?"

"Oh. Sorry. Adrian Carr."

"Mr. Carr, do you mind if I come in? Ask you a few questions?"

"I'm not sure how I can help you. I didn't know her very well."

I give him a tight smile. "It won't take long."

He steps aside in the narrow hallway. "Of course."

"Thanks."

The carpet sinks under my feet. There is a row of footwear along the hallway, and I notice for the first time that he's not wearing shoes.

"Sorry, yes. I'm a bit of a neat freak. Would you mind?" He nods at my shoes.

I slip them off and stand in my socks inside the door. A cool snake of evening air wraps around my ankles.

"Come in, come in." He walks ahead down the hallway, waving me into a living room. Cozy. No TV. A coffee table sandwiched between two pale sofas.

He sits down on one of them and waits until I sit across from him.

"So, what can I do for you?"

"You didn't mention that you lived across from Eleanor Costello."

He frowns. "You never asked. Sorry, Detective, have I done something wrong?" He appears genuinely concerned, rests large hands on his knees.

"No. It's a strange coincidence is all."

"I'm afraid I didn't really know Eleanor Costello. I know that seems odd, but she only used the house a few weekends a year and often I was away then. And work? It's the first time I've worked at that university. As I said, I'm covering for Dr. Burke."

"When was the last time Eleanor was down here?"

He spreads his hands. "I really don't know, Detective. I'm sorry."

I meet his eyes. Hold them.

"Okay. But you've met Dr. Burke? The lecturer you're covering for?"

He gives a short laugh. Shakes his head. "Look, I've just got in. I'm parched. Would you like some tea, Detective? Then, I promise, I'll answer all the questions you want."

I nod. "Sure."

He moves swiftly from the sofa, pads out of the room, toward the kitchen.

"Do you take sugar, Detective?" he shouts back down the hall.

"One, please," I return. I take out my phone. Check for any more updates on Lorcan's whereabouts, Nicole's. There's a text from Baz.

"More dead ends," it says. "Nicole Duarte walked into a Garda station on the Southside this afternoon. She's fine. Was staying with friends."

I can read Baz's frustration in the space around the words. He's thinking of time lost, energy spent. Me, I feel a tired kind of peace. She's okay. One less victim. I sit back down, drop my head into my hands. Eyes closed. Deep breath. She's okay. I tuck my phone back into my coat. Get up, move to the window, push back the curtain.

Across the street, Eleanor's house sits dark and lonely among the warm yellow lights of the street. Adrian Carr would have had a good view of comings and goings, if he chose to look. I let the curtain swing closed. On the mantelpiece, a ceramic skull, the planes and pockets of personality marked out in black lines. Phrenology, a shrink's paperweight.

There are dull thuds coming from the kitchen, cupboards opening, closing, the knock of mugs on the counter. My eyes move over the grate, no fire, a single log, half burned, the singed bark peeling upward like a curling lip. For a brief moment, I smell charred flesh again. Amy Keegan. I swallow, turn away.

Under the coffee table, there are stacks of books. A mottled blue spine calls me closer. My breathing catches, changes gear. I bend. Read the word. "Chagall." The same book was found in the Costello home. I remove it. Spread open the first page. *La Mariée.* The image of a young couple, the bride luminous in reds and whites pushed forward on a dreamy blue. Eleanor. Shallow, quick breaths. I look up, around the room, a certificate behind me on the wall, an acknowledgment of qualification. I move cautiously toward it, half knowing what it will say.

"Dr. Jeremy Burke." His name swirls in gold letters. Eleanor Costello's therapist. I blink white stars from my eyes. I'm in his house. I see it, free and full, all the dots line up, all the pieces stumble into formation. The affair, the manipulation, the shared dark fantasies, the collusion, the need for more, the abuse of her husband, torture, murder. Amy Keegan, a pawn, a vulnerable young woman trying to understand her own issues, wrapped up tight from the moment she reached out.

My throat closes. Hand goes to mouth. Press the panic down. I edge away from his name, my fingers already pressing dial on Baz's number. The clink of cutlery comes down the hall. *Get out. Get out!* my head screams. I clamber over the coffee table, pull the door back.

And he's there. Two mugs of tea and a knowing smile.

"You going, Detective?"

Heat prickles along my hairline.

I drop the dialing phone into my pocket, hope that Baz is on the other side.

"Toilet," I say. "I should've gone in Eleanor's. I wasn't expecting to bump into one of her work colleagues here. It's a long trip back to Dublin."

His eyes narrow. He raises the mugs, indicating for me to wait, leaves them on the table. Next to the open art book, the painting of the young bride.

He turns. "I've always loved that painting. How the blue makes her stand out." He looks back at me, frowns. "Here, let me take your coat. Seems silly to still be wearing it when you've no shoes on?"

I clear my throat. "No, thanks. It's okay."

He makes a tsking sound, steps behind me. "It's no trouble. Otherwise, it'll be no use to you outside." His fingers unhook the coat from my shoulders. He lays it on the back of the couch.

"There. The toilet," he says, "is up the stairs, second door on the left."

"Thanks," I murmur, lips sticking.

He stands in the doorway, watching me. I move quickly, increase the distance between us, but halfway up the stairs it hits me. Sweet, rotting smell. The cloying scent of blood and a faint sting of bleach cuts through the warmth of the house. Smell. The most primitive of senses. My mouth dries. A fluttering pulse starts up at the base of my throat. A check behind shows me Burke bent over the tea, flicking calmly through the art book.

I move over the landing, into the darkness, away from him. Finding the toilet, I turn on both taps, leave them running. There is no air up here, as if the windows haven't been opened in years. The bathroom window is locked. Hammered shut with crooked, rusted nails. I pull at the collar of my blouse. Sweat gathers under my arms, across my back.

I take a deep breath, try to get some control, but suddenly the thrum of Dublin city is in my ears, the sound of my feet on gravel as I inch round the back of Tracy Ward's home. The smell of blood is in my nostrils, the rise of hatred like acid on my tongue. I swallow. Chase my breath, catch it, get it under control.

Creeping out of the bathroom, I hurry into another room. A bedroom. Clammy, stale air, stiff with body odor. The windows, again, like in the bathroom, are hammered shut. A prison. There's another door, by the landing, directly over the living room. I edge closer, but something stops me from entering. Someone's on the other side. I feel it. I press my ear against the door. There are no sounds, no groans, no murmurs for help, but cold or warm, there is a presence behind that door. Another person. Another victim? My hand appears ahead of me, reaching for the door handle, fingers trembling.

"Detective?"

I suck in the sticky air. Turning, I see him behind me. He comes up the last few steps, stands on the landing, facing me, not more than two strides away.

"Your tea's getting cold," he says. He moves aside, holds his hand out in the direction of the stairs, and looks at me expectantly.

In the darkness, it's difficult to make out his expression, but his fingers are white and stiff on the banister, as if at any moment he could tear a chunk of wood away.

"I need you to open this door."

I'm sure I see his nostrils flare, his mouth tighten.

He takes a step forward. "It's not worth your trouble."

"Is there someone in this room?" I ask, forcing a hardness into my voice.

He takes another step closer and I'm up against the door. He looks at me with an expression of pure disdain. His top lip lifts, twitches.

"Yes, Detective. There is."

"Are they alive?"

I hold his eyes, too afraid to look away, too afraid to move. He's close, close enough for me to feel the heat of rage fizzing under his skin.

"Are they alive, Dr. Burke?"

His eyes close, like a father asking the gods for patience. A slow sigh, blown warm into my face.

"Define 'alive,' Detective. Are they aware of every aching strip of flesh? Alive? I believe he's probably never been more so."

My brain stumbles. *He.*

"He?"

And there it is, stirring in the black of his eyes. Circling in on itself, hollowing out its core, a living mix of evil and anger pulled back, readying itself.

He doesn't answer. I'm unworthy of response. I've judged him. And his victims. Wrongly.

Straightening, I try to summon an air of control. "Why don't we go downstairs? Talk this through. My team will be here any moment."

There it is again. A flare of disgust.

"Your team. Your team," he laughs. "Fuck. Who do you think I am? I don't make the same mistakes, Detective, but clearly, you do. Where is your fucking team?" he spits.

His hand moves. Swift. Blur. And then, there is a knife, the wide blade almost white in the darkness. "Open the door," he growls.

I know there is terror on my face. The scar at my temple aches. My throat is screechingly dry. I reach back and grasp the door handle. The round bulb of wood presses into my wet palm. The door swings easily inwards, and the smell of blood both pungent and bitter rises, the primitive centers of my brain screaming: *Run!*

Burke keeps the knife tight to his side. His eyes are stones of hatred, polished evil. Scornful. His arm trembles in anticipation, as if the weapon demands use. He moves forward, head low, and I stumble back into the room.

My feet slip on plastic sheeting and I put a hand out to steady myself against a dresser. Burke steps across the threshold, closes the door, and flicks on a light. The room is blue, soft baby blue with dark skirting boards. A glance behind shows me the window dressed in blue floral curtains. In my mind, Amy Keegan turns tired, bruised eyes toward a streak of sunlight before a hand reaches out, turns her to look at the camera, to face the horror of her death. And now, Burke's latest victim lies pale and still on the same bed.

Lorcan Murphy. All his limbs are tied down, his body covered in knife wounds. A terrified sound groans out from somewhere, and it takes me a moment to know it's risen from my own throat. *I'm sorry!* I want to shout. I'm sorry I couldn't see the answers soon enough.

"Lorcan," I say. Calm. Easy. Reassuring. "Lorcan? It's Detective Sheehan. Help is on its way."

His eyes flicker, and a swift flutter of relief beats in my throat. He's alive.

Burke's voice cracks across my thoughts.

"He's alive because I wish it," he says, as if reading my mind.

Anger loosens my tongue. "And what about Eleanor? Amy?"

Burke leaves the knife on the dresser, opens the top drawer, and removes a camera. He sets it on a tripod, points the lens in my direction.

"We were childhood sweethearts, you know. That takes something." He gives me a serious look, pride full in his chest. "Eleanor had such an engaging way with her. Addictive. Flypaper. Everyone flew to her and got stuck. She tortured her husband for months. Stupid bastard. With me, she thought she pulled the strings, thought I'd pull her up to that beam, then let her drop, safe, to the floor. No harm done."

His eyes glaze for a moment; pleasure plays at the corners of his mouth. He's remembering. Remembering how good it felt to see the realization dawn on Eleanor's face that it was he who held the power.

Even without light, I'd know the moment he looks at me. Really looks at me. I feel his eyes on me and I can't help shrinking back against the window.

"She thought I'd let that rope go. But I didn't."

He returns to the camera. Presses a button at the side and a red light blinks on.

There is no engagement on his face. He has stepped away from the mask, retreated into his true self. He reaches into the dresser again, takes out a length of blue rope. He winds the thick band of nylon around his hands and approaches me as a hunter might approach an animal he means to kill. And he does mean to kill me. The desire is darkening in his eyes; it moves there like a living thing, writhing in the dark pools of his pupils. I glance to Lorcan. His eyes are open. Watching. Panic carved into his face. His mouth, swollen and bruised against his gag, stretches white as he tries to speak.

I wait until Burke is almost upon me, then push off the wall. I duck under his arms, but my chance to escape vanished the moment I stepped into his home. His hands come over my head, the rope taut between them. The rough band rises swiftly to my neck and I'm pulled back onto his chest. He's heaving now with excitement. Exertion. The chase. The capture. The power. The rope rips against my neck. Skin broken. Raw, fresh pain. Pressure builds against my temples.

My hands scratch, scrape, dig against my throat. My feet kick, slip, slide over the crackling plastic. I feel his arms jerk backward, a sudden tightening of the rope, and my body twitches in response. Tiny bursts of light are popping across my vision. I am underwater, alone with the sound of my heart. Not even my breath reaches me through the fog. My arms are slack, floating at my sides. Darkness covers me. Warm, then deliciously cool.

I AM ANCHORED TO the ground. There is wetness on my face. Tears. Blood. I taste salt, metal in my mouth. I try to scream, but my tongue tangles, chokes on soggy fabric. I try to look, to see, but my eyes are so heavy. The curve of my eyelids weighs down on my vision. I smell sweat and blood. Something sharpens in my mind and it drags me through the fog of unconsciousness. I draw in dank, stinking air through my nostrils, chase the tinnitus from my ears, and slowly my body comes back to the room.

I turn my head, and a burst of pain flowers across my neck and into my cheek. My hands are above my head; I flex my fingers, feel the cold metal of the radiator against my knuckles.

I can sense my attacker. Know he's moving somewhere in the room, an arm's reach away. I make myself see, stretch open my eyes. Lorcan is somewhere above me on the bed. He doesn't move, but when I hold my breath, I can hear the shallow chug of his breathing.

"Ah, you're back." Burke's voice is hoarse. A mix of anger and anticipation.

A sinking sensation pulls at my vision, and the room begins to darken. I blink, swallow down a wave of nausea, and make myself focus.

"Feeling unwell?"

There are new pains spreading over my chest and abdomen, a throbbing bruise in my right leg.

He approaches, knife already in hand, already bloody. "That would be the loss of blood."

His words have the effect of calling forth pain. I glance down. Blood is pooling around me, swelling out from my limbs. The dark fabric of my blouse is wet with it. A rush of faintness swoops through me, and I let my head drop to my chest, gasping. But he is on me, gripping my face between his fingers.

"Come on, Detective. I thought you were made of stronger stuff. Maybe a little pick-me-up is all you need. Pain has a beautiful way of sharpening the senses."

He draws the knife along my face, from my cheekbone to the edge of my jaw. Pressure lighter than the trace of a finger. Razor-sharp. The point of the blade continues, rests at the top of my throat. I can feel the blade moving to the thrum of my pulse. He won't slice through the artery, though. That would be too merciful.

The knife lifts, falls to the plastic sheeting, and he takes up the rope, wraps the ends between his hands. He holds it to my face. I struggle beneath him, but pain tears through my leg and abdomen; fresh blood runs from my shirt. He smiles; then his face twists and the rope slams against my neck.

I can't breathe. My tongue pushes against the gag; my nostrils flare. I can't breathe. I can feel the pulse of every blood vessel in my head, my lungs tight, rigid, waiting for air. He leans in against my throat. His face contorted, red with rage. My feet kick out at nothing; my hands flex, grasp the air, tug at their bindings. Each movement wins me more pain. My neck strains; something snaps in my shoulder; a bone cracks in my hand.

Darkness comes, coils around my vision, closes me up. My limbs are so heavy, leaden beyond my control. I am drifting. Away. Floating away.

THERE IS MOVEMENT, somewhere in the darkness. Lights. Voices. Someone is crying. Feet pad close by. Hands, cold hands, lift my face, my eyes. Air steals into my mouth, sharpness into my chest.

"We got you, Frankie. We got you," a voice whispers near my ear. "Jesus. Can we get a medic over here, please?"

CHAPTER 30

I PUSH THE BUTTON and the treadmill slows, then stops. My leg throbs; the injury objects to rehabilitation, and I stand for a moment until the dull ache subsides. The bonsai has followed me to work; I've decided it prefers the shade of the office over the shifting light of the flat. The foliage, although sparse, is a minty green, and there are new buds pushing into life along the branches, proof that desk life suits it, or that Steve, a witness to my neglect, has taken to tending to it when my back is turned.

There's a soft knock on the door and I glance at the window. The sky is darkening. I imagine him in his cell, watching his cut of sky, only the sounds of the city slipping into his room and only the sound of his guilt answering back. A trail of sweat runs down my back, soaks my blouse. I pull the material away from my skin and lean for a moment against my desk, catch my breath.

"Come in!" I call out.

Baz steps in. "You all right, Sheehan?"

I smile, take up the case file, pass it to him.

"I'm great."

And I am. Frankenstein's monster has fewer stitches holding him together, but I'm at peace for the first time in months. My broken shoulder will mend; my leg will mend. The scar along my cheek is shallow and already shriveling to a thin line.

"Are you sure you're up to this?"

"Yes. I owe it to them. To Peter, to Amy. Tracy. Rachel. Even to Eleanor, to some extent."

Burke's confession was only half there. There are some mysteries a killer likes to keep to himself. Burke was never going to paint a full picture, but it turns out broad strokes are enough. Prussian blue was used first by Eleanor, Burke's longtime lover and patient.

Eleanor used the compound to counter any exposure to thallium, but soon it became an infatuation for both of them. An obsessive trigger of the power and control they had over Peter. When I think of the color, I can't help the twist in my mouth. Their use of Prussian blue sneered at Peter Costello. Sneered at Peter's love of art and of Chagall.

Eleanor became a victim of the monster she helped create. Photos found at Burke's house charted the course of their destructive relationship. As teens, Burke, tall, angular, standing behind Eleanor, arms locked around her shoulders, Eleanor's body folded against his chest. Smiling. Always smiling. Then later, Eleanor, in the kitchen of her aunt's house, wedding band loose on her finger, holding a glass of champagne, toasting the camera.

Eleanor was the spark that ignited a conflagration in Burke, and eventually she was choked by his desire for absolute control. The Black Widow site was an easy and playful way to connect with potential lovers and, for Burke, victims. Amy tested out her fantasies on the wrong platform.

He doesn't want to talk about Tracy's murder or his attack on Rachel because he fluffed them. Early, rookie mistakes, rushed and amateurish. Not the control he sought. He thinks it matters. And to him it does, but we have his profile, his DNA. We don't need his confession; his history leaves filthy fingermarks all over his crimes, and now we can trace them. Once we had a match on his prints, we found them all over the Tracy Ward case. The pigment found under Tracy's nails was placed there by him. This was his calling card. A deliberate tag marking all his victims, even his accomplice, Eleanor Costello.

The evening I was attacked, Baz got the call that Nicole had returned home. She'd needed a break, had spent a week bingeing and partying with a friend. She sometimes needed to decompress; she's a lot on her shoulders, she'd said. She had deliberately avoided my calls. She'd been frightened. Eleanor's murder had swerved too close for her liking and she'd wanted out. I should've been angry, but I couldn't rouse it in me. It was one less victim to add to the list.

I take up the crutch, position it under my uninjured shoulder, and move out of my office and onto the case-room floor. At the case board, I stop and take in the path of our investigation. Priscilla Fagan had her brother cremated, a move that was no doubt to save him from sharing a patch in the ground with his abusive wife. That was not the eternity she wanted for her flesh and blood.

She came to the hospital, hard-faced and red-eyed. She placed a bunch of stiff flowers on my side table and thanked me for showing Eleanor's true face. Her final comment came to me with the sweet taste of a reprieve: "He's free from her games now, at least."

It takes me a while to get down to the car. Baz opens the passenger door, then moves round to the driver's side.

"Don't get used to the driving seat," I say as I ease myself into the car.

He smiles. "Wouldn't dream of it. I know you, remember?"

"Like fuck you do."

"You know, I don't need this shit. I'm gonna put in for a move. Maybe Ballistics," he says. The corner of his mouth lifts.

I look out the window, suppress a smile. "Best place for you."

We drive the rest of the way in silence.

Baz found me. He picked up that call. Right before I slipped the phone into my pocket, right before I went up those stairs. He heard me mention Eleanor's aunt's house. Heard Burke's replies. Baz didn't paint any grisly pictures of when he found me. He didn't need to: I could read the scene playing out in his eyes.

Outside the court, the press are waiting. Waiting to get a shot at the middle-class doc who liked to play rough with his victims, who liked to "say it with knives." Garda cars pull up, clear the entrance for the blacked-out van. In a rush of uniforms and shouts of hatred, Burke is escorted from the vehicle, hands clasped in front, cold steel round his wrists. He's led swiftly inside, away from the questioning public to face justice.

"You said to me once that it was about winning. No matter the cost," Baz says, his eyes fixed on the door of the court. "At the time, I don't think I understood."

He turns, smiles at me. "But now? Now I do."

My teeth find the inside of my cheek. I look away. Cost? Lorcan Murphy survived. Or parts of him did. He needed his spleen removed; there's permanent nerve damage in his left hand. He's moved. Cork or Kerry. Somewhere in the bowels of the country where he can continue lecturing without Eleanor Costello haunting his every move. I visited him before he left. Gray pallor, the shine gone from his smile, a shifting anxiety in his eyes that I recognized. "It gets better," I said. "I'm fine," he answered. And then he was gone, a ghost of himself, but I could see his pain clinging to his shoulders like a goblin. I don't want to think of cost.

Baz swings the car round and heads down a side street. Clancy is waiting at the back entrance. Face, as usual, like a smacked arse, a fag hanging loosely from his lips.

"He looks happy," Baz says.

"Ecstatic," I say. And I can't help the smile.

I get out of the car and Clancy winces on my behalf.

"Christ, Sheehan. This is becoming a fucking habit."

"Well, if one of you lazy articles could take the beating next time, I won't be complaining," I reply.

"Serves you right for being such a pushy bitch." He gives me a rare smile. "He got close, though, Frankie. Too close."

I rub the top of my thigh.

"All of this will fade. Will heal." I lean into the crutch and meet his eyes. "Too close is not nearly enough to stop me."

ACKNOWLEDGMENTS

A **BOOK IS ONLY** alive and finished in the mind of a reader, so my first thanks go to you. Thank you for reading *Too Close to Breathe*.

Thank you to my wonderful agent, Susan Armstrong, and to all the team at C&W Agency, especially Emma Finn, Jake Smith-Bosanquet, Alexandra McNicoll, and Alexander Cochran. Thank you to Zoe Sandler at ICM Partners for her advice, belief, and enthusiasm, and thank you to Stephanie Kelly for her clever editorial input, and to all the team at Dutton.

Thank you to my sister, Ann Kiernan, for always replying with "try again," for being a patient sounding board, a kind reader, and a constant cheerleader.

Thank you to friends and critique groups who read and commented on the manuscript.

Special thanks to those members of the Garda Síochána who have been so generous with their time, help, and expertise when I was researching this book. Any inaccuracies in police procedure are my own.

Lastly, thank you to Matthew: keeper of balance, provider of sanity, and defender of "time to write."

ABOUT THE AUTHOR

Olivia Kiernan is an Irish writer living in the UK. She was born and raised in County Meath near the famed heritage town of Kells and holds an MA in creative writing awarded by the University of Sussex. *Too Close to Breathe* is her first novel.